# THE LIBERTINES

ANONYMOUS

Carroll & Graf Publishers, Inc.
New York

Copyright © 1989 by Carroll & Graf Publishers, Inc

All rights reserved

First Carroll & Graf edition 1989

Carroll & Graf Publishers, Inc.
260 Fifth Avenue
New York, NY 10001

ISBN: 0-88184-562-0

Manufactured in the United States of America

# Part I

What a deep satisfaction it is to be free of the vain pleasures, frivolous amusements and dangerous passions that are so prevalent in the world today. Having regained my senses after so many perversions and aberrations and having won a tranquillity by abstaining from the former objects of my desires, I still shudder at the thought of the perils I escaped. On the other hand, their remembrance enhances my feeling of security.

Many, many times have I thanked the Almighty for His mercy in rescuing me from the abyss of libertinage into which I had plunged and giving me the determination to write down my transgressions for the edification of my fellow-man.

I am the fruit of the lasciviousness of the reverend fathers of the city of R.... I use the plural, because all boasted of having conceived me. Here I hesitate for fear of being censured for revealing the mysteries of the Church. But away with such scruples. A monk is still a man, and as such, he is able to propagate the species. And he acquits himself quite well in spite of the prohibitions.

I know, dear Reader, that you are impatiently waiting for a detailed account of my birth, but I am afraid that you will have to be indulgent and let me tell it in my own way and when I think is the right time.

To begin, I was living with a kindly peasant whom I considered my father for many years.

Ambroise, for that was his name, was a gardener of a villa that the priests owned. It was in a little village not far from the city. His wife, Toinette, gave still birth to a child on the very day I came into the world. The dead infant was secretly buried and I took its place. As is well known, money works miracles.

As I developed into a gawky youth, still believing myself to be the son of Ambroise and Toinette, I began to have vague doubts about myself. My inclinations were certainly not those of a peasant's son, but rather those of a monk.

Toinette was the proof. She was an attractive and lively woman. There was something very seductive about her Junoesque figure, sparkling black eyes, and retrousse nose. For a woman of her station, she dressed with an uncommon elegance. When I saw the coquette on Sundays in a robe that half exposed her two opulent breasts, I cheerfully would have forgotten that I was her son.

There is no doubt that I had the tastes of a monk. Prompted soley by instinct, there was not a pretty girl on the street that I did not try to kiss and caress. Although I did not know what the end of the matter would be, I sensed that there would be more if only the lasses had given me permission to experiment with them.

One afternoon while I was dozing in my bed – it was a hot August day – I was awakened by jolts coming from the next room. Not knowing what to make of the racket which doubled in intensity, I put my ear to the thin partition which separated my room and heard pants, grunts, and unintelligible sounds.

'Ah, not so fast, my dear Toinette. More slowly, please. Oh, you darling – you are killing me with bliss. Faster, now! That's it. My God! I must be dead.'

I was both disturbed and mystified by what I had heard. And, to tell the truth, I was slightly afraid. But my fear soon gave way to curiosity, and my ear was again pressed to the wall, through which I distinguished the same noises. Toinette and a man were repeating to each other the same expressions I had heard before. I was so determined to learn what it was all about that I would have gone into that room without knocking. It was not necessary, however.

Wondering about the best way to satisfy my aroused curiosity, I spotted a knot hole in the wall. Through it, I had a perfect view and what a sight met my eyes! There was Toinette without a stitch of clothing stretched out on her bed and Father Polycarpe, Procurator of the monastery, also naked as the day he was born, lying at her side. What were they doing? They were doing what our original parents did when God ordered them to people the earth, but only with a great deal more lubricity.

The spectacle caused in me strange feelings, a blend of misgivings and desires I had never experienced before. Whatever they were, I would have given anything to be in the monk's place. How I envied him! From the expression on his face, he was in a state of heavenly bliss. Now flames were coursing through my veins; my face was all red; my heart was pounding madly; and the pike of Venus that I was holding in my hand was so hard that it could have punched a hole in the partition. The monk seemed to have completed what he was doing, for he got up from Toinette, leaving her exposed to my feverish regards.

Her eyes were languid and her cheeks flushed. Seemingly exhausted, her arms were dangling lifelessly down the sides of the bed and her bosom was rising and falling. From time to time, she clutched her buttocks while emitting little animal snorts. Rapidly, my eyes took in every part of her delicious body, every one of which my imagination was covering with passionate kisses. I sucked the pink tips of her rounded, large breasts and licked her flat velvety stomach, but the spot that held my attention the longest – I could scarcely tear my eyes away from it – well, you know what it was. What a spell that charming sheath cast over me! What a fascinating flower! The bits of white foam that partially flecked it only enhanced the vivid colour as did the ring of black curly hair. I instinctively realised that that was the centre of lust. Never have I seen a woman in such a lewd position.

Apparently, the monk had regained his forces, for he began a new assault. But his ardour exceeded his abilities. When he withdrew the limp sword from the sheath, the frustrated Toinette grabbed it and began to shake it vigorously. She seemed to have been successful for the man of God was twitching as he had before.

I was bewildered as to what was causing the monk's convulsions. For some reason, my hand wandered to my prick and I was soon experiencing a completely new sensation that increased in intensity and ended with an explosion so powerful that I sank back on my bed with exhaustion. The white fluid I had seen on Toinette's fringed aperture was all over my trousers. Recovering from my ecstasy, I returned to the peephole, but I was too late. The last card had been played and the game was over. The two were now putting their clothes back on.

For days afterwards, I was in a sort of stupor, still amazed at what I had witnessed. It was a turning point in my life. For the first time, I recognised why the sight of a pretty woman aroused such sensations in me. Now the reason for the transition from rapture to tranquillity was no longer an enigma.

'Ah,' I cried to myself, 'how blissful they were. Joy transported them both. The delights they must have had! Yes, they were supremely happy.'

Thoughts of this kind absorbed me for some time.

'Well,' I continued to myself, 'aren't I big enough to do the same thing to a woman? I think I could give Toinette more delights than Father Polycarpe because I have so much more of that white stuff in me. But then again, I am so ignorant as to how to go about it. Maybe it goes automatically once you are on top of a woman.'

Suddenly, it occurred to me to tell my sister Suzon all about it. A few years older than I, she was a very pretty little blonde with indolent eyes. But they caused as much effect on men as a brunette's fiery, sparkling ones.

Strangely enough, I had never attempted to experiment with Suzon, because I lusted after every girl I saw. Maybe it was because I did not see her often. Her god-mother, one of the wealthiest women in the city, had sent her to a convent for her education for a year and she had just finished her schooling. Now that she was home, I was inflamed with the desire to indoctrinate Suzon and enjoy with her the same delights that Father Polycarpe had with Toinette.

Now Suzon appeared to me in a new light. She had charms that I had never noticed before. Her bosom, rounded and firm, was whiter than a lily. While I was mentally sucking the tiny strawberries at the tips, my mind was on that centre, that abyss of bliss.

Animated at such a dazzling prospect, I set out to find Suzon. The sun was setting and the fog was coming in. I flattered myself that when it was dark, all my desires would be fulfilled. In the distance, I saw her picking flowers in the field. When she spotted me, little did she realise that I was intending to pluck the most precious blossom of her bouquet. As I hurried to her, I was turning over in my mind how to let her know what I wanted from her. My indecision slowed my steps.

'What are you doing, Suzon?' I asked as I tried to kiss her.

'Can't you see that I'm picking flowers,' she replied with a laugh as she escaped my arms. 'It's Godmother's birthday tomorrow.'

Now I was not so sure of my conquest.

'Why don't you help me get up a bouquet,' she suggested.

As a reply, I threw some flowers at her face and she retaliated the same way.

'Suzon,' I sternly warned her, 'if you do that again, I'll... you'll pay for it.'

To show that she did not give a fig for my threats, she hurled another handful at me. At that, I lost all my timidity. Also, I was not afraid of being seen for it was getting dark. I threw myself on her and she pushed me back; I kissed her and she slapped me on the cheek; I forced her to the ground and she writhed like a snake; I held her tightly in my arms, kissing her breasts through her bodice, and she struggled like a wild cat; I put my hand under her skirt and she screamed like a banshee. She defended herself so successfully that I had to abandon my efforts. I released her with a laugh to show that I bore her no ill will.

'Suzon,' I said meekly, 'I didn't want to hurt you. I just wanted to teach you something you would like.'

'I can imagine,' she replied in a shaking voice. 'Look, there's Mother coming, and I'm going to...'

'My dear sister,' I quickly broke in. 'Please don't say anything. I'll do anything in the world for you if you keep quiet.'

Her little kiss on my cheek was her tacit assent. When Toinette came up, she did not say a word and the three of us returned home to supper.

When Father Polycarpe had been to call, he had given new evidence of the monastery's bounty for Ambroise's alleged son: I had just been given a complete new outfit of clothing. His conscience bothered him at times. Such prodigality towards me could have aroused suspicions about the legitimacy of my birth in certain circles. But the local peasants were simple souls, and they were not allowed to learn more than what was good for them. As for the others, who could suspect the ulterior motives of the benevolent monks? They were truly beloved in the village. They were helpful to all and consequently enjoyed respect and affection.

But now I should return to myself.

I had a roguish air, but it was not held against me. My eyes were mischievous and my long black hair falling down to my shoulders set off the clearness of my fair complexion. And now I was neatly dressed.

As I mentioned, Suzon had made a bouquet for Madame Dinville, her god-mother, who was the wife of a councillor in a neighbouring town. She was in the habit of coming to her chateau to drink the fresh milk and breathe the fresh air as a cure for the ailments caused by too much champagne and other excesses.

Suzon, dressed in her best which made her even more desirable in my eyes, asked if I would like to go with her to the chateau. I was more than happy to accept the invitation. When we got there, we found the lady of the house in the pavilion ejoying the cool of the evening. Picture to yourself a woman of medium height, brown haired, white skin, unattractive features, but alert and sparkling eyes that had that come-hither look, and a generous bust. It was the latter which first caught my attention, for I have always had a weakness for those celestial globes. One of the supreme delights in this vale of tears we call life is to have one in each hand. But enough of that.

When she saw us approach, she gave us a wave of her hand in welcome, but she did not change her position on the canape on which she was reclining, one leg on the couch and the other on the ground. Her skirt was so short that it was almost possible to see what every red-blooded man desires to regard. Also, she had on a flimsy, almost transparent bodice. With my memories of Toinette and Father Polycarpe fresh in mind, I regarded her avidly.

'Good evening, my dear child,' Madame Dinville

cheerfully greeted her god-child. 'So you have come to see me, and you were not forgetful of my birthday. Thank you ever so much for the flowers. Come over here and give me a kiss.'

Suzon did as she was bid and planted a kiss on each cheek.

'But,' she asked, looking at me, 'who is that nice looking lad with you. A young girl like you with a beau already. Shame on you.'

As I lowered my eyes, Suzon explained that I was her brother.

'Welcome, then,' she said. 'In that case, I'd like to get to know you better. Give me a kiss, too.'

When I was close to her, it was she who kissed me and full on the lips. Her tongue darted into my mouth, as her hand played with the locks of my hair. I had never kissed that way before, but it sent thrills running up and down my spine. Bashfully looking into her eyes, I saw sparks of passion, and I lowered my glance. I was reassured after a second kiss of the same nature. After all, it was nothing but a friendly greeting, but I was a little surprised at its vivacity.

She resumed her conversation with Suzon, which consisted mostly of admonitions to come and kiss her again.

Out of deference, I respectfully stood apart.

'Well,' Madame Dinville remarked not without sarcasm. 'So the boy is not going to kiss me again.'

I again advanced and put my lips to her cheeks, not daring to do what had so exhilarated me. But I was a little bolder than the first time. I could see that the lady was getting simultaneous enjoyment from my caresses and those of her protégée, but it soon became obvious that she was getting more pleasure from me.

We were seated on the divan, chatting, and Madame Dinville loved to prattle. While Suzon was gazing out into the garden, the lady amused herself by curling my hair with her fingers, pinching cheeks, and giving me playful slaps. All that excited me and gave me the courage to touch her neck. She did not reproach me, and my hand descended down to her bosom, where it rested on a delightfully pneumatic breast. I was overjoyed. Finally, I was in possession of one of those glorious orbs I had always so desired. And I inwardly knew that I could do with it as I wished.

I was about to put my mouth on it, when misfortune occurred. A servant announced the visit of the village bailiff, an ugly, wizened monkey of a man.

Startled by the interruption, Madame Dinville pushed me away, saying: 'What do you think you are doing, you little scamp.'

Thinking all was lost, I turned a deep red. Noticing my embarrassment, she gave me a smile which seemed to say that she was not really angry and that the bailiff's unexpected appearance was as displeasing to her as it was to me.

The bore came up to us. After coughing, spitting, sneezing, and wiping his nose, he delivered a wearisome speech felicitating the lady on her anniversary. To top it all, he had invited all the tiresome dignitaries of the village to come and pay their respects. I was furious.

While Madame Dinville was responding to all sorts of stupid compliments, she turned to Suzon and me and said: 'My children, you'll have to come and dine with me when we can be alone.'

She looked me straight in the eyes when she said that.

I am sure I would have acquitted myself with her if it had not been for those damned callers. What I felt for her was not love, but the violent desire to do with a woman what I had seen Father Polycarpe do with Toinette. The date Madame Dinville suggested for our dinner – the following day – seemed an eternity away.

On our way back home, I tried to set Suzon straight about my intentions with her the day before.

'You got me wrong, Suzon,' I earnestly told her. 'I hope you don't think I wanted to harm you yesterday.'

'It certainly seemed like it. What did you want to do with me then, Saturnin?'

'I just wanted to give you pleasure,' I simply replied.

'What!' she exclaimed in surprise. 'You thought you would give me pleasure by putting your hand under my skirt?'

'Of course. And to prove it, let's go somewhere where we won't be seen.'

I looked at her closely to learn what reaction my proposal might have produced in her. Apparently, it had left her cold.

'Please give me a chance,' I pleaded. 'I assure you that you won't regret it.'

'What is this bliss that you seem to prize so highly?' she asked, seemingly still mystified.

'It is the union of a man and a woman. They hug each other tightly until they both swoon at the same time.'

This time, my words had some effect, for her bosom was heaving.

'But,' she protested, 'Father held me the way you

describe and I didn't have any of those sensations.'

Her comment was a good omen.

'That's because he didn't feel the same way about you that I do.'

'What do you want to do?' she asked in a trembling voice.

'I'm going to put something between your legs,' I boldly informed her.

She blushed and remained silent.

'You see, Suzon, you have a little hole there,' I continued, pointing to the spot.

'Who told you that?' she asked with lowered eyes.

'Who told me that...?' I repeated, slightly embarrassed at the question. 'It's... well, all women have one.'

'How about men?' she demanded.

'Men,' I answered authoritatively, 'have a projection that fits in perfectly with the slit of the woman. Putting them together is what produces the raptures. I'll show you mine, but only on the condition you show me yours. We'll touch each other, and then you'll find out what fun it is.'

Suzon was now as red as a beet. I had impressed her, I knew, but she was still reluctant. I had failed this time, because we were now at home, but I was confident that the next time I would have better luck.

We were scarcely in the house when we saw Father Polycarpe arrive. I guessed that he had come to have lunch with us, for he knew that Ambroise was away. Not that Ambroise ever bothered him, but one feels more easy with the husband absent if he has intentions on the wife.

Confident that I was going to enjoy the same

spectacle this afternoon that I had the previous day, I decided to let Suzon share the pleasure with me. Only after lunch did I extend her the invitation. If anything could persuade her to accede to my wishes, this would be it.

The monk and Toinette, believing us too innocent, were not constrained by our presence. I saw the Father's hand slip down and then up Toinette's skirt, and it appeared that she was spreading her legs to provide him easier access. Then one of her hands disappeared and it was not difficult to imagine what she was doing to him. Now they were so excited that they could not hold themselves back, and they told Suzon and me to go and take a walk. I knew what that meant.

We immediately rose from the table, leaving them the freedom to do other things. I was envious of the fun they were going to have. Before offering her the tableau, I tried first to gain my ends with Suzon without having to resort to that ammunition. I tried to escort her to a grove whose thick foliage provided protection against prying eyes. She was still reluctant.

'Look, Saturnin,' she said ingenuously. 'Tell me more about what you were talking.'

'Do you like to hear such things?' I asked.

Her silence was assent.

Looking deeply into her eyes, I took her hand and pressed it to my breast.

'But, Saturnin,' she said worriedly, 'maybe it will hurt.'

'How can it hurt?' I replied scornfully, delighted at having one last feeble resistance to overcome. 'On the contrary. It is the most enjoyable thing imaginable.'

'Maybe you would make me a baby,' she murmured.

That observation jolted me somewhat. I did not think that Suzon knew so much, and I was unable to give her a satisfactory answer.

'Do you mean pregnant?' I asked. 'Is that how women get swollen bellies?'

She assured me that it was so.

'Where did you learn about that? I guess it's your turn now to tell me a few things.'

'I think I can trust you, Saturnin, but if you ever tell a soul what I am going to say, I'll hate you for the rest of my days.'

I swore to her that I would never breathe a word.

'Let's sit down here,' she said, refusing to go with me into the arbour. 'Now, I'll tell you what I know. You thought you were going to teach me something, but you are going to find out that I have more knowledge than you. But don't think I didn't like what you said to me. And a girl is always pleased to feel that a boy wants her.'

'I thought you were in a convent,' I cried. 'Is that what the nuns taught you?'

'I learned many things there,' she admitted.

'Well, hurry up,' I impatiently urged her.

'One night,' she continued, taking her time, 'I was awakened from a deep sleep by a naked body crawling into my bed. I started to scream, but a hand was clapped over my mouth, and a voice said: "Suzon, I mean you no harm, so keep quiet. It's your dear Sister Monique." This nun had just assumed the veil and she was my best friend. "Mother of Jesus," I whispered, "why are you here in the dead of night?" "Because I love you," she replied, amorously embracing me. "And why are you naked?" I inquired. "It's so hot that I couldn't stand any covers. Besides, there's a terrible storm. Don't you hear it? I get frightened stiff at the sound of thunder. Take me in your arms, my dearest, and let's put the sheet over our heads so that we won't see the lightning. That's fine. You have no idea of how terrified I am, Suzon."

'Since I am not afraid of thunder or lightning, I did my best to comfort Monique who, in the meantime had stuck her tongue in my mouth and was rubbing my thighs with hers. Also, she was gently slapping my derriere. After a time, I felt her twitch violently, and my legs were wet with a sticky liquid. She was sighing and groaning which I thought was due to her fear of the tempest. I caressed her more in order to calm her. When her spasms ceased, I told her I was tired and I was going back to sleep.

'"So you're going to let me die of fright!" she whispered in my ear. "You won't see me alive tomorrow if you leave me by myself. Give me your hand."

'I did as I was asked, and she guided it to the slit you were talking about. Then she requested me to tickle the little button near the entrance with my finger. Because of my affection for her, I did that, too. After a time, I expected her to tell me to stop, but she didn't say a word. All she did was spread her legs apart and pant. At times, she moaned and wiggled her backside. Thinking that it was hurting her, I stopped.

'"Ah, Suzon," she murmured in an anguished voice, 'finish it, finish it, I beg you.' Her voice was so urgent that I went back to my curious task. "Oh, oh!"

she sobbed, her entire body vibrating as she embraced me more tightly, "Hurry! Faster! Oh yes, that's it. I am dying!" Her body stiffened, and I felt again that fluid on my thighs. With a sigh, she relaxed and remained motionless.

'You have no idea, Saturnin, how puzzled I was at what she made me do.'

'Didn't you have any feelings yourself?' I asked Suzon.

'More than you know,' she replied. 'I realised that for some reason, I had caused her intense pleasure, and that if she did to me what I did to her, I would have the same raptures. But I didn't have the courage to suggest it to her, even though I was burning with desire. So I put my hand back on her hole, and that gave me much pleasure. Then I took hers and placed on several parts of my body, but not on the spot where I most wanted it to be. Monique well knew what I wanted, but she mischievously refused to do what I wanted.

'Finally, taking pity on me, she kissed me and said: "I can guess, darling." She lay herself on me and I eagerly pressed her body close to mine. After obeying her command to spread my legs, she inserted her finger into the aperture where I had given her such esctasy in hers. By degrees, I felt the bliss intensify with each jab of her finger. Then she ordered me to raise my buttocks in time with the insertions of her finger. I was in heaven, Saturnin, or at least, I was dead. When it was over, and we were lying without a sign of movement, she still on top of me, and I felt the same liquid dribbling out of me.

'I thought it was blood, but I was so exhilarated that I did not mind. In fact, I couldn't wait to start all over again. But Monique said she was exhausted. After a few moments, I lost patience and straddled her. Rubbing my button against hers, I soon had another spasm of rapture.

'"Well," Monique asked me, "are you sorry that I came into your bed? Are you angry that I woke you up?" I replied that I owed her so much for teaching me what pleasure really is. She answered that I was not in her debt, for I had paid her for what she had given me.

'"Tell me, dear Suzon, and don't hold anything back," she said, "but haven't you ever had any idea of what we have just done?" I told her no. "You never put your finger in your little cunt?" she wanted to know. I replied by saying that I did not know what the word "cunt" meant. "It's that little slit we titillated each other with," she informed me. "Didn't you know that? I see that I knew more than you when I was your age."

'"I never knew that such delights existed," I admitted. "You know Father Jerome, our confessor. It is he who always prevented me. I am always scared stiff when I go to confession with him. Without fail, he wants to know if I have done anything impure with my friends, and he expressly forbids me to do anything to myself. I was stupid enough, I know now, to believe him." Monique then wanted to know how he explained those lewd acts he prohibited. I told her he said I should not put my finger you know where and look at myself naked in a mirror. And lots of things like that. Monique said that he was nothing but an old lecher.

'"Well, I'll tell you more what goes on in the confessional," I said to Monique. "I always took his acts as marks of friendship, but after what you told me,

I know better." Monique was all ears. "He tells me to come closer to him so he can hear better, and then he kisses me on the mouth. After that, he looks down into my bodice, and as I am talking, he sticks his hand inside, all the way down to the nipple. Then he pulls out one of my breasts and starts rubbing it. That gets him so excited that I can't understand a word he is saying.

'"I remember one day, he covered my whole bosom with a hot, viscous liquid. I dried myself with a handkerchief which I had to throw away afterwards. Father Jerome said it was sweat from his fingers. What do you think, Monique?"

'"I had the same experience with him," Monique replied. "The old goat. That's the reason why I no longer go to him for confession. I'll tell you more about him, but you have to promise to keep your mouth shut. If you blab, I am ruined."

'Saturnin, I know I am breaking my promise, but I'll tell you what Monique confided in me only if I have your solemn oath to keep it to yourself.'

Without hesitation, I crossed my heart, so eager was I to hear the rest of a story with such an enchanting beginning.

What follows is tale of Sister Monique as my sister Suzon rendered it to me.

## *The Story of Sister Monique (as told by Suzon)*

'We women,' Monique began by telling me, 'are not the mistresses of our hearts. Seduced from birth by pleasure, we cannot control ourselves. But I don't envy those who let themselves be swayed by wise counsel. They pay dearly for their austerity. The rewards for their virtue are imaginary. It is old women no longer able to satisfy a man who preach these false doctrines. But let them talk, Suzon. When a girl is young, she should obey no laws except those dictated by her heart. Follow its advice.

'You would think that a convent would be the ideal spot to stifle any nascent lasciviousness, but that is the very place where I discovered it.

'I was very young when my mother came to this convent after the death of her fourth husband. Although I did not say anything, I was dismayed at the thought of life in a nunnery. One could not even get a glimpse of a man. What a deprivation! Then I began to reflect on the difference between man and woman. What is there about a man, the sight of whom makes a girl's heart beat more quickly? Is he prettier than we women are? No, that cannot be it, for Father Jerome, ugly and disagreeable as he is, arouses certain sensations in me when I am with him. There is something about a man that produces this reaction, and I did not know what it was. I made vain efforts to break the bonds with which my ignorance shackled me.

'Alone in my room with the door locked, my sole thoughts were concentrated on men. Taking off my clothes, I voluptuously examined my nudity. I cast inflamed looks on every part of my body in the mirror. To extinguish the blaze within me, I lay down on the bed and spread wide my legs, but that did not help. In my overheated imagination, there was a man whom I welcomed with outstretched arms because he would put out the fire in my cunt. Never did I dare put my finger on it, in spite of the unbearable itching, for fear of doing some damager to it.

'At times, I almost succumbed to temptation. I touched it with the top of my finger, but frightened at what might happen, I quickly withdrew it. Then I covered it with the palm of my hand. That was no good.

'Finally, I was no longer able to restrain myself. I determined to do it, no matter what might result. When I bravely stuck my finger in, the bliss was so great that I nearly died. When the first rapture was over, I did it again and again until my hand was so tired that I could barely move it.

'Overjoyed with my discovery, I felt that my eyes had been opened. If my finger could produce such ecstasy, the finger men have between their legs would give even greater satisfaction. I was now sure that this was the only true way to pleasure, and I was wracked with desire to view that masculine organ which promised so much.

'To attract a male, I became a true flirt, dressing

myself as seductively as I could, smiling enigmatically, casting inviting regards, and so on, but... alas!... there was no male on whom I could exert my charms.

'In the sitting-room, I waited with girls whose brothers would come to visit them. When they appeared, they were not oblivious to what I was inwardly offering them.

'One day, there was a handsome lad whose lively black eyes returned my regard. I felt a delicious sensation running through me. He tried to avert his glance, but it always returned to me. When his sister was not looking, he made certain signs to me. I had not the faintest idea of what they meant, but I pretended that I understood. When I smiled back, he became even bolder. With his hands stretched apart, he made it clear that he had an organ of such and such a length by pointing to the bottom of his stomach.

'Although modesty advised me to leave at such obscenity, I could not, for the gesture set me on fire. Besides, modesty is a weak opponent against desire.

'Verland, for that was his name, sensed what I was feeling. Then he joined his middle finger with his thumb and inserted the index finger of his other hand into the circle that was formed, and with inaudible sighs, he pushed it in and out. I understood.

'At that moment, his sister was called, and she left, saying she would be right back. Taking advantage of her temporary absence, he explained himself more clearly. Although the compliment he paid me was not very elegantly phrased, I shall always remember it with pleasure. Women are usually more flattered by a simple and straightforward declaration than by meaningless insipid gallantries.

'"We don't have much time," he exclaimed. "You are charming and I have a hard prick that is yearning to get into you. Tell me how I can sneak into this convent."

'Not only was I stunned by his words, but also his actions. He darted his hand through the bars of the grille and grabbed my breast which he feverishly fondled. I stood there as if petrified, absolutely unable to stop him. Just at that moment, his sister appeared and surprised us. She vilified us both, and I never saw Verland again.

'The whole convent soon knew about the escapade. Every time the girls saw me, they whispered, tittered, and looked at me knowingly. The pretty ones were kinder, for they realised that their homely fellow-students were simply jealous of me. No fellow would ever make an advance towards them.

'Naturally, the story reached the ears of the Mothers Superior who met to discuss what punishment should be meted out to a wanton who allowed her breasts to be touched. In the eyes of those withered mummies with tits so shrivelled that they could throw them over their shoulders, I had committed an unpardonable crime. It was a grave misdemeanour and I deserved expulsion. How I would have liked such a sentence!

'But my mother appealed to them, saying that if I were allowed to stay, she would force me to take the veil. As I had foreseen, the offer was accepted. I barricaded myself in my room, but the nuns forced open the door. I bit, scratched and kicked them and tore their wimples from their heads. I defended myself so effectively that the six sisters, including the Mother Superior, had to give up.

'Nevertheless, my rage was supplanted by fatigue. I was dispirited as I had been courageous, and I burst into tears. The thought of the jeers and mockery I would have to undergo plunged me into gloom. Then I determined to go to my mother for advice and help.

'As I opened the door and stepped out into the corridor, I tripped on an object on the floor.

'Fumbling in the dusk on the floor to learn what it could be, I found it. You can imagine my feelings when I saw an instrument which was a faithful reproduction of what so preoccupied me, namely, a prick.

'"What in heaven's name is that?" I asked the sister who was keeping guard on my room.

'"You'll soon find out," she calmly replied. "Because you are so attractive, many handsome young chevaliers will be more happy to instruct you in its usage. This is an artificial prick, my dear, and a prick is the name for the male organ. It is called the member *par excellence*, because of the pleasure it gives. If women would render it the adoration it deserves, the real thing, I mean, they would call it a god. Indeed, it is a deity worthy of worship, and the cunt is its domain. Pleasure is its element and it unerringly seeks it in the most hidden recesses. Penetrating and probing, it locates it and then dives into it, receiving and giving raptures. In the cunt it is born, lives, dies, and revives in order to continue its relentless task. But by itself it is nothing. Without the sight or thought of a cunt, the proud pike becomes flabby, cowardly, shrivelled, and ashamed to show itself. But when it meets its partner, it is arrogant, ardent and impetuous. It threatens, attacks and breaks down every barrier."

'"Just a moment," I interrupted the sister. "You

forget that you are talking to a beginner, and your eulogy of this merely confuses me. One of these days, I believe I shall worship this god, but I don't know much about it yet. Could you speak in simpler language so that I can understand?"

'"Gladly," the nun answered. "When inactive, the prick is soft, limp and short. But when men see a woman they want or get erotic fantasies, it is transformed. We can bring about this change by opening our bodices and letting the men see our breasts or revealing to their eager eyes a slender waist or a shapely leg. It's not necessary to have a pretty face. More often than not, it is a trifle that catches their attention, and then their imagination gets to work. It gives firmness to flabby breasts, flatness to swollen bellies, sleekness to wrinkled skins, and the flush of youth to withered cheeks. Then the prick swells, stretches out, and hardens, and the longer and harder it is, the more delight a woman receives from it, because it fills the hole more fully, penetrates more deeply, rubs more vigorously, and produces more divine raptures."

'I told her how deeply indebted I was to her for her information. And I said that I would display my legs and breasts on every possible occasion.

'"Be careful," she warned me. "That's not the way to arouse men. It's more of an art than you think. Men are funny. They don't like to feel they are indebted to us for the delights we give them. They think they are doing us a favour. And they always want something left to their imagination. And a woman loses nothing by indulging them. When a man wants a woman, she, to him, is the most desirable object in the world. There is nothing he wants more. As soon as Monsieur sees the Madame or Mademoiselle who strikes his fancy, he burns with a yen to insert his prick into her cunt. But he won't tell you that. He merely says that he is in love with you."

Delighted with what Sister Monique told me, I was more impatient than ever to hear the end of her story, and I urged her to continue. After catching her breath, she began to discuss the contrivance she had picked up.

'I had often heard of the dildo, and I knew it was the instrument with which the mothers superior consoled themselves for lack of men. It is an exact imitation of a prick and designed to perform its function. It is hollow and can be filled with warm milk to take the place of semen. After a bit of practice in using it, you can scarcely tell the difference from the real thing. The milk squirts when you squeeze it at the right moment and inundates you just like the man's juice.

'Apparently, in the ruckus with the nuns, the instrument had been jostled out of one of their pockets. I went back in my room and locked the door. As I held the article in my hand, all my grief and anxiety disappeared. Although its size frightened me, it also fascinated me. I could not wait to try it out. A sweet warmth ran through my body in anticipation of the pleasure I was going to enjoy. Already I was shuddering and panting.

'Without taking my eyes off the dildo, I undressed with all the eagerness of a young bride about to enter the nuptial couch and then I got into bed with the instrument in my hand.

'But, my dear Suzon, you can imagine my despair

when I found that I could not get it in. In my desperate efforts, I thought that my poor little cunt was going to be ripped open. The pain was intolerable when I spread open the lips and tried to insert the contraption. But I did not give up. Then I was struck with the happy idea that some sort of grease would facilitate the entrance. I took some cream, which I rubbed both on the dildo and my cunt. That helped. I did not mind the indescribable hurt, so great was my pleasure. But it was so big that I could not get it all the way in. In desperation, I gave it one last mighty shove, but it bounced out, leaving me in frustrated agony.

'"Ah," I cried. "If only Verland were here. No matter how big his is, I would be able to take it. Yes, I would suffer anything, even help him torture me, and die happy as long as it was in me. The pains would be delights. I would hug him as hard as I could, and he would do the same to me. I would cover his lips and eyes with burning kisses. He would eagerly respond to my transports, and I would idolize him, adore him. Our souls would become one through the union of our bodies. Ah, Verland, why aren't you with me? You could do anything you want with me, anything. Why don't you come, you cruel monster. I'm all alone, alas, with nothing but a deceptive replica, a poor substitute, which serves merely to augment my despair and frustration.

'"Cursed instrument," I said, addressing the dildo and shaking it with a vengeance, "go and service some other poor creature, for you are of no use to me. My finger is a thousand times better than you."

'Immediately, I reverted to my finger and gave myself so much bliss that I forgot about the dildo.

Falling back with exhaustion, I fell asleep with my thoughts on Verland.

'The next morning, I got up, dressed, and to commence my emancipation, I ripped to shreds my veil which I regarded as a symbol of servitude. That done, my heart was lighter for I felt it was the first step to liberty. As I was pacing up and down my room, my eyes fell on that damned dildo. I picked it up and sat on my bed, where I began to investigate it closely. I could not help but admire its beauty. Caressing it, I was impressed by its length. It was so thick that I could barely wrap my fingers around it. What a shame it was so big that I could not make use of it.

'Although I realised I could not utilize it, I still lifted up my skirt and attempted to insert it. It caused the same burning pain as the night before. But it so excited me that I again had to resort to my finger. Never before had I masturbated so hard. My finger went in and out like a piston. When I had finished, I had an idea that I was very proud of. Since I had nothing to lose, I decided to depart from the convent in a burst of glory. I was going to take the device to the Mother Superior and enjoy her reaction.

'Going to the nun's suite, I relished in advance the consternation the sight of the dildo was going to cause her. Finding her alone, I saucily addressed her.

'"You realise that after what happened yesterday and the way you affronted me, I cannot honourably remain in the convent."

'She looked at me with surprise, and since she did not answer, I felt free to continue.

'"If I did something wrong, I would have deserved to be punished, but I did not. It was that vile Verland who wronged me, and I had no chance to defend myself. A simple reprimand would have been sufficient. You did not have to try and take me by force."

'"A reprimand?" she drily asked. "A simple reprimand for an action such as yours? You had to be made an example of, and if it were not for the consideration we have for your mother who is a saintly woman, you would have been expelled."

'"You don't punish all the wrongdoers," I accused her heatedly.

'"If you tell me who they are, I'll see that they will get what is coming to them," she answered.

'"You know I would not stoop that low," I retorted, "but among them are some of your nuns who so brutally tried to inflict indignities on me yesterday."

'"You're going too far," the Mother Superior cried. "Your heart and mind are depraved and corrupted. In addition to your base conduct, you are calumniating the chastest of women, models of virtue and piety."

'After permitting her to finish the eulogy of the sisters, I coolly took the dildo out of my pocket and presented it to her.

'"Here you are," I told her. "Here's evidence of the chastity and saintliness of at least one of your sisters."

'As she fingered it, I carefully examined her features. Returning my scrutiny, she blushed. From the look in her eyes, I had no doubt that the dildo belonged to her.

'"Oh, my dear child," she sighed, casting her eyes upwards, "how is it possible that there are women so abandoned by God in this house of the Lord to make use of such an infamous instrument. I can't get over it. But do not tell anyone about this matter. If you do, I'll have to take stern measures and make an investigation, but I would prefer to keep it under cover. But, my dear child, do you still want to leave us? Why don't you go back to your room, and I'll take care of everything. I'll say that it was all a mistake. You won't have to worry about the other girls. And I'll have a long talk with Mademoiselle Verland." Casting another look at the dildo, she muttered: "How cunning the devil is. What a diabolic, foul instrument. May God forgive her who made use of this."

'As she was finishing her speech, my mother entered the room.

'"What's this all about, Madame?" she asked, addressing the Mother Superior. "And you, Monique," she said, turning to me, "what are you doing here?"

'Not knowing what to say, I stuttered, turned red, and lowered my eyes. When my mother kept after me, the Mother Superior broke in and defended me with spirit. If she did not say that I was completely blameless, she made it clear that I had done nothing seriously wrong. My only error was my imprudence to let a young man slip his hand through the grille and grab my breast. And he would never again be permitted in the confines of the convent. She concluded by stating that it was Mademoiselle Verland who was in fault for having spread the story which should have been kept quiet, if not for the reputation of her brother, at least for mine. She would see to it there would be no disagreeable consequences for myself. I could not ask for anything more. I emerged from the escapade with my reputation unsullied. My mother was smiling with tenderness at me.

'Souls zealous for the glory of God are able to reap

advantage from everything. Although I was in the clear, my mother and the nun agreed that I would have to do the sacrament of penitence with Father Jerome.

'When I was locked up with the priest, I was reluctant to confess my sins and he had to force them out of me. Heaven knows what pleasure the old lecher had in hearing them. I did not tell him everything, for I did not think God considered it a sin if a poor girl tries to satisfy her desires by herself when they become too strong. Besides, whose fault is it that those erotic desires are planted in her? If she attempts to quench the flames that are consuming her, she uses the means nature has given her, and there is nothing wrong in that.

'In spite of the harmless secrets I revealed to Father Jerome, he refused to give me absolution, guessing correctly that I was holding out on him. When he permitted me to go, it was already night. I was so exhausted after the ordeal that I sat down on the *prie-dieu* near the altar and there fell asleep. During my slumber, I had the most charming dream. I was with Verland who was holding me in his arms. When he pressed me with his thighs, I spread open mine and lent myself to all his delightful movements. He was fondling my breasts in a delirium of joy, squeezing and kissing them.

'The bliss was so great that I woke up and, to my wonderment, I was really in the arms of a man. But it was not Verland. I could not see who it was for I was held tightly from behind. It did not matter, for I was ecstatic. Something hard and hot was penetrating me. Suddenly, I felt myself drenched with a hot fluid. Then I became aware that a similar liquid was gushing forth from my body in delicious jets and blending with what he was pouring out a second time. I fell forward senseless on the *prie-dieu*.

'This joy, if it lasted forever, would be a thousand times more delightful than the promised in heaven, but alas, it ended all too quickly.

'I was seized with terror at the thought that I was alone at night in the chapel with a man I did not know. Who could he be? But I was too frightened to make an attempt to learn his identity. In fact, I could not move. I closed my eyes and trembled like a leaf. My tremors became more violent when I felt my hand being pressed and kissed. Still, I could not move. But I was somewhat relieved when a deep voice whispered in my ear: "Don't be afraid. It's only I."

'The voice which I vaguely recalled having heard before restored my courage sufficiently so that I was able to ask who he was, but I still did not dare look at him. My assailant informed me that he was Martin, Father Jerome's valet. This discovery dispelled my fears, and I was now able to turn my eyes on him. Martin was a little blond fellow, quite good looking, and with flashing eyes. I could see that he was as nervous as I. He seemed unable to make up his mind whether to attack me again or take flight. He regarded me as if it were up to me to make the decision for him. I don't have to tell you that I certainly was not angry with him, and my eyes reflected the raptures I had just enjoyed. Perceiving that I bore him no rancor, he threw himself in my arms which warmly received him.

'We did not worry in the slightest about being surprised. Since love forgives anything, we felt no sense of impropriety when he stretched my body on the steps of the altar, lifted my skirt, and ran his hand over my legs and thighs. Just as stimulated as he, I extended my hand gropingly to his prick, and, oh wonder, for the first time in my life I had the ineffable pleasure of fondling that noble organ. How delicious my sentiments were. Slender but long, it was just the thing for me. Now I felt a voluptuous itch as I squeezed the beloved rod. I regarded it lovingly, fondled it some more, put it on my breast, brought it to my mouth, sucked, and tried to swallow it.

'During this time, Martin had his finger in my cunt in which he stirred as in a kettle of soup, then pushing it in and out, renewing and increasing my raptures at every motion. His kisses covered my stomach, my Venus mount, and my thighs. Abandoning them, he wetted my breasts with his tongue and gently nibbled the nipples. Of course, I made no attempt to resist these amorous attacks. Letting myself fall back, I dragged him down on me. Clutched firmly in my hand was the object of all my desires which I attempted to introduce into myself to obtain more solid pleasures. What we had been doing was merely the *hors d'oeuvres* of the main meal. Animated by the same urge, he pressed himself to me and began to shove.

'"Stop, dear Martin," I pleaded with him between my sighs. "Not so fast. Just a moment."

'Writhing under him, I spread my legs wide and wrapped them around his back. My thighs were next to his, my belly was glued to his, my bosom was squashed by his chest, our mouths were pressed together, our tongues were searching for one another, and our exhalations blended.

'"Oh, Monique," he panted. "What a wonderful

position! It is perfect for love-making."

'I was too engrossed in savouring to the full the thrill I was experiencing to answer him.

'Impatience prevented me from enjoying it at greater length. I had a sudden spasm at precisely the moment Martin did, and our bliss vanished. We were still locked together, but desire and pleasure refused our invitation to return.

'It is time, Suzon,' Monique continued, 'to tell you what that holy water was that Father Jerome sprinkled on you that time he was giving you absolution.

'My first reaction, when Martin slipped out of my arms, was to touch the spot which had received the most vigorous punishment. Inside and out, it was covered with the effusion that had caused my raptures. But now it had lost its warmth, and it was as cold as ice. It was fuck, as one calls the white matter that is discharged from the prick and the cunt. The emissions were the result of the reciprocal friction of our sexual parts. And a man or a woman can produce it by themselves with the hand. And fuck was what Father Jerome wetted you with.'

'What?' I asked Monique. 'Is that what you just spilled?'

'Of course,' she casually replied. 'And didn't you ever feel your cunt all moist? That dampness is fuck, my little one. The pleasure you experienced is much less than that enjoyed with a man for what he gives us, mingling with what we give him, penetrates us, inflames us, kills us, revives us, and sears us. Oh, what raptures, dear Suzon! But let me tell you the rest of my story.

'My clothing was all rumpled, as you can well

imagine after such strenuous activity. I straightened out my dress as best I could and asked Martin what time it was.

'"Oh, it's not late," he assured me.

'But I heard the bell ringing, announcing that it was time to go to bed.

'"I have to go, Martin, but before I do, tell me how you happened to be here and how you dared do what you did."

'"You know tomorrow is All Saints' Day and I had come here to put up some decorations. Then I noticed you and I said to myself that there is a pretty girl offering her prayers to God. But I wondered why you were here at such an hour, and when I came up to ask you, I saw that you were asleep. You were snoring, too. I stood there just looking at you for a long time and my heart went pit-a-pat.

'"I determined to take advantage of this unexpected opportunity. When I opened your bodice, I saw two petite hemispheres that were as white as snow. I couldn't help but kiss very gently their pink tips. Seeing that that did not awaken you, I felt the urge to do more. So I lifted your skirt and, damn it, I gave a shove, and well... I fucked you, as you well know."

'Although a little shocked at his crude language, I was charmed by the ingenuous way he explained his actions.

'"Well, my friend," I asked him, "did you enjoy yourself?"

'"You have no idea," he answered, giving me a kiss. "So much so that I am ready to start all over again, that is, if you are willing."

'"No, not now." I told him. "I'll be missed at bed

count. And besides I am exhausted. But you have the key to the chapel. If you would like to come here tomorrow at midnight, leave the door unlocked and wait for me. All right?"

'"Oh, yes," he enthusiastically replied. "We'll have the place to ourselves at that hour. You can be sure I'll be here impatiently waiting for you."

'I gave him like assurance. Prudence won out over desire, and I turned a deaf ear to his plea for "one more little time". I consoled his grief by reminding him of the delights that he would have the next night. After exchanging kisses, I returned to the dormitory without being seen.

'You can imagine my impatience to examine my body and learn what condition it was in after the assaults it had undergone. I had such a burning sensation between my legs that I could hardly walk. Locking the door and drawing the curtains, I lit a candle and investigated myself with one leg on the bed and the other on the floor. I was surprised to find that the lips of my cunt which were so firm and chubby had become flaccid and shrivelled. The hair covering them smelt of his effusion and were now a mass of crinkly curls. The interior was an angry red and very tender. In spite of its sensitivity, it itched so much that I had to stick my finger in, but the sharp pain made me withdraw it immediately. I rubbed it against the bed post, covering it with the traces of Martin's virility. That so excited me that I forgot my suffering and tiredness. Gradually, my eyes became heavy, and I fell into a deep sleep broken only by the delicious dreams of what I had experienced.

'The next day, no mention was made of my absence

from classes and meals. When I went to Mass, I held my head high and regarded disdainfully the girls without paying any attention to the muffled whispering and looks cast in my direction. When I saw Martin enter the chapel, I forgot everything. More than one of my fellow students would have willingly exchanged the spiritual nourishment they were receiving for the raptures Martin could have bestowed on them.

'The regards I cast at my lover were more adoring than those I gave the altar. In the eyes of a woman of the world, Martin would be nothing but an impudent rascal, but with his youth and native charm, he was the epitome of love to me. I saw that he was running his eyes over all the girls, trying to pick me out. I did not want him to spot me, but I was pleased that he made the attempt. The sight of him made me all the more impatient for the rendezvous we had agreed on for that night.

'The hour that I so ardently yearned for finally came. The chimes sounded midnight. Trembling with anticipation, I tip-toed down the corridor. Although everybody was sound asleep, I felt as if the eyes of the world were on me. The only illumination to guide my steps was my love.

'As I quietly made my way down the hall, I was seized with a sudden fear that perhaps Martin might not keep his promise. If he did not show up, I thought that I would die of grief.

'But my dear Martin was there, waiting for me. He was as eager as I was punctual. I was very lightly dressed for it was warm, and also I had noticed the previous night that too much clothing was a nuisance.

'No sooner was I at the door than my heart began to

beat more rapidly. I was incapable of speech. All I could do was whisper "Martin" to announce my arrival to my lover. He swept me into his arms, and I returned caress for caress. We remained locked in each other's arms for interminable minutes. Recovering from these initial transports, we commenced to arouse one another to greater ones. I put my hand on the source of my desires while his hand groped to the spot where he knew I was eagerly awaiting him.

'We quickly stripped, making a bed of our discarded clothing, and lay down on it. Our ecstasies came in rapid succession for more than two hours. We gave ourselves up to each one as if we never would have another again. In the blaze of sensuousness, one abandons oneself completely. Excess is not enough. But Martin's forces were not the equal of mine, for finally he had to give up the battle.

'Our bliss lasted barely a month, but during that time, what rapturous nights we spent!

'Now hear me, Suzon,' Monique told me earnestly. 'Promise again that this is a secret between you and me. Nobody must ever know about it.

'I loved well but not wisely, but a girl loses her head with such an attractive boy as Martin was. The anxiety I suffered was a dear price to pay for the delicious pleasures I had tasted. How I repented those sweet hours! The consequences of my weakness seemed so horrible that I could do nothing but wail and sob the whole day long.'

'What was it?' I asked Monique.

'I noticed that I missed my period,' she replied. 'To my dismay, eight days passed without any sign of it. I heard that when it is that late, it is almost a sure sign of pregnancy. I was nearly out of my mind with worry, for I was positive that I was going to be big with child.

'Well, Martin had caused my condition and he would have to rescue me from my condition. My melancholy discovery did not prevent me from seeing him, however. Although I was anxiety-ridden and nervous, my love for him was still as powerful as ever. When he was in me, I momentarily forgot my woes. Besides, nothing worse could happen to me by going on with him as before. I had reached bottom which, in itself, was a sort of comfort.

'One night, after having received from Martin those tokens of affection that never abated in intensity, he heard my sad sighs and felt my hand, which was in his, shaking. He perceived that I was distressed. He worriedly asked what was wrong, and when he learned the cause of my melancholy, he tenderly commiserated with me.

'"Ah, Martin, you have ruined me. Don't say that my love for you has cooled, for I bear in my belly a proof which is driving me to despair. I am pregnant."

'His astonishment gave place to profound reverie, and I did not know what to make of it. Martin was my sole hope in the cruel circumstances. What was I to think of his hesitation? Was he considering ways to extricate himself from the situation? Perhaps he was thinking of flight, leaving me to face the consequences alone. Inwardly, I prayed that he would stay with me, for I would rather die loving him than hating him. At that thought, I started to shed warm tears. But he caused them to stop when he promised to do everything he could to help me. I felt as if I had been called back from the dead.

'Overjoyed at his reassurance, I was curious to learn how he was going to rid me of my burden. He told me that he was going to give me a potion he had found in his master's closet. Sister Angelica had used it successfully, he said.

'I was all ears at his casual remark. I was more than eager to learn about what had gone on between the monk and the sister. For the latter I nursed a mortal hatred because of her treatment of me the day of the incident with Verland. I had always thought her as pure as the driven snow, but it seemed that I was wrong. Apparently, she had been able to conceal her real propensities under a mask of unremitting devoutness. So she had been carrying on with Father Jerome.

'Martin told me all the details. While snooping among Father Jerome's effects, he came across a letter from Angelica in which she informed her lover that she was in the same embarrasing state I was. And Father Jerome had given her a phial of the liqueur he was going to purloin and give to me. Sister Angelica wrote him back, acknowledging the receipt of the potion and informing him that it had worked perfectly. The danger was gone and they could resume their relationship.

'"My dear friend," I urgently said to Martin. "Bring me that medicine tomorrow without fail. You will rid me of all my worries, and I'll be able to get my revenge on that hateful Angelica."

'Not realising what my imprudent request would cost, he brought me the next night the potion along with the damaging letters.

'I couldn't wait to read them, but I reflected that if I

lit a candle, I might be noticed, and so I restrained my impatience to read them until morning. When the sun cast its first rays into my room, I eagerly perused them. They were written in a passionate tone in which she described her erotic fury, using expressions and terms I never would have believed her capable of. She showed no restraint in revealing her feelings and ardour, for she counted on Father Jerome burning the missives, as she counselled him, but he was unwise enough not to have followed her advice. And I had some powerful ammunition in my hands.

'For some time, I pondered ways to make best use of this incriminating evidence in order to bring about the downfall of my foe. It was too risky for me to hand them over to the Mother Superior myself since I would have to explain how they came into my possession. And having someone else deliver them was also out of the question.

'I considered leaving them under her door, but I discarded that idea, too. Martin would come under suspicion, and he was too precious to lose. Finally, I decided to postpone my plans for revenge for the time being, that is to say, when I would be out of danger.

'I had asked Martin for an armistice of eight days, after which the elixir was to have had its effect. When the period was over, I could carry out my plans. And my success exceeded my fondest hopes. The Mother Superior found the letters slipped under her door. Summoning Sister Angelica to her apartment, she found her guilty on the spot. Perhaps she might have shown some mercy if it had not been for the rage that devoured the Mother Superior. She was envious of Sister Angelica. Although she did not lack, as I have mentioned, the means to blunt the points of the needles of the flesh, a dildo is a poor substitute for the real thing. And the Mother Superior could not forgive Angelica for having had the genuine article.

'Angelica was ordered to expiate in solitary confinement in a remote cell for an indefinite period and on a diet of bread and water.

'It was not long before I repented of what I had done. I had flattered myself that the storm would fall only on Sister Angelica, but it went farther than I had expected. Father Jerome, irritated at seeing his favourite mistress taken away, suspected that his servant, my lover, was the root of it all, and blamed him for the whole affair. He kicked Martin out of the convent and I never saw that delightful boy again.

'That's my story, Suzon,' she ended. 'Please keep it to yourself. Now you know the pleasures I enjoyed. If he were only here, I would suffocate him with my kisses.'

The memory of Martin excited her, and her recital produced the same effect on me. Unconsciously, we began games which compensated for her loss. They reminded her of the enjoyment that she had had with him. Momentarily deceived that I was only a young girl, she imagined that I was he. On me, she lavished the same compliments and endearments she had employed with her lover.

For myself, I could not imagine any greater pleasure than I was having with Monique. In her desire to recapture the past, she showed me the favourite position she and Martin had assumed. Our heads were at opposite ends. I learned later that the posture is commonly known as the sixty-nine. In that stance, we embraced each other until our fluids exuded. A momentary pause, and then we experienced new raptures. We were enchanted with one another, and it was only exhaustion that put an end to our games.

Both delighted, we separated with the mutual promise to repeat our revels the next day. Our games stopped only when I left to come here.

## *In Flagrante*

Since Suzon had not been bashful about telling me her actions with Monique, my hopes for success rose immeasurably. But I determined not to rush matters so as not to ruin my chances. I tried to conceal my agitation, but it did not escape the eyes of Suzon.

I asked if Sister Monique was pretty.

'She is as beautiful as an angel,' Suzon declared. 'Her waist is slender, her skin white and satiny, her creamy complexion is set off by deep blue eyes and crimson lips, and she has the most adorable bosom in the world.'

'I feel sorry for her, now that she has lost you,' I remarked. 'I don't envy her, having to spend the rest of her life in a nunnery.'

'That's where you are wrong,' Suzon corrected me. 'She took the veil only a short time ago just to please her mother, but she has not yet made the final vows. Her fate depends on her brother who was seriously wounded in a brawl in a brothel. If he dies, which seems likely, Monique will be the only child, and her mother would not want to see the family come to an end.'

'A brothel!' I exclaimed. 'What is that?'

'I'll tell you what Monique told me,' Suzon answered. 'She seems to know everything about things like that. It's a place where girls and women of easy virtue gather. Their calling is to accept the attentions of lustful men and lend themselves to their caprices for a fee. That is how they earn their living.'

'Oh, I would give anything to live in a city with places like that!' I cried. 'Wouldn't you, too, Suzon?'

She did not answer, but I could see from her expression that she shared my desire.

'I bet that Sister Monique would like to work in such a place,' I added.

'I think so, too. She's mad about men,' Suzon concurred.

'How about you?' I asked suggestively.

'I can't deny that I have a yen for men,' she replied demurely. 'I adore them, but there are too many risks in having anything to do with them.'

'Oh, it's not as dangerous as all that!' I pooh-poohed.

'Come, come, Saturnin. If two women make love together, neither of them can get pregnant.'

'How about the lady next door?' I argued. 'She's been married a long time. She does it all the time with her husband, and she has never had a child.'

This example seemed to shake her convictions.

'Listen, dear Suzon,' I declared excitedly, for I had just been struck with a brilliant idea. 'Sister Monique told you that when Martin put his prick into her, she was flooded with his fluid, and I am sure it was that juice that made her pregnant.'

'Perhaps, but what is the point?' Suzon asked, averting her face to conceal the desire I felt was rising in her.

'What I am trying to say,' I went on, 'is that if this

ejaculation in the woman causes pregnancy, the man can prevent it by withdrawing his prick just before it comes out.'

'That's not possible,' Suzon demurred, although her eyes were sparkling with excitement. 'Didn't you ever set two dogs in action, one on top of the other? Even if you beat them with a club, they won't separate. They are joined so closely that it is impossible. Isn't that the same with a man and a woman?'

The objection took me aback for the example was apt. Suzon was looking at me as if asking me to give her a convincing rebuttal. She seemed to regret having pointed out a difficulty that I could not overcome. I wracked my brain.

Suddenly, I recalled that Father Polycarpe the preceding day had no trouble in getting off Toinette. I would have told Suzon about this, but I thought it preferable to let her see for herself.

'Come with me, Suzon,' I said confidently, 'I am going to show you how wrong you are.'

I got up, helping her do the same but first shoving my hand under her skirt. She pushed it away, but she was not angry.

'Where are you taking me?' she demanded as I led her down the path. The little wanton thought I wanted to bring her to some spot where we wouldn't be seen, and I think she would have liked nothing better. But to be sure, I wanted her to regard Toinette and the reverend father who must have been up to their tricks for he had not yet left. I answered that we were going to a spot where she would see something that would amuse her.

'And where is that?' she persisted.

'To my room,' I replied simply.

'To your room,' she repeated. 'Oh, I would never go there with you. You'll try to do something to me.'

She allowed herself to be persuaded when I swore that I would not do anything without her consent.

We reached my chamber without being seen. As we tip-toed down the hall, hand in hand. I could feel that Suzon was trembling. Putting my finger to my lips as a sign not to speak, I put my eye to the knot-hole in the partition, but they were not there yet.

'What are you going to show me?' she whispered, intrigued by my mysterious air.

'You'll see in good time,' I told her, and turned her on her back on the bed. I inserted my hand between her legs and was up to her garter, when she fiercely said that she would make a fuss if I did not leave her alone. She went so far as to pretend that she was going to go out, and I was simple enough to believe her. Dismayed, I began to plead with her, and in spite of my babbling incoherence, she consented to remain.

Then I heard the door of Ambroise's room open. I took heart and waited until Suzon's curiosity would do for me what I was not able to accomplish myself.

'There they are,' I jubilantly whispered to my companion, pulling her back to the bed near the peephole. Peering through it, I saw the good father beginning the game by fondling Toinette's magnificent breasts which had popped out of her bodice. Now they were motionless, locked in each other's arms. They were so totally absorbed in each other that it seemed that they were going to celebrate the great rite of contemplation.

I waited until they had made some progress before

nodding my head for Suzon to come and look. Bored with meditation, Toinette freed herself from the monk and let her chemise and dress drop to the floor in preparation for the ceremony. Oh, what a delicious sight it was! And because of Suzon's presence, it stimulated me all the more.

Burning with curiosity when she noticed my attentiveness at the aperture, she came up to me.

'Let me have a look,' she whispered, giving me a nudge.

I gladly relinquished my post, unable to wish for anything better. Remaining at her side, I watched carefully for the emotions that the spectacle was going to produce on her face. She blushed, but her eye remained glued to the hole.

While she was avidly regarding the scene in the adjoining room, my hand crept up her legs and met merely a token resistance. Now my hand was in the vice of her thighs, but as the amorous combat she was watching increased in intensity, she gradually relaxed them. I could have counted every stroke Toinette and Father Polycarpe exchanged by the twitches I felt on Suzon's satiny buttocks. Finally, I reached my goal. Now, without the slightest sign of objection, she spread her legs in complete surrender to allow my hand to do as it wished.

Taking advantage of the occasion, I put my finger on the sensitive spot, but it was so tight that it could barely go in. I felt her quiver as my finger worked its way in. She gave a start at each sign of progress.

'Now I have you, Suzon,' I thought triumphantly.

Immediately, I flipped up her skirt and what met my delighted eyes was the loveliest, the whitest, the most perfectly rounded, the firmest, the most delicious derriere it is possible to imagine. Never before or since had I paid my devotions to such an alluring altar. I paid those adorable hemispheres the worship due them with a thousand impassioned kisses. Never shall I forget that divine behind.

But Suzon possessed other charms which piqued my curiosity.

Getting back on my feet, I undid her bodice and released two little breasts, hard, firm, and seemingly fashioned by love itself. Rising and falling, they begged for a male hand to control their violent heavings. Mine came to their succour and tenderly squeezed each in turn and then both together.

Unable to tear her eyes away from the spectacle she was viewing. Suzon lent herself automatically to my manipulations. Her submissiveness charmed me at first, but her prolonged concentration on the performance taking place in the next room soon began to irritate me. I was burning with a fire that only she could extinguish, but she refused to leave her post.

I wanted to see Suzon completely nude in order to be able to take in all at once her exquisite body that I was kissing and fondling. To my experienced mind, that was all that was required to satisfy my desires.

Quickly, I summoned up enough courage to strip the unprotesting Suzon of every stitch of her clothing, and then I did the same to myself. Now that both of us were stark naked, I tried every which way to assuage my passions, but she remained unresponsive. Repeated kisses and tender but energetic caresses failed to stir her. Her thoughts were elsewhere.

Even though our position was uncomfortable, I

tried to take her from behind. Although she spread her legs and buttocks dutifully, my prick could not get in. I inserted my finger into her adorable little cunt, and when I withdrew it, it was dripping with the love liqueur. Again I tried to penetrate her with my prick, but my efforts were fruitless.

'Suzon,' I muttered, enraged at her preoccupation with our neighbours which prevented me from obtaining the satisfaction I was yearning for, 'enough is enough. Come now. We can have as much pleasure as those two.'

When she turned her eyes to me, they were glistening.

Taking her tenderly in my arms, I bore her to my bed and turned her on her back. Without my asking, she widened her thighs. My eyes were fixed on a tiny crimson button rise peeping out from a tuft of golden fleece which partially concealed a mound whose delicate tint the most skilful brush would have difficulty in reproducing.

Motionless but eager, Suzon awaited the marks of my passion which I was burning to bestow on her. But I was so incredibly clumsy, going either too high or too low, that my efforts proved in vain. Finally, her dainty little hand acted as a guide, and I felt that I was now on the right track. But I experienced an unexpected pain on the path that I believed was strewn with flowers.

A little squeak and start proved that Suzon was sharing my suffering. But neither of us was disheartened. Suzon seconded my exertions by trying to widen the road, and I shoved in all the harder. It seemed that I was half way there. Suzon, whose cheeks were flushed a bright pink, was panting heavily. The perspiration on our bodies mingled. From Suzon's sensuous expression, I could see that rapture was supplanting pain as it was with me. I was wallowing in the anticipation of approaching bliss.

Heavens! Why do such divine moments have to be ruined by the cruelest of misfortunes? We were both bucking in an erotic frenzy, when my bed, which I proudly thought was to be the site of my victory and delight, betrayed me. The slats under the mattress gave way under our vigorous bouncings, and we crashed to the floor with a frightfully loud thud.

The tumble could have helped me by forcing open the last barrier, but Suzon was terrified and made violent efforts to free herself from me. In a rage of desire and despair, I held her only more tightly, an action which was to cost us dear.

Toinette, alerted by the din, opened my door, entered and caught us *in flagrante*. What a sight for the eyes of a mother! She was petrified with astonishment and indignation. She was so dumbfounded that she could not budge. She regarded us with eyes inflamed not by anger but lust. Her mouth opened to speak, but no words came out.

Suzon was now in a dead faint. Wrathfully I glared at Toinette, and pityingly, looked at Suzon. Emboldened at my mother's immobility and silence, undoubtedly caused by amazement, I decided to salvage as much as I could from wreckage. I nudged Suzon who was showing some signs of returning life by heaving deep sighs, fluttering her eyelids, and wiggling her backside. Now she was at the peak of pleasure and flowing like a torrent. Her ecstasy soon aroused a similar sensation in me.

At the supreme moment, Toinette grasped me by the shoulders and I spurted on Suzon's stomach.

Father Polycarpe, also curious as to the cause of the ruckus, entered the room and was equally stupefied at what he saw: naked Suzon lying on her back with one arm over her eyes and the other over the seat of shame. It was an ineffective attempt to conceal her charms from the eyes of the lascivious man of God. It was such an enticing picture that I could not tear my glance from her. And my prick, regaining its pristine virility, stood up proudly.

In spite of fear, fury, and surprise, nothing had cooled my ardour. Looking down, I could see my prick, hard as iron, throbbing madly. There was longing in Toinette's eyes as she regarded it, and there was forgiveness in her expression as she looked at me. I was barely aware that she was ushering me out of the room. When I realised what she was doing, I felt some misgivings and uneasiness. Naked as I was, I followed her docilely. Not a word was exchanged between us.

When we were in her room, I noticed that she carefully locked the door. A sudden sense of fear snapped me out of my stupor, and I wanted to escape. Searching for some place of refuge and not finding any, I flung myself on the bed. Realising the cause of my terror, Toinette tried to reassure me.

'Don't worry, my dear boy,' she soothingly said. 'I don't mean you any harm.'

I did not believe her and kept my head buried under the pillow. She started tugging at me, and I could not resist, because do you know where she grabbed me? By the prick! There was no help for it; I had to emerge from my hiding-place.

When I came out into the open, my eyes popped open when I saw that Toinette was just as naked as I. She was as bare as a new-born infant.

She had my virility still in her hand, and she made it clear that she was not going to release it. Her expert fondling made it rise again. I don't think it ever was so hard. All thoughts of Suzon were gone, for all my desires were concentrated on the woman before me, particularly, on one special fringed spot.

Still clutching me, she lay on the bed, forcing me down on top of her.

'Come, my little Adonis,' she coaxed with a kiss on my cheek. 'Put it into me.' As I promptly obeyed, she sighed with deep satisfaction, 'That's perfect.'

Without any difficulty whatsoever, I was soon down to the very bottom of her. The flood I released in her was so copious that I nearly fainted as Suzon did. What a woman she was! A young man like me could not desire a better one for the first time. That I had cuckolded my father did not bother me in the slightest.

What food for thought this recital must give to those readers who had never experienced such erotic frenzies. But they can go their own moral way. As for myself, I like to fuck.

I was about to do a repeat performance, to which Toinette was more than agreeable, when we were disturbed by a loud screech coming from my room. Realising what was happening, she quickly got out of bed, dressed, and after telling me to hide under the bed, she ran out of the room, yelling at Father Polycarpe.

No sooner had she gone than my eye was on the peep-hole. Through it, I saw the monk apparently trying to ravish Suzon. Although she was now dressed, her petticoat and the priest's robe were both up to their waists. Apparently, the shrieks were caused by the amazing diameter of the monk's organ which was far too thick ever to effect passage into a dainty little cunt like Suzon's.

The skirmish ended with Toinette's appearance in the room. With a lunge, she was on the assailant and his victim, snatching the latter from the priest's arms and giving her several sound smacks on her bottom. Then she shoved Suzon out of the chamber.

One would have thought that she would be furious with Father Polycarpe, but she looked at him, panting heavily. One should keep in mind that a monk is always saucy and impudent. Nevertheless, Father Polycarpe felt a sense of humiliation at having been caught in the act with Suzon, and he inwardly quaked at the reproaches he was sure Toinette was going to rain on his head. He turned red and white and averted his eyes. Strangely enough, Toinette seemed similarly embarrassed.

From my observation post, I expected to witness some violent crisis, but nothing like that occurred. Although the monk was abashed, his prick did not go soft. But then, does the virility of an ecclesiastic ever go soft?

Although Toinette was beside herself with rage, she could not help stealing glances at the monstrous member. At the ravishing sight, her anger subsided to desire. His fears allayed, the monk approached her, and putting his pride in her hand, he whispered loud enough for me to hear: 'If I can't fuck the daughter, at least I'll have the mother again.'

Toinette, always ready to forgive an insult that was a

promise of pleasure, became again a willing victim of the divine's amorous attack. Tumbling on my messed-up bed, they sealed their reconciliation with mutually abundant discharges. At least they seemed copious from the way they were convulsing at the end.

The reader undoubtedly will ask himself what that imp Saturnin was doing while he was watching the events. Did he merely look without some fantasies being aroused?

I was still undressed and excited from the marks of affection Toinette had favoured me with, and the present spectacle stimulated me even more. What do you think I did? I masturbated, of course.

Enraged at not being able to participate in the game, I shook myself in a frenzy and discharged at the moment when the rise and fall of my mother's behind began to subside.

'Well,' commented the monk, 'how do I compare with Saturnin?'

'Did I do anything with Saturnin?' Toinette innocently asked. 'He's hiding under my bed. Just wait until Ambroise comes. He'll give him what he deserves.'

You can imagine with what little pleasure I heard that exchange of dialogue. I continued to listen, but more attentively.

'Now, don't get all worked up,' Father Polycarpe advised her. 'You know as well as I that he is not to stay here forever. He's old enough, don't you think? I'll take him with me when I leave here.'

'I hope he has not found out about us, for he is a real blabbermouth,' she answered. Suddenly, she let out a little squeal and pointed to the wall. 'My god! I never noticed that hole before. The rascal could have seen everything.'

Thinking that she would come to verify her suspicions, I hastily crawled back under the bed from where I was careful not to emerge a second time, despite my desire to hear the conversation which was getting more and more interesting. Impatiently, I bided my time to learn the outcome of their talk, and I had not long to wait.

Somebody entered my prison to release me. I shook with fear lest it be Ambroise, who really would have given me a walloping. But it was Toinette who brought me my clothes and ordered me to get dressed immediately. Although tempted to taunt her on her antics with Father Polycarpe, I held my tongue and quickly obeyed. When I was presentable again, she curtly commanded me to go with her. When I inquired as to where she was taking me, she simply replied that we were going to the parish priest.

I was not pleased with the prospect of seeing that old goat again. In fact, I was quaking in every limb. On more than one occasion, my bottom had received the honour of his attentions, a chore he did not dislike performing, and I was frightened lest he grant me the same favours. But I did not dare voice to Toinette my trepidations. But why she was taking me there, I did not know. Since I saw no alternative, I meekly followed her.

I entered the room and my fears were dispelled when Toinette, presenting me to the awesome character, asked if he would be good enough to keep me for a few days. The phrase 'a few days' reassured me.

'Good,' I thought. 'After a few days, Father

Polycarpe will take me away with him.'

At first, I was delighted at the prospect, but Suzon suddenly crossed my mind. She would be lost to me forever. The thought agonised me, and I was overcome with grief. The experiences and emotions I had just undergone had driven her out of my mind. But now my heart was rent at the idea of leaving her.

In my mind, I saw again all the beauties of her adorable body, her thighs, her rounded buttocks, her swan-like throat, and her firm little white breasts that I worshipped with my kisses. I recalled the delights I had enjoyed with her and compared them with those Toinette had given me. With the latter, I had fainted, but I knew I would have expired on Suzon if we had not been interrupted. What a happy death it would have been! What was going to happen to her, I wondered. How was Toinette going to get revenge on her? Was Suzon going to miss me? Perhaps she is weeping now. She is sobbing and cursing me, the cause of all her misery. I am sure that she hates me. Shall I be able to continue living with the knowledge that she detests me? I, who adore her, would cheerfully suffer the agonies of hell to spare her the slightest sorrow? Such were the gloomy thoughts that threw my soul into turmoil. My melancholy was dispelled at the sound of the dinner bell.

## *The Cure*

Let us leave Suzon for a while. We shall meet up with her again, for she plays an important role in these memoirs. Let us go and have something to eat, and I'll acquaint you with some of the characters who are to figure in my life. We'll begin with the Cure.

The Cure was one of those figures whom it was impossible to regard without laughing. He was no more than four feet tall, with a moon-shaped face illuminated by deep red cheeks that did not come from drinking water, a squashed nose with a ruby tip, little brown darting eyes surmounted by bushy brows, a narrow forehead, and a frizzled beard. Add to all that a mocking air, and you have the Cure. In the village, he was noted for certain talents which are worth more than a handsome face.

Next comes the Cure's housekeeper, Madame Françoise. She was an old witch, as malicious as an old ape and more wicked than a senile demon. Her face showed her fifty years, but women being what they are, she admitted to only thirty-five. She used so much rouge she looked like a bedizened Jezebel, her nose dripped with tobacco snuff, her mouth was a slit from ear to ear, and the few teeth she had left in her gums were wobbly. In her earlier years, she had served the Cure in more ways than one, and in gratitude, he kept her on.

Being in complete charge of the menage, everything went through her hands, including the money, most of which remained stuck to her fingers. She never spoke of the Cure except in the collective pronoun. *We* shall do this and *we* need that.

Under the protection of this grotesque pair lived a girl, ostensibly the ecclesiastic's niece, but it was common knowledge that the relationship was much closer than that. She was a big girl with a beautiful pale complexion only slightly pocked, an admirable bosom, a prominent nose, and tiny but ardent eyes. She was not overly endowed with intelligence.

From time to time, a certain rogue of a theologian came to the presbytery to spend a week or so, less out of friendship for the Cure than his interest in the niece. Later, I'll tell you my role in that affair.

Mademoiselle Nicole, which was the name of the amiable lass, was adored by all the boys, but she gave her preference to the bigger and older ones. Unfortunately, my age and size were against me. It was not that I had not attempted on several occasions to launch a spearhead against this winsome creature, but I was always disdainfully rebuffed. The gift I offered was heartlessly refused. She would not let me prove that I was more of a man than I appeared. To add insult to injury, my amorous attempts were always reported to Madame Françoise who passed them on to the Cure, and the latter showed me no mercy with the rod. I raged at my size, which was the cause of all my woes.

I was getting discouraged at my lack of success with Nicole and with the thrashings I regularly received from the Cure. I did not think I could hold out. But every time I was near the girl, my desires were relit, and I knew that sooner or later something was bound to happen. It did, but before giving an account of it, I have to tell you about Madame Dinville.

I had not forgotten that this lady had asked me to dine with her the next day, and I decided to keep my promise because there was a chance I might find Suzon there. I reasoned that I had been turned over to the Cure because Father Polycarpe suspected that Toinette had given me something other than a beating for my escapade with Suzon and he did not want me to get too accustomed to such chastisements. Toinette had as much reason to remove Suzon from the monk as he had to get me away from Toinette.

As I walked to the chateau, I planned, if Suzon was there, to seduce her behind the bushes in the garden. I was already anticipating the bliss.

Finding the door open, I entered. A deathly silence prevailed. There was not a soul to be seen. Going down the deserted corridor, I opened each door in turn. Each time I went into a room, my heart beat faster in the hope of finding Suzon.

'She will be in this one,' I said to myself, 'and if not, in the next one.'

Sunk in these reflections, I finally came to a chamber that was locked but with the key in the door. I hesitated, but then I thought I had not come this far just to retreat. I boldly opened it. The first thing I saw was a large bed in which apparently someone was sleeping. As I was about to leave, I heard a woman's voice ask who was there. At the same time, the bed curtains were opened and Madame Dinville stuck out her head. I would have fled if the view of her breathtaking breasts had not deprived me of all powers of locomotion.

'If it isn't my little friend Saturnin,' she gaily greeted me. 'Come over here and give me a kiss.'

At this invitation, I became as audacious as I had been timid, and I ran into her outstretched arms.

'I like that,' she remarked in a tone of satisfaction after I had acquitted myself well of a duty which went beyond the bounds of courtesy. 'I like it when a young man is so prompt in obeying.'

Scarcely had she finished these words, when I saw come out of the dressing-room a little simpering figure. He was singing out of tune a popular air and marking the rhythm with little comical pirouettes that perfectly matched his ridiculous voice.

At the appearance of this harlequin whom Madame Dinville addressed as Abbot, I felt embarrassed at the thought that he might have witnessed my passionate kisses. But from his demeanour, he apparently had no suspicions. I now regarded him irritatedly as an intruder whose presence was going to postpone or prevent the raptures I was eager to enjoy.

Carefully examining him, I pondered his appellation of Abbot, for he was dressed like a Paris fop. But then the only ecclesiastics I knew were of the small-town class.

This diminutive Adonis, whose name was Abbot Fillot, was the son of the collector of a nearby town. He was very rich, but God only knows how he got his money. From the way he talked, it was obvious that he was filled with more fatuity than doctrine. He had accompanied Madame Dinville to this bucolic retreat to spend some time with her. To her, there was no difference between an abbot and a schoolboy.

Madame Dinville pulled the bell cord and, to my delight, Suzon appeared. My heart throbbed at the sight of her, and I was so grateful that my hopes had been realised. She did not see me at first, because I was partially hidden behind the curtains of the bed. It was a situation that the Abbot was beginning not to like, for he was smelling a rat.

When Suzon came forward, she immediately spotted me. The colour of her cheeks changed from a pale pink to a deep red. She turned her eyes to the floor, and she was so agitated that she could not speak. I, too, had lost the power of speech. Madame Dinville's charms, which she made no attempt to conceal, had inflamed my imagination, but they now paled in comparison with Suzon's.

If it came to a choice between Dinville and Suzon, how could anyone fail to pick the latter? But I was not given a choice. To have Suzon was only a faint hope, and the enjoyment of Madame Dinville was a sure thing. Her looks assured me so, and her words, although somewhat restrained by the presence of the Abbot, did not belie what her eyes were saying.

After dismissing Suzon to do some errands, Madame Dinville became bolder with me. When I felt her hands on me, I was both confused and disturbed. My desires were divided – one was for pure sensuous pleasure and the other for enjoyment which had something deeper to it. I was so upset that I did not notice the disappearance of the Abbot. Madame Dinville had seen him leave the room, but thinking that I had observed him, too, she did not think it necessary to mention it to me.

Reclining back on her pillow, the lady of the house gave me a languorous regard which told me clearly that she was mine if I wanted to take her. Tenderly, she took my hand and put it between her thighs which were lasciviously opening and closing. Her halfshut eyes were reproving me for my timidity. Under the impression that the Abbot was still in the chamber, I maintained an insane stubbornness that ended by irritating her.

'Are you asleep?' she asked sarcastically.

I told her that I was not asleep, an artless reply that delighted her. For her, I now had the charm of innocence, always appealing to lustful women. Ignorance and naivety gave pique to pleasure.

My continued indifference made Madame Dinville realise that her method of attack was ineffective and that some other stimulant was required to rouse me. Releasing my hand, she stretched her arms with a pretended yawn and exposed to me some of her charms. Her action dispelled the sluggishness I had felt since Suzon's departure. Returning to life, I sensed tingles running through my body. Suzon vanished from my thoughts. Now my regards and desires were concentrated on Madame Dinville. She immediately perceived the effect of her stratagem. To arouse me further and to encourage me, she said she wondered what had happened to the Abbot. I looked around, but I did not see him. That was the last thing that had been holding me back.

'He's gone,' she remarked and added, 'it's rather hot in here.'

With that, she threw off the covers, exposing a dazzling white thigh at the top of which was the edge of a chemise that seemed to have been placed there expressly to prevent my eyes from going any higher, or rather, to excite rather than to satisfy my curiosity. In spite of the covering, I did get a glimpse of a spot of vermilion which made me almost wild.

I shyly took her hand, and rapturously kissed it. There was fire in my eyes and sparkles in hers. One thing led to another without a hitch, but it was ordained that I was never to take full advantage of the opportunities offered me. That damned chambermaid Suzon had been asked to summon appeared just at the wrong moment. I promptly ceased what I was doing. The soubrette, standing at the door, was laughing her head off.

'What's so funny?' Madame Dinville asked, pulling the sheet back over her.

'Hee, hee,' giggled the maid. 'Monsieur the Abbot.'

'Well, what about him?'

So she was laughing at something that had happened to the Abbot, and not at us.

At that moment, the Abbot returned, concealing his face with a cambric handkerchief. The maid's titters increased when she saw him.

'What's wrong with you?' Madame Dinville demanded of him.

'See for yourself,' he answered, showing us a face that looked as if it had been worked over with a rake. 'That's the work of Mademoiselle Suzon.'

'Suzon!' Madame Dinville cried in surprise.

'That's what she did just because I tried to kiss her,' he replied coldly. 'Her kisses are expensive.'

I could not help but be amused at the free and easy manner with which the Abbot spoke of his misfortune, and he bore with indifference Madame Dinville's gibes.

As she dressed, the Abbot, in spite of the sad state of his face, flirted with her, made outrageous remarks, helped her arrange her hair, and told stories that made her laugh until tears came to her eyes. We then went down to dine.

We were four at the table, Madame Dinville, Suzon, the Abbot, and I. The one who cut the most miserable figure was I, seated opposite Suzon. The Abbot, next to her, maintained his composure in spite of Madame's continued banter. I could see that Suzon was confused, but from her furtive looks at me, I guessed that she would have preferred to be alone with me. Her wistful regard drove all thoughts of Madame Dinville from my head, and I impatiently awaited the end of the repast so that I could try to find some way to slip off with Suzon.

When we rose from the table after coffee, I made a little nod to her. She understood and was the first to leave the room. I was about to follow her, when Madame Dinville stopped me, saying she would like the Abbot and me to escort her on her promenade. A stroll at four o'clock on a hot summer afternoon! The Abbot found the proposal ridiculous, but it was not to win his approval that she made it. She knew what she was doing. Aware that he was too vain of his fair complexion to expose it to the rays of the sun, she foresaw correctly that he would decline, which he promptly did. I, too, would have liked to get out of it in order to be with Suzon, but I could not think of any plausible excuse. As a result, I made the sacrifice.

Slowly we walked, not in the tree-lined paths but

among the open garden beds where the rays of the sun were the hottest. The only protection Madame Dinville had was a little fan. I had nothing, but I suffered my tortures stoically. The Abbot was laughing at our foolishness, but he soon became discouraged after we went around several times. I still could not guess what Madame Dinville had in mind. Also, I could not understand how she was able to stand the burning heat which I was beginning to find unbearable. Little did I realise what rich reward I was to get for my faithful service.

Our stubbornness in continuing the walk soon bored the scoffing Abbot and he retired. When we were at the end of one of the paths, Madame Dinville led me into a pleasantly cool little arbour.

'Aren't we going to go on with our stroll?' I innocently asked.

'No, I think I've had enough sun,' she replied.

She regarded me searchingly to learn if I guessed the reason for the promenade, and she perceived that I had no idea of the blessing she was intending for me. She took my arms which she squeezed affectionately. Then, as if she were extremely tired, she rested her head on my shoulder and put her face so close to mine that I would have been a fool not to kiss. She made no objection.

'Oh, oh,' I thought to myself. 'So that's her game. Well, nobody will disturb us here.'

In truth, we were in a sort of labyrinth whose obscurity and turnings and windings would conceal us from the sharpest eyes.

Now she sat down under a bower on the grass. It was the ideal setting for the purpose I was sure she had in mind. Following her example, I seated myself at her side. She gave me a soulful look, squeezed my hand, and reclined on her back. Believing that the moment had come, I started to ready my weapon when all of a sudden she fell sound asleep. At first, I thought it was only drowsiness caused by the heat and that I could easily rouse her. But when she refused to wake up after repeated shakings, I was simple enough to believe in the genuineness of a slumber that I should have suspected because of its promptness and profundity.

'My usual luck,' I swore to myself. 'If she fell asleep after I had quenched my desires, I wouldn't mind, but to be so cruel at the moment when she had raised my hopes so high is unpardonable.'

I was inconsolable. There was sadness in my heart as I regarded her. She was dressed like the previous day, that is to say, with the diaphanous blouse which revealed her unbelievable breasts, that were so near and yet so far. As the strawberry-tipped orbs rose and fell, I longingly admired their whiteness and symmetry.

My desires were almost at the breaking point, and I felt the urge to wake her up, but I dismissed the desire for fear that she would get angry. She would have to awaken eventually, I reflected, but I could not resist the urge to put my hand on that seductive bosom.

'She is sleeping too soundly for her to awaken at my touch,' I said to myself, 'but if she does, the worst that she can do is scold me for my boldness.'

Extending a quivering hand to one of the inviting mounds, I kept an anxious eye on her face, ready to retreat at the first sign of life. But she slumbered peacefully on as I lifted her blouse up to her neck and let my fingers graze the satin-smooth contours. My hand was like a swallow skimming over the water, now and then dipping its wings in the waves.

Now I was emboldened to plant a tender kiss on one rose-bud. She still did not stir. Then the other was given the same treatment. Changing my position, I became even naughtier. I put my head under her skirt in order to penetrate into the obscure landscape of love, but I could not make out anything for her legs were crossed. If I could not see it, at least I was going to touch it. My hand slowly crept up the thigh until it reached the foot of the Venusberg. The tip of my finger was already at the entrance to the grotto. I had gone too far, I decided, but having reached this point, I was more miserable and frustrated than ever. I was so anxious to see what I was touching. Withdrawing the intruding hand, I sat up again and regarded the visage of my sleeping beauty. There was no change in her placid expression. It seemed that Morpheus had cast his most soporific poppies on her.

Did my eyes deceive me? Did one of her eyelids twitch? I felt a sense of near panic. I looked again, this time more closely. No, the eye I thought had momentarily opened was still tightly shut.

Reassured, I took new courage and began to gently lift up her skirt. She gave a slight start, and I was positive that I had awakened her. Quickly, I pulled the skirt back down. My heart was pounding as if I had narrowly escaped a disaster. I was terror-stricken as I sat again at her side and feasted my eyes on her admirable bosom. With relief, I saw that there was not a sign of returning life. She had just changed position, and what a delightful new position it was.

Her thighs were now uncrossed. When she raised

one knee, the skirt fell on her stomach, revealing her hirsute mound and cunt. The dazzling sight almost intoxicated me. Picture to yourself a rounded leg encased in a frivolous stocking held up by a dainty garter, a tiny foot in a saucy shoe, and thighs of alabaster. The carmine red cunt was surrounded by a ring of ebony black hair and it exuded a scent more heady than the rarest incense. Inserting my finger in the aperture, I tickled it a little. At this, she opened her legs still wider. Then I put my mouth to it, trying to sink my tongue to the very bottom. Words cannot describe the straining erection I had.

Nothing could stop me now. Fear, respect and caution were thrown to the winds. My passion was like a torrent, seeping away everything in its path. If she had been the Sultan's favourite, I would have fucked her in the presence of a hundred eunuchs armed with sharp scimitars. Stretching my body over her and supporting myself with my hands and knees so that my weight would not arouse her, my member gradually disappeared into the hole. The only part of me touching her was my prick which I gently pushed in and pulled out. The slow but regular cadence enhanced and prolonged my ineffable bliss.

Still carefully watching her face, I gently kissed her full lips from time to time.

But the raptures I was experiencing were so great that I forgot my caution and fell heavily on the lady, furiously hugging and embracing her.

The climax of my pleasure opened my eyes which had been shut since I had entered her, and I saw the transports of Madame Dinville, joys which I was no longer able to share. My somnolent friend had just clutched my buttocks with her hands, and raising hers which she convulsively wiggled, she dragged me down hard on her quivering body. I kissed her with the last of the passion I had left.

'My dear friend,' she moaned in a failing voice, 'push a little more. Don't leave me half way to my goal.'

I felt renewed vigour at her touching appeal and resumed my enjoyable task. After barely five or six strokes more, she really lost consciousness. For some unknown reason, that excited me and I quickened my tempo. In a matter of seconds, I reached the peak again and fell into a state like that of my partner. When we revived, we showed our appreciation of each other with warm kisses and tight embraces.

With the fading of passion, I felt I had to withdraw, but I was embarrassed for I was unwilling for her to see the sorry condition my prick was in. I tried to hide it, but her eyes were fixed on me. When it was out, she grabbed it, took it into her mouth, and began to suck it.

'What were you trying to do, you silly boy?' she murmured. 'Were you ashamed to show me an instrument you know how to use so well? Did I conceal anything from you? Look! Here are my breasts. Look at them and fondle them as much as you want. Take those rosy tips in your mouth and put your hand on my cunt. Oh, that's wonderful! You have no idea of the pleasure you're giving me, you little rascal.'

Animated by the vivacity of her caresses, I responded with equal ardour. She marvelled at the dexterity of my finger as she rolled her eyes and breathed her sighs into my mouth.

My prick, having regained its pristine rigidity from her lips on it, wanted her more than ever. Before putting it in her again, I spread open her thighs to feast my eyes on that seat of delight. Often these preliminaries to pleasure are more piquant than pleasure itself. Is there anything more exquisite than to have a woman willing to assume any position your lascivious imagination can conjure? I experienced an ecstatic vertigo as I put my nose to that adorable cunt. I wished that all of me were a prick so that I could be completely engulfed in it. Desire begat even more violent desires.

Reveal a portion of your bosom to your lover, and he insists on seeing it all. Show him a little firm white breast, and he clamours to touch it. He is a dipsomaniac whose thirst increases as he drinks. Let him touch, and he demands to kiss it. Permit him to wander farther down, he commands that you let him put his prick there. His ingenious mind comes up with the most capricious fantasies, and he is not satisfied until he can carry them out on you.

The reader can imagine how long I was content nuzzling that appetising aperture. It was a matter of seconds until I was again vigorously fucking her. She eagerly responded with upward thrusts to match my powerful lunges. In order to get farther in, I had my hands on the cheeks of her derriere while she had her legs wrapped around my back. Our mouths, glued to each other, were two cunts being mutually fucked by two tongues. Finally came the ecstasy that lifted us to the heights and then annihilated us.

It has been said that potency is a gift of the gods, and although they had been more than generous with me, I was squandering my divine patrimony, and I had need of every drop of the heavenly largesse to emerge from the present engagement with honour.

It seemed that her desires were increasing in proportion to the loss of my powers. Only with the most libertine caresses was she able to turn my imminent retreat into still another victory. This she accomplished by getting on top of me, letting her full breasts dangle above my face and rubbing my failing virility with her cunt which seemed possessed of a life of its own.

'Now, I'm fucking you!' she joyously cried as she bounced up and down on me. Motionless, I let her do what she wanted with me. It was a delightful sensation, the first one I had ever enjoyed in that way. Now and then, she paused in her exertions to rain kisses on my face. Those lovely orbs swayed rhythmically above me in time with her repeated impaling of herself. When they came close to my mouth, I eagerly kissed or sucked the rose nipple. A streak of voluptuousness shuddering through my body announced the imminence of the supreme moment. Joining my transports to hers, I gushed just at the moment she did, and our juices mingled with the perspiration on our bellies.

Exhausted and shattered by the assaults I had launched and withstood for more than two hours, I felt an overwhelming desire for sleep and I yielded to it. Madame Dinville herself rested my head on her abundant bosom, wanting also to enjoy some rest, but with me in her arms.

'Sleep, my love,' she murmured as she wiped the perspiration from my forehead. 'Have a good sleep, for I know how much you need it.'

I dozed off immediately, only to awaken when the sun was sinking on the horizon. The first thing I saw when I opened my eyes was Madame Dinville. She looked at me cheerfully, interrupting the knitting she had occupied herself with during my slumber to dart her tongue in my mouth.

She made no attempt to conceal her desire for a resumption of the sport, but I had little interest. My indifference irritated her. It was not that I was disinclined, but if it had been left up to me, I would have preferred repose to action. But Madame was not going to have it that way. Holding me in her arms, she overwhelmed me with proofs of her passion, but they did not arouse me, even though I tried my best to stoke the dead fires within me.

Disappointed at her lack of success, she employed another ruse to relight my extinguished flames. Lying on her back, she raised her skirt to her navel, revealing the object of the desires of most men. She well knew the effect such an exposure would produce. When she suggestively jiggled her buttocks, I felt something stirring in me and I placed my hand on the gift she was offering me. But it was only a token gesture of passion. As I was negligently titillating her clitoris, she was feverishly massaging my prick in a hysterical cadence dictated by her feverish eagerness. When my prick finally stood up, I saw her eyes sparkle in triumph at her success in reviving my ardour. Now aroused by her caresses, I promptly bestowed on her the tokens of my gratitude which she zealously accepted. Grasping me around the waist, she bumped up and down under me so violently that I ejaculated almost automatically, but with such raptures that I was angry with myself for having ended the joy so promptly.

Now it was time to leave the arbour which had been the scene of such transports. But before returning to the chateau, we took several turns in the labyrinth to allow the traces of our exertions to disappear. As we were strolling, we naturally chatted:

'How happy I am with you, dear Saturnin,' she remarked. 'Did I live up to your expectations?'

'I am still relishing the delights you were good enough to grant me,' I gallantly replied.

'Thank you,' she said. 'But it was not very wise of me to have surrendered to you the way I did. You will be discreet, won't you, Saturnin?'

I retorted that if she thought I was capable of betraying to others what joys we had, she must not have a very high opinion of me. She was so pleased with my astute response that she rewarded me with a long, lingering kiss. I am sure that I would have been rewarded much more richly had we not been in a spot where we could be seen. As an additional gratitude, she pressed my hand to her left breast with a meaningful expression.

Now we quickened our pace as the conversation languished. I noticed that Madame Dinville was anxiously looking from side to side and wondered why.

But who would have thought that after such an exhausting afternoon, she still wanted more? She wanted to crown the day with one last engagement, and she was on the lookout for some stray servant. The reader will probably think that she had the devil in the flesh, and he would not be far off the mark.

She tried to revive me with her tongue and mouth,

but the poor thing was lifeless. Sad but true. To attain her goal, what did she do? That is what we are going to find out.

As a youngster just getting to know the ways of the world, I flattered myself that I had made an auspicious debut and that I would be lacking in respect if I did not see her to her rooms. That done, I felt I could take my leave by giving her a final kiss for the day.

'What's that?' she demanded in a surprised tone. 'You're not leaving, are you? It's only eight o'clock. You stay here. I'll arrange things with your Cure.'

The thought of avoiding Mass appealed to me and I was agreeable to her interceding for me. Making me sit on the bed, she went to lock the door and returned to take her place at my side. She looked at me intently without uttering a word. Her silence disconcerted me.

'Don't you want to any more?' she finally said.

Because I knew I was finished, I was so embarrassed that I could not force out a word. To admit my impotence was unthinkable. I lowered my eyes to conceal my shame.

'We're all alone, dear Saturnin,' she said in a coaxing voice, bathing my face with hot kisses which just left me cold.

'Not a soul in the world can spy on us,' she continued. 'Let's take off our clothes and get into my bed. Come, my friend, down to the buff. I'll soon make the stubborn little prick stand up.'

Taking me in her arms, she actually carried me and deposited me on the couch where she disrobed me in a feverish impatience. She soon got me in the desired condition, that is to say, naked as the day I was born. More out of politeness than pleasure, I let her have her way with me.

Turning me on my back, she started sucking my poor prick. She had it in her mouth up to my testicles. I could see that she was in ecstasies as she covered the member with a saliva that resembled froth. She did restore some life to it, but so little that she could make no use of it. Recognising that that treatment was of no avail, she went to her dressing-table and got a little flask containing a whitish fluid. This she poured on her palm and vigorously rubbed it on my balls and prick.

'There,' she said with satisfaction when she finished. 'You aren't through yet by any means.'

Impatiently I waited for the fulfillment of her prediction. Little tingles in my testicles raised my hopes for success. While waiting for the treatment to take effect, she undressed in turn. By the time she was naked, I felt as if my blood was boiling. My penis shot up as if released by a powerful spring. Like a maniac, I grabbed her and forced her on the bed with me. I devoured her, scarcely permitting her to breathe. I was blind and deaf. Sounds like those of an enraged beast came out of my mouth. There was only one thought in my mind, and that was her cunt.

'Stop, my love!' she cried, tearing herself from me. 'Not in such a hurry. Let's prolong our pleasures and elaborate on them. Put your head at my feet, and I'll do the same. Now your tongue in my cunt. That's it. Oh, I'm in heaven.'

My body, stretched out on her, was swimming in a sea of delight. I darted my tongue as deep as I could into the moist grotto. If possible, I would have sunk my entire head into it. Furious sucking on her taut clitoris produced a flow of nectar a thousand times more delectable than that served by Hebe to the gods on Mount Olympus. Some readers may ask what the goddesses drank. They drank from Ganymede's prick, of course.

Madame Dinville was clutching my backside with both her arms while I squeezed her pneumatic buttocks. Her tongue and lips wandered feverishly over my prick while mine did the same to her nether parts. She announced to me the increasing intensity of the raptures I was causing her by convulsive spasms and erratically spreading and closing her thighs. Moderating and augmenting our efforts, we gradually progressed to the peak. We stiffened as if collecting all our faculties to savour the coming bliss to the full.

We discharged simultaneously. From her cunt gushed a torrent of hot delicious fluid which I greedily gulped down. Her mouth was so filled with mine that it took several swallows to get it all down, and she did not release my prick until she was sure that there was not a drop left. The ecstasy vanished, leaving me in despair at the thought it could not be recaptured. But such is carnal pleasure.

Back in the pitiable state from which Madame Dinville's potion had rescued me, I beseeched her to restore me again.

'No, my dear Saturnin,' she replied. 'I love you too much to want to kill you. Be content with the joy we just had.'

Not overly eager to meet my Maker at the expense of another round of pleasure, I followed her example and put on my clothes.

Feeling that Madame Dinville was not displeased with the way I had comported myself, I asked her if I would be permitted to play our games again with her.

'When do you want to come back?' she answered, kissing me on the cheek.

'As soon as I can and that won't be soon enough,' I declared spiritedly. 'How about tomorrow?'

'No,' she smilingly refused me. 'I have to let you get some rest. Come and see me in three days' time.' (She handed me some pastilles that she said would produce the same effect on me as the balm.) 'Be careful how you take them. Also, I don't have to tell you that you are not to say a word about what we did.'

I swore eternal secrecy, and we embraced one last time. So I departed, leaving her under the impression that I had presented her with my virginity.

As I made my way silently down the dimly lit corridor and passed through the antechamber, I was stopped by someone. It was Suzon. I was struck dumb with astonishment. It seemed that her presence was a reproach for my infidelity to her. In my feelings of guilt, I imagined that she had witnessed all that had occurred. Taking my hand in hers, she stood motionless without saying a word. My inner turmoil prevented me from looking at her. Uneasy at her silence, I raised my eyes and weakly asked the reason for her silence. When she refused to reply, I saw that she was shedding tears. The sight was like a stab in my heart. It also relit the flames that the caresses of Madame Dinville had just extinguished. Regarding Suzon with love in my breast, I wondered what I had seen in the older woman.

'Suzon,' I said with distress in my voice. 'Am I the cause of your tears?'

'Yes, it is you,' she sobbed. 'You heartless boy. You

have broken my heart and I am going to die of grief.'

'Me!' I protested. 'How can you reproach me this way? What have I done? You know that my love for you is as deep as the ocean.'

'So you love me, eh?' she replied bitterly. 'It would be better if you spoke the truth. I suppose you swore the same thing to Madame Dinville. If you love me, as you say, why were you with her? You didn't even try to find me when I left the dining-room. Is she more desirable than I? What have you been doing with her all this time? I bet you were not thinking of your Suzon who loves you more than life itself. Yes, Saturnin, I adore you. You have inspired in me a sentiment so profound that I would expire if you did not reciprocate it. But you don't say anything. I see it all now. Your conscience did not bother you when you dallied with my rival. I shall hate her until the end of time, for I know that she is in love with you and you have returned her affection. All you were thinking about was the pleasure she was holding out to you and forgetting the sorrow you would cause me. I can't get over it.'

I had to recognise the justice of her accusation, for indeed I had used the same terms of endearment with Madame Dinville as I had with Suzon.

'Suzon,' I said brokenly. 'Your harsh words are killing me. Please stop. Don't crush the one who worships you. And your tears plunge me into despair. Yu can't imagine how much I love you.'

'Ah,' she sighed. 'You have given life back to me. From now on, I forbid you to think of anyone but me. Since yesterday, you have been constantly in my thoughts. Your face has been following me everywhere

I go. Now listen, Saturnin. If I agree to forgive you for the wrong you did me, it will be on the condition that you promise never again to see Madame Dinville. Do you love me enough to make such a sacrifice?'

'Oh, yes!' I cried eagerly. 'I'll gladly give her up for your sake. All her charms put together are not the equal of one of your kisses.'

As I uttered those pacifying words, I gave her an impassioned kiss which she did not rebuff.

'Saturnin, now tell me something and be honest about it,' she softly said as she tenderly squeezed my hand. 'I am sure that my god-mother wants to see you again. When did she tell you to come back?'

'In three days,' I admitted.

'And you'll come, won't you?' she said sadly.

'Tell me what I should do,' I asked helplessly. 'If I come, she'll be annoyed at my indifference, and if I don't, I won't be able to see my beloved Suzon.'

'I want you to return,' she told me firmly, shaking her pretty little head in determination, 'but she mustn't see you. I'll pretend that I am sick and stay in bed. That way, we can spend the day together by ourselves. But you don't know where my bedroom is. Follow me. I'll show you.'

I let myself be led, but as I walked behind, I had the foreboding that something terrible was going to happen.

'Here is the apartment I have been given,' Suzon informed me. 'You won't be too unhappy with me here?'

'Ah, Suzon,' I sighed, 'what delights you are proferring me. We shall be together, just you and I, and we'll give ourselves up to all the raptures of our love. We shall have bliss such as you have never dreamed of.'

She did not reply, seemingly in a deep reverie. Wondering if I had said something wrong, I urged her to speak.

'I understand you perfectly,' she cried agitatedly. 'Yes, we'll abandon ourselves to our amorous caprices, but you can't look forward to them very much if you are able to wait three days.'

The reproach struck home.

The impossibility of proving her wrong dismayed me. My whole being was tortured. How stupid of me to have squandered all my resources on Madame Dinville! How I now regretted the pleasures I had showered her with. Desolate and crushed, I inwardly cursed her.

'Dear God!' I silently cried from the depths of my heart. 'Here I am with Suzon and I would give my life's blood to be able to make her happy. Here she is, just waiting for me, and I am helpless. I am drained dry. What can I do to take advantage of this unparalleled opportunity?'

Suddenly, I remembered the pastilles Madame Dinville had given me. Not doubting that they would have the same prompt effect as the lotion, I swallowed several of them. The anticipation of soon being able to satisfy Suzon's urges made me embrace her with an ardour that deceived us both. Suzon took it as a sign of my desire for her, and I believed it evidence of the revival of my virility.

In the expectation of imminent bliss, Suzon fell back on her bed. Inwardly praying that I would not disappoint her, I mounted her and placed my prick in her hand. Although it was still limp, I was confident that her dainty little hand would aid the action of the pills and the organ would soon be in the wished for state. She squeezed it, she massaged it, and she sucked it. Nothing happened. I exerted myself a hundred times more vigorously than I had with Madame Dinville, but it was to no avail. It was as dead as a door-knob.

'Here I have my dearest Suzon, the object of all my desires, in my arms, and I might as well be a corpse,' I reviled myself. 'I kiss her saucy breasts, those two adorable orbs, that I worshipped yesterday and that now leave me cold. Have they changed since then? No. They are as smooth, firm and full as they were. Her skin is still a delight to touch. Her open thighs should arouse me again to a fury. I have my finger in her delightful little cunt, but that's all I can put into it.'

As I heard Suzon sigh at my lethargy, I damned the gift that Madame Dinville had made me. I was sure that she foresaw something like this would happen when I left her and that she wanted to keep me in the same state of impotence until I saw her again.

I was on the verge of telling Suzon everything, when I was startled out of my wits. An invisible hand noiselessly opened the bed curtains and gave me a resounding smack on my behind. Gripped with terror, I abandoned Suzon to the specter, for I was convinced that it was a ghost, and fled for my life.

When I got back home, I was still shaking. Once in bed, I pulled the covers over my head.

Fright coupled with exhaustion soon brought me sleep. The next morning I awoke, but I was so fatigued that I could not get out of bed. Surprised by the lassitude that I could attribute only to the gymnastics of the previous day, I realised for the first time how necessary it is to ration one's self in amorous engagements and how dearly one pays for blindly heeding those lustful sirens who drain you dry and suck your marrow. How stupid to have such reflections only when it is too late, and remorse is no consolation.

But youth is resilient. I gradually regained my strength, gave up my lugubrious meditations, and turned my thoughts to the events of last night. I felt a sudden surge of anxiety as to the fate of Suzon with the phantom. With a sense of horror, I wondered what terrible things could have happened to her.

'She's probably dead,' I said to myself mournfully. 'She's so timid and shy that she surely died of fright. And I'll never see her again except in her coffin.'

Crushed by such thoughts, I burst into tears. At this moment, Toinette entered my room.

I shook when I saw her, for I believed she had come to confirm my worst fears. Her silence, however, gave me hope that my suspicions were unfounded. Perhaps Suzon had made good her escape as I had. The grief I had felt at Suzon's demise gave place to curiosity as to what had happened after my hasty departure. But Toinette had merely come to find out why I had not appeared for breakfast.

The two days of rest that Madame Dinville had prescribed for me were over and the third day had come. Although I felt my native vigour restored, I had little inclination for more gambols at the chateau. The recollection of what had happened there stifled my desires before they were born. Just so that I would not get any sexual urges, I gulped down the rest of the pastilles Madame Dinville gave me. They put me to sleep for several hours, and when I awoke I found myself with an erection, the like of which I never had in my life. My prick was throbbing and aching for satisfaction.

At the same time, I was exceedingly embarrassed. Yes, the reader can laugh. He can remind me that four fingers and one thumb were all that was necessary to assuage my pain. All right! Go ahead and say it: 'Dom Bougre, you have four fingers and a thumb, an infallible cure for the intemperance of the flesh. So why don't you use them? What do the priests do when there are no complaisant nuns or parishioners around? You do not always have a brothel or a devout at your disposal. So they masturbate until they are blue in the face. Simpletons assume that their pallor is the result of their austerity, but now you know what it comes from. So why not have recourse to the same remedy they employ?'

I was aware of all that. But I had been so crushed and impotent the past three days, that I was reluctant to relieve myself in such a solitary way. Nevertheless, I could not help myself. My fingers slowly embraced the quivering engine. Rubbing it up and down, I stopped just at the moment when all my pains would be dissolved. It became a game with me to see how long I could prolong the pleasurable agony. As I amused myself in this fashion, I pictured in my mind a shy young *grisette* who has not yet tasted the delicacies of love and who is unaware of your appetite for her. When I kissed her on the mouth, I saw her blush. She made no attempt at resistance when I unbuttoned her blouse and regarded her delightful breasts rising and falling. Then my hand descended to a hot little cunt that, in the beginning, fiercely defied my attacks.

Pleasure is sparkling, bubbling, and ephemeral. If it can be compared to anything, it would be those flames that suddenly jet out of the ground, dazzling in their brilliance, and disappear just at the instant you believe you have divined their cause. Such is pleasure. It shows itself momentarily and then vanishes.

The only way to capture it is to fool it, trap it, and force it to stay with you as you jest with it, then let it escape, summon it back, let it flee, call it back once more. That is the only method to enjoy it to the full.

I was so preoccupied with my diversion I did not notice night had fallen. I had ejaculated several times and was about ready to fall asleep when somebody in a nightshirt passed the foot of my bed.

At first, I thought it was the theologian I mentioned when I gave my description of Nicole.

'If that's who it is, he's probably on his way to fuck Nicole,' I said to myself. 'Well, I'm going to follow him.'

I sprang out of bed, dressed only in battle costume, that it is to say, a nightgown. Gropingly, I made my way in the dark to the corridor which I thought led to Nicole's room. I spotted the door slightly ajar and went in. With the utmost circumspection, I made my way to the bed where I expected the lovers to be engaged in amorous games.

I listened carefully, expecting to hear the usual erotic sighs, groans, and pantings. There was someone breathing heavily, but she appeared to be alone. Maybe the theologian had lost his way, I hopefully wondered.

I ran my hand over the body, and at the first touch, I discovered that it was feminine. I kissed her on the mouth.

'Ah,' she murmured in a voice that I could barely hear, 'I've been waiting for you so long that I fell asleep. But now that you are here, hurry up and get on top of me.'

Needing no further urging, I was soon atop my Venus. But there was a noticeable lack of enthusiasm on her part when she embraced me. Perhaps it was my tardiness that had incurred her displeasure, but I congratulated myself on the good luck that fortune had bestowed on me. Now I was going to get my revenge on that disdainful, haughty maiden who had so often rejected my advances. She thought I was somebody else, and that delighted me.

Kissing her full on the mouth and on her eyes, I gave myself up to raptures that had been denied me for what seemed an eternity. I gently massaged the resilient breasts, for Nicole possessed one of the most charming bosoms imaginable, delectable in their firmness and sauciness. Venus herself would have envied those hemispheres. I was in raptures. To reward her for the joys she was affording me, I spent in her a torrent the likes of which I wager she had never before felt. From her ohs and ahs, and from her spasms, I gathered that she had not expected such a royal munificence.

Scarcely had I crowned my labours with an initial transport than I felt myself incited to second effort, and I merited the praise she lavished on me. From her groans, I gathered she was in the mood for a third act to make this night stand out. Although I was still in good shape to give her the satisfaction she desired, the fear of being surprised by the theologian slightly dampened my enthusiasm. I was at my wits' end to give her an excuse for my procrastination. But as her desires became more urgent, I felt that the devil could take the hindmost and I proceeded again.

But two discharges slightly dispel the erotic fumes. Illusions vanish and the mind returns to normal. The shadows disappear and values resume their true value. It goes without saying that beautiful women win out over their less favoured sisters. For the latter, I have a bit of advice. If you give your all to a man, ration your favours. Don't splurge them. If you leave nothing more to be desired, interest is lost. Passion is extinguished by a too complete satisfaction. There should be always left something to be desired or wanted. But if you can hold out the prospect of something more, you can compete on equal terms.

It was indeed delectable to run my hand over the beauties of my elusive nymph. But I was astonished to find a difference from those I had manipulated with so much pleasure several moments before. Her thighs which I had found so firm and velvety were now wrinkled and flabby. The cunt that was so deliciously tight was now a yawning chasm and the delightful breasts, pointed and taut, were sagging and pendulous. The transformation flabbergasted me, but I thought it was just my imagination. In spite of the change, I was now ready for the third assault. Just as I was prepared to launch the attack, my partner and I were interrupted by a racket from the adjoining room which I assumed was that of the venerable Françoise.

'You wretch!' a voice cried.

At these words, my little sweetheart whose cunt I had already started to penetrate shoved me away.

'My God!' she exclaimed. 'What is happening to our daughter? Go and see what is the matter! It sounds as if she is being murdered.'

So Nicole had a daughter, I thought to myself. Strange.

I was so nonplussed that I could not move. As the hubbub grew louder, my bed partner, impatient at my refusal to budge, got out of the couch and lit a candle.

Now I saw who she was. It was not Nicole, but that hag, Françoise. Never shall I forget that horrible moment. I still become petrified at the recollection of the sight of that spook. Beside myself with rage, I now realised I had gone into the wrong room. And it was the Cure whom she had been expecting.

'God! What am I going to do?' I said to myself in a panic. 'How am I going to get out of this mess? If Françoise notices that it was with me she had her amusement, she certainly will tell the Cure, and what a whipping I shall get!'

Inwardly, I urged her to hasten and separate those dear enemies, but not to forget to leave the door open.

The bitch had locked it. I yanked at it with all my might, but it refused to open. Reduced to despair at my perilous condition, I tried to keep on my feet, but I sank to the floor. I was too young and inexperienced to realise that pleasure and misery are so closely interwined that in the depths of misery, one should not lose hope for a change in fortune. Often when you feel crushed by the cruel blows of fate, chance puts an end to them in the most unexpected manner.

At the moment when I was shivering with fear under

the bed where I had taken refuge, the wheel of fortune turned. The racket became noisier when the combatants saw Françoise, from whose hands fell the candlestick holder. The first thing she saw was the Cure who she thought was in her room. I could see the tableau in my mind.

There was the Cure wearing only his underpants and a nightcap on his head. His eyes were glittering and his mouth frothing as he viciously pummelled the squawling lovers, Nicole trying to protect herself by crawling under the covers. The theologian also under the blankets was not without courage for he occasionally stuck his head out and got in a punch on the face of the roaring Cure. And let us not forget the shrew in her nightgown, her eyes glazed with astonishment, slumped in a chair.

Judging from the sounds I heard, the theologian, for fear of being recognised, had bounded from under the covers and tried to escape in the darkness, for the candle had gone out when Françoise dropped it. The Cure was hot on his heels.

At that moment, I heard the door of my room quickly open and close and somebody throw himself on the bed. Trembling like a leaf, I thought it was Françoise and that the Cure would come to join her. But all was calm, except for the soft sighs of the one lying on the bed.

Now I was confused. What was I to make of those sobs? Why was Françoise weeping like that? Why did she come back? Would the Cure come or not, I wondered. Uncertainty is one of the cruelest of tortures. At times, I was tempted to try an escape, but the fear of discovery held me back. There was another more compelling reason that kept me in the chamber: I had another immense erection.

'So you're going back to your room with a stiff prick like that,' the devil whispered in my ear. 'You're both heartless and stupid. How can you abandon Françoise to her sorrow, when you have the ability to console her? It's the least you can do for her. Didn't she overwhelm you with her caresses? And you are unwilling to dry her tears? She's old and ugly, I agree with you, but she still has a cunt, doesn't she?'

'By God!' I muttered. 'He's right. A cunt is a cunt, no matter the age of its owner.'

Mephistopheles continued his exhortation: 'The storm is over, and there is nothing more to fear. Get into bed with her.'

Blindly I obeyed the injunction. Although I climbed into the couch with all care, Françoise gave a little squeal of fright. With my groping hands, I found her cringing in the far corner of the bed. It was too late to beat a retreat, and I put my hand between her thighs.

To my amazement, they had returned to their former delectable condition. They had changed back to a silken smoothness that was a delight to the touch. Now I was at a peak of erotic excitement. My hands wandered over her delightful resilient breasts, her belly that was as flat and smooth as a young girl's, and down to the cunt, and what a cunt! As I expected, there was no protest at my exploratory fondling. Her charms were so appetising that I had to put my mouth on all of them.

My ardour aroused hers in turn, for her whimpering gave place to sharp little cries of pleasure.

'How did you happen to find me here?' she

whispered, calling me by the theologian's name, as she opened her legs to make my entrance easier. So she was mistaken about the identity of her lover. But I was at such a pitch of excitement that I could not stop now. And from the way she responded to my jabs in her cunt, I knew that she was in ecstasies. Our mingled sobs and pants made a sweet harmony as we kept perfect time with our movements.

After the preliminary raptures had subsided, I recalled how she had addressed me. Was Françoise capable of sharing the theologian with Nicole? I ran my hand again over the body next to me, expected to find the same wrinkles and flaccidity, but no... the body was still as deliciously supple and firm as ever. 'What does this mean?' I asked myself in puzzlement. 'Is my partner Françoise or not?'

The moon briefly appeared at the window, and with its light, I saw who it was. Heavens! It was Nicole. She probably had also escaped from the other room and come here to hide, counting on Françoise's forgiveness. And she undoubtedly imagined that her lover had done the same. To my mind, that was the only logical explanation for her mistake.

With such thoughts in my mind, I felt rise within me all the passions I formerly had for her, but I regretted the resources I had wasted on Françoise.

'My dearest Nicole,' I whispered, attempting to imitate the theologian's voice, for I intended to continue with the deception, 'what good fortune that we should find ourselves together here. Let's forget that disagreeable incident by fucking.'

'What delights you give me,' she replied, quivering with pleasure at my caresses. 'Yes, let us calm ourselves in the only way possible. Let come what may, as long as I have that in my hand,' she continued, clutching my prick, 'I am not afraid of death itself. Besides, I locked the door and we won't be disturbed.'

Reassured by this precaution that love prompted, I began to fondle her beauties with renewed zest. My prick which she kept tightly in her hand was of a stiffness that overjoyed her.

I urged her to put it in her, but she was in no haste to comply. However, she did not release it.

'Wait a moment, my dear friend,' she said when I attempted to insert it myself. 'Wait until it gets even bigger and harder. I have never felt it in such a condition. Did it grow during the night?'

From this naive question, I gathered that the theologian was not as well endowed as I.

'I am sure that this is going to be the night of nights,' she gasped as she finally put the impatient member in her. 'Now push, push as hard as you can.'

It goes without saying that her injunction was unnecessary. I shoved in with all might and main. As I did so, I covered her sensuous lips and abundant breasts with hot kisses. For several moments, I was so blissful that I had to stop to savour the enjoyment.

'Go on,' she coaxed me, wiggling her buttocks so lasciviously that I was roused out of my ecstatic stupor.

I deepened my jabs so that she gave out little screams as she surged up to meet me. She panted that she thought it was going all the way to her heart. Her passionate responses plunged me into a torrent of rapturous fury. Flames seared every hidden recess of my body.

'Come, now is the time to gush out your elixir! You are a god from above, and I beseech you to let me remain in this state of bliss for an eternity. How is it that one does not die from such transports?'

I was as overjoyed with her as she was with me. What a difference between a hag and a girl! Youth makes love because of love, and age does it out of habit. You old people should leave fucking to the young. For you, it is a chore, and for us it is a delight.

Although there was not the slightest danger of my prick going soft, Nicole took every precaution to prevent such a sad occurrence. Her fiery efforts resulted in an unprecedented rigidity. She would not have surrendered me for a kingdom, and I would not have given her up for all the riches in the world.

Our simultaneous gushes were copious and relieving and the raptures ineffable. But it was not long before we hastened in pursuit of that which had just escaped us. Imprudence, though, is one of the characteristics of love. Intoxicated by ecstasy, you are unable to conceive that it can be lost. And we were betrayed by our blind desire for each other.

Our bed was right next to the wall separating our room from the one adjoining it, and we had not the slightest suspicion that Françoise was occupying it. Nor did we have any inkling that the sounds of our amorous gambols would penetrate through the partition and wake her up, enabling her to guess what was going on.

In a flash, she was at our door. When she found it locked, she called:

'Nicole!'

We were petrified by the terrifying voice. At our

silence, she began to screech, but after realising that that did not help, she remained silent. In spite of the knowledge that she was at the door, our desires outweighed our fears and we resumed our games. When she heard the bed creak, she began to shriek again.

'Nicole,' she screamed. 'You're nothing but a slut! Aren't you ever going to stop?'

Nicole seemed perturbed, but I comforted her by saying that since we were discovered, we might as well be hung for a sheep as a lamb. She tacitly agreed by joining her movements to mine. Slapping me on the backside and darting her tongue in my mouth, she got on top of me and began to fuck with all the valour of a brave soldier who is oblivious to the shells bursting around him. As we neared another climax, the hag's screams of frustration merely piqued our raptures. When it was over, we panted to each other that never before had we experienced such a thrill.

Five times in a very short period was not bad for a convalescent like myself. Although I felt that I was not yet completely *hors de combat*, I decided that wisdom was the better part of valour. The old bitch could get really angry and resort to severe measures such as ringing the tocsin on us. We would be in a pretty kettle of fish if she did that. We would have to come out of the room naked, hardly suitable for a youth and a maid.

The sagest course was to beat a retreat, which I did by going out through the window. But before regaining my bed, I thought I would be a fool to leave Nicole believing it was the theologian who was the hero of the exploits she had admired so much. I was vain, I admit, but if the reader puts himself in my place, I am sure he would do exactly as I did.

'My dearest Nicole,' I cooed in her ear. 'I hope you have not been dissatisfied with me.'

She assured me fervently that such indeed was not the case.

'I bet you never thought that that funny little fellow you always looked down on was capable of such feats,' I continued. 'How wrong you were about him, and he certainly did not deserve the treatment he got from you. Now you have learned that size is not everything. Good-bye for now, dearest Nicole. My name is Saturnin and I am at your service.'

With a final kiss, I left her with a baffled expression and a drooping jaw.

As I said, I think the reader, in my place, would do the same thing.

Still somewhat stunned by the bizarre adventures that had befallen me, I impatiently awaited the coming of morning to learn what the results, if any, might be. Because of my exhilaration at the theologian's humiliation, I did not sleep a wink.

With the exception of Nicole, on whose silence I could count, nobody could cast the slightest suspicion on me. I was chuckling in advance at the figure they would cut when I saw them. The Cure would look solemn and be in a vile mood, but I would not be among those who would feel the back of his hand.

Françoise would scrutinise carefully all the pupils, one by one, eyes scarlet with suppressed fury. Among the bigger fellows, she would spot a likely candidate for revenge, not for the joys she had but for those Nicole had received. Because of my size, I would be the last to be suspected. Nicole probably would not show her face, for if she did, she would be blushing, have a guilty look, and regard me with longing eyes.

I was so preoccupied with these happy reflections that I did not notice dawn spreading its rosy fingers in my room. Only then did Morpheus close my eyes and keep them shut until noon.

When I awoke, I was extremely surprised to find Toinette at my bedside. I turned pale and trembled with fear that my part in the night's escapade had been discovered.

'Don't you feel well, Saturnin?' she asked.

I did not answer.

'If you are sick, I suppose you can't go with Father Polycarpe, who is leaving today. He was planning to take you with him.'

The mention of departure dissipated all my trepidation.

'I never felt better in my life,' I shouted exultantly as I sprang out of bed and dressed before giving Toinette time to wonder at my sudden transition from depression to jubilance. When I had my clothes on, I followed her out of the room.

I left the Cure's house without the slightest regret. The thought that I would never see Suzon or Nicole again did not bother me in the slightest.

Father Polycarpe was delighted to see me, and Ambroise gave me an affectionate embrace. Seated behind the Reverend Father on his mount, I waved farewell to Ambroise and Toinette.

Now I entered a new stage in my life. Destined from birth to augment the number of those holy swine whom the credulous stupidly nourish, I was perfectly suited by nature for this calling which experience perfected me in.

It is now my intention to recount some extraordinary events. If the reader argues that they are so improbable as to be untrue, allow me to assure him that they are veritable down to the last detail. All I am doing is describing what is done behind the seminary walls by mean, debauched, and corrupted monks who laugh at the gullibility of believers under their hood of religion. As hypocrites, they do in secret all that they condemn in public.

Since I became one of them, I have often reflected on the life they and I lead.

How is it that men of such varying characters and temperaments should come together in a monastery? There you find indolence, profligacy, mendacity, cowardliness, dishonour, and intoxication.

I pity those poor souls who believe that there is religion and piety behind those walls. If only they knew what goes on! The rampant iniquity would astound them, and they would despise those so-called holy men as they justly deserve. I am now going to lift the veil.

You have met Father Cherubim, that man of God whose vermilion bloated visage was the incarnation of lust. You knew him before he assumed the masquerade of the black serge cowl. What was his way of life?

He never went to bed before having downed nine or ten bottles of the best wines. It was not unusual to find him the next morning sprawled out under the dining-table he had been unable to leave. He abandoned the world, for God had showed him the way and he took it. I do not know if it was the Lord or one of His mundane deputies who effected this miracle, but I do know that Father Cherubim could more than hold his own with the most intrepid imbibers. That is how you knew him and he has not changed in the interim.

Perhaps you also glimpsed Father Modesto, puffed with his own self-importance. How has his character changed since he began wearing the triple cord around his pot-belly? You believe his words, but I know how he lies. Listen to him talk. In eloquence, Cicero is only an unconvincing babbler by comparison. He is more subtle than the most profound theologians. In his own eyes, he is another Saint Thomas, but in mine, he is nothing but a pompous ass. If you knew him as well as I do, you would agree with my opinion.

Now take Father Boniface, the crafty snoop who always walks with his head humbly bent down as if he were in silent communication with the Almighty. But watch out for him, for he is a snake in the grass. When he comes to call on you, keep an eye on your wife and daughters and send away your sons. If you are not present when he is there, your whole family will be fucked and buggered.

You have made the acquaintance of Father Hilary.

When you are with him, keep your hand on your purse, for he is the biggest swindler that ever lived. He will tell you of the urgent needs of the monastery in such a heart-rending fashion that tears will well in your eyes. The wretched friars are almost starving and the roof is about to collapse on their shaved pates. How could you allow such a piteous state of affairs to continue? Of course, you could not. In a burst of generosity, you open your purse until it is completely empty. Thus Father Hilary robs, pillages, and steals for the Church.

What a gang of rogues they are! You would think they would have changed for the better after they had taken the orders, but such is not the case. The drunk is still a drunk, the libertine still a libertine, and the thief still a thief. I'll go even further than that and aver that their vices are accentuated once they have donned the cowl, for they have unlimited opportunity to indulge in their caprices. How can they resist?

Although these monks hate and loathe each other, they are held together by common bonds. Even though rent by civil war, they present to the world a united front that is a model of discipline. And when it comes to stripping the gullible of their worldly goods, they have no peers. It is the same with the superstitions they invented and foisted on their flocks. In these efforts, they join forces with a common zeal.

After what I had seen of monkish frolics while living with Ambroise, I came to realise that the wearing of the cowl was the easiest way to gain admittance into the temple of pleasure. My mind reveled at the prospects such a calling would afford me.

With such thoughts, I eagerly donned the robe the

Father Prior gave me the day I arrived at the seminary.

I had learned enough Latin from the Cure to distinguish myself during my noviciate, but what good did it do me? I was made a porter.

As a writer who sticks to his facts, I should lead my reader, year by year, through my theologic career from novitiate to full priesthood. There would be many things to tell, but, alas, they would be of little interest. But I will mention a few amusing bagatelles.

After several years in the monastery, I was disabused of the high hopes I held when I entered it. If the monks had their fun, they certainly did not let a neophyte like me share it. Torn between repentance for having taken up a career which did not meet my expectations and eagerness for priesthood, I kept on the thorny path mostly because of the Prior who was the soul of kindness. More than once he told me that my abilities were unusual for the son of a gardener.

My first years in the seminary were not pleasant. There were the snubs I received from the other novices about my humble birth. There was no sex. Although Toinette came to see me, how could I enjoy her under the eyes of the ever present superiors? The loss of my beloved Suzon hurt even more. Although I knew that she was living with Madame Dinville, I had no news from her. I truly loved her, for there was an indefinable something about her. Every time I thought of our childish love-making, I was plunged into despair.

As I was attempting to console myself in my grief, there was one who was moved by my unhappy state.

'What are you doing, Saturnin?' he asked sympathetically.

As a matter of fact, I was masturbating. In those

unhappy days, my prick was the only thing that enabled me to forget my woes.

I thought I was alone while indulging in this voluptuous diversion. But a monk with an impish sense of humour was observing me. He was not a friend of mine. On the contrary, he never made any attempt to conceal his distaste for me. On this occasion, he came upon me so suddenly that I was frightened out of my wits. I thought I was lost for I was sure he would spread the story of what I was doing.

'Well, well, Brother Saturnin,' he remarked, rubbing his hands and raising his eyes heavenward, 'I never dreamed that you could stoop so low, you the learned theologian and the model of piety.'

'All right,' I brusquely interrupted him. 'That's enough of your sarcasm. So you caught me playing with myself, and I suppose you will see to it that everybody knows about it.' I took up where I had left off. 'Bring anyone you want here and laugh to your heart's content. I'll probably be on my tenth discharge by the time you are back.'

'Brother Saturnin,' he answered with the same sangfroid, 'I understand. There's nothing wrong. All the novices do it, and I did it when I was one.'

'If you don't get out of here, I'll...' I sputtered, clenching my fist.

My threat caused him to burst out into gales of laughter.

Extending his hand to me, he said in the most cordial tone imaginable: 'Take it, my friend. I never thought you had such spirit. Also, I feel genuinely sorry that you are so unhappy that you have to masturbate. You deserve better than such a feeble solace. I think I can find for you something more substantial and satisfying.'

His open and candid speech disarmed me, and I warmly shook his hand.

'I don't know what you have in mind,' I said, 'but I gratefully accept your offer.'

'All right,' he replied. 'Button up your trousers and don't expend your ammunition, for you'll have need of it later. At midnight, I'll be at your cell. For the moment, I won't say anything more. Don't follow me when I leave here, for nobody must see us together. It would cause talk. So, until later, then.'

I was slightly stupefied after Father André had left, so much so in fact, that I no longer had any interest in continuing with my game.

'What did he mean by "substantial"?' I wondered. 'If it's just some other novice, he can keep him for himself. That's not my cup of tea.'

My reasoning was that of an idiot, for I had never tried to get pleasure with a partner of my sex. Prejudice prevents us from so many delights. The thought of it disgusted me at first, but when I later tried it, I found it most appetising.

I happened to think of Giton. Is there anything more appealing than that pretty lad? His skin is like velvet and his rounded rump is as alluring as the most enticing little cunt. Yes, dear reader, you think I am breathing hot and cold by praising the cunt and then the male bottom. I suppose I am fickle.

Follow my advice, young fellow. Take your pleasure where you find it. My preference is to fuck a pretty, willing woman, but who in his right mind would reject a delicious pair of buttocks if they were offered him?

Take the famous philosophers of ancient Greece, for example, as well as some of the most distinguished men of our time – they will tell you the same thing.

As midnight sounded, there was a scratch at my cell door. It was Father André.

'I'm ready, Father,' I warmly greeted him. 'But where are we going?'

'To the chapel,' he curtly answered.

'Oh, no,' I balked. 'I'm not going there. Or are you making fun of me?'

He told me not to be a fool, and I meekly followed him.

Inside the chapel, we climbed up behind the organ, and, there, to my amazement, I found a table groaning under the weight of the finest food and wines.

The guests consisted of three monks, three novices, and a girl of about eighteen who seemed as lovely as an angel in my eager eyes. Father Casimir, who was the host of this cheerful gathering, gave me a cordial welcome.

'Greetings, Brother Saturnin,' he boomed as he wrapped me in his arms. 'Father André has spoken very highly of you, and that is why you have been invited here. I don't think he mentioned our way of life here. Simply said, we eat, drink, laugh, and fuck. Are such diversions to your taste?'

'Good Lord, yes,' I instantly replied. 'You'll see that I won't be a wet blanket on your festivities and that I shall avail myself of the offered pleasures as eagerly as anyone.'

'Well, let's get the party going!' Father Casimir cried, and turning again to me, he said: 'I am going to seat you between me and this adorable little girl.'

Father Casimir, who was now uncorking a bottle, was of medium height, dark complexion, sharp features, and had the pot-belly from good eating that is common among prelates. Whenever he was near a good-looking boy, his eyes glistened with the lust of a bugger and he whinnied like a rutting stallion. And he had a clever and novel way of getting what he wanted without ever leaving his study. The novice who surrendered himself to him was rewarded with the favours of his niece, who willingly paid her uncle's obligations.

'We have chosen this spot for our orgies, because it would be the last place anyone would suspect,' he explained to me.

Father Casimir's niece was brunette, petite, and lively. Perhaps the first sight of her did not inspire immediate desire, but she knew how to guide a man's eyes down to an absolutely magnificent bust. She laughed easily, and she had something of the coquette that made her irresistible.

As soon as I was next to the charming maiden, I experienced the confused sensation I had when I happened on Father Polycarpe and Toinette. Also, my long period of continence had whetted my lubricity. For the first time in ages, I sensed life beginning to stir in me again, and I was confident that I was soon going to enjoy the pleasures of flesh. My confidence was confirmed by the merry, mischievous eyes of my partner.

I soon had my hand on her thigh which I pressed to mine. Then it went under her skirt. She took the intruder in her hand and guided it to the spot where I wanted it. The possession of a site that had been denied me for an eternity produced a shudder of pure joy in me. It was noticed by everybody.

'Get going, Brother Saturnin,' they encouraged me. 'You have it made.'

Perhaps I would have lost my self-assurance at their friendly jeers had not Marianne, for such was the name of the delightful creature, given me a warm kiss, unbuttoned my trousers, and squeezed my neck. In her other hand she now had my prick which was stiff as an iron rod.

'My reverend fathers,' she cried exultantly as she displayed my pulsating masculinity on the table, 'yours are nothing but little sausages compared to this prodigy. Have you ever seen its like?'

There was a muted murmur of undeniable admiration. All congratulated Marianne on the delights she was going to enjoy, and her eyes shone with enchantment at the prospect.

Now Father Casimir called for silence. After congratulating his niece on her acquisition, he addressed me:

'I don't have to vaunt the charms of my niece to you, Brother Saturnin, and she is all yours. I think you'll find the texture of her skin softer than velvet and her breasts inviting cushions. And, according to general opinion, there is no cunt in the world like hers. But to have her, there is one little condition which, I am sure, will give you great pleasure.'

My desires were stimulated to the breaking point and I cried: 'Anything, anything at all. Just tell me the stipulation. I'll give you my life's blood if you want it.'

'Don't you know what I want?' he exclaimed in unfeigned surprise. 'All I want is your adorable bottom.'

'Oh!' I cried. 'Whatever in the world do you want that for. Besides, I am bashful about even showing it to you.'

'What I'll do with it is my affair,' Father Casimir replied.

So eager was I to get on top of Marianne that I made no further objection and quickly dropped my trousers. I was in her in a flash and Father Casimir was in me. The pain I experienced in the rear was more than compensated by the bliss I enjoyed in the front. Also, I sensed that Marianne was suffering with as much pleasure from my organ as I was from her uncle's.

The three of us, with myself in the middle, were now bucking in perfect cadence. I felt like a conductor between uncle and niece. She was squeezing me, biting me, and scratching me as she felt the explosions I was causing in her. Her spasms astonished the company.

Father Casimir, who had long since abandoned the field, was also amazed at the ferocity of our combat. Everybody was ranged around us in a respectful silence. For myself, I was piqued that Marianne was standing up so doughtily against my repeated assaults, for I knew that I was at the peak of my powers after such a long abstinence.

As for her, she was annoyed at her inability to drain me.

Thus we continued the conflict, literally drenching ourselves with our emissions which were now starting to show flecks of blood.

After we had discharged simultaneously the seventh time, Marianne shut her eyes, let her arms droop, and remained still as she awaited the *coup de grâce* of my eighth ejaculation. After submissively receiving it and savouring it to the last drop, she sprang up and shook my hand to contgratulate me on my victory. In turn, I filled two bumpers with champagne, one of which I handed her, and we exchanged toasts in honour of the armistice.

After the finale, everyone returned to his place. I was again between Marianne, who had her hand on my prick, and her uncle, who had his on my rump.

Now the conversation turned from praises of our exploits to the subject of sodomy. Father Casimir vigorously defended it, eruditely citing its adherents who included Jesuits, philosophers, cardinals, and monarchs. Then he inveighed against those who frowned on pederasty, charging them with stupidity and blind prejudice.

His eloquent peroration was greeted with the praise it deserved. Then we made merry, drank and fucked, before the party broke up. We agreed to celebrate again in a similar fashion in a week's time. Such festivities were not possible every night for the monastery's revenues were not that great.

One day, after having held my first Mass, the Prior asked me to dine with him in his rooms. When I made my appearance there, I found him with some elders, all of whom greeted me with fulsome praise. The reason for the accolade was not clear to me.

We sat down to an excellent repast, and under the influence of the fine wines, the friars' tongues loosened, uttered words like 'cunt' and 'fuck' with a lack of restraint that astonished me. The Prior noticed my surprise.

'Father Saturnin,' he said to me, 'you are to feel as

free with us as we are with you. Now that you are a full-fledged priest, you are one of us. Now the time has come to reveal important secrets that have been withheld from you until now. You realise they could not have been imparted to young men who might leave us and have no scruples about baring mysteries that have to remain known only to the initiate. And it is to fill that obligation that I have asked you come here.'

This solemn exordium caused me to pay close attention to the words of the Prior.

'I don't think you are one of those prudes who are shocked by the thought of fucking, which, as you know, is as natural to a man as drinking or eating. We are priests, to be sure, but our penises and testicles were not amputated when we entered the monastery. But the imbecility of the founders of our order who laid down the rules of celibacy and the cruel insistence of our flocks that we follow those mandates have forbidden us the most natural of functions. If we were to conform to their tyranny, we would burn with flames that would be extinguished only with our deaths. But we don't accept that. We show an austere face to the outer world and indulge ourselves in the seclusion of the cloister.

'In a number of well regulated convents, there are some nuns who are willing to assuage the concupiscence we inherited from Adam, and in their arms we hurl ourselves to lessen the tortures of continence.

'Your words astound me,' I exclaimed.

The others burst out laughing.

'Why should we be such fools and give up the sweetest delight life has to offer?' the Prior continued. 'And we aren't about to. Here we have a refuge where we can escape the atrocities the outer world wants to inflict on us.'

'Have you no fear of being found out?' I inquired.

'None whatsoever,' he assured me. 'There is no chance of discovery. Who would ever think of snooping into a tranquil little corner such as ours? The eyes of the world pass us by. If you, who have been here nine years, had no idea of what was going on, how would an outsider have even an inkling?'

'When can I join you to console those lovely nuns you mentioned,' I eagerly asked.

'It won't be long before you give them the solace they are pining for. But these recreations are reserved only to full-fledged priests. We have to be sure of the discretion of those we accept into our inner circle. You are now one of us, and you join us whenever you wish.'

'Whenever you wish!' I cried. 'I'll take you at your word. Let's go right now.'

'Not so fast,' he said with a smile at my impatience. 'We have to wait until evening. That's when we go to assuage our desires in the piscina where the sisters have their retreat.'

'Now, Father Saturnin, I have another surprise for you. It is something you never even suspected. Ambroise is not your father.'

My jaw dropped at that revelation.

'Yes,' continued the Prior, amused at my dumbfoundedness. 'Ambroise and Toinette are not your parents. You are of much more distinguished lineage. You came into the world in our piscina from the womb of one of our sisters.'

Recovering from my surprise, I replied: 'Father, all along I had the feeling that I was not really a gardener's son. But I am slightly bitter that you withheld this truth from me so long. I would have been overjoyed with the knowledge, and you could have been sure that I would have kept the confidence. Is my mother still living?'

'We had our reasons for not telling you,' he said gently. 'Yes, your mother is alive and well, and in a few hours, you will be embracing her. It will not be a pleasure that you had lost, but one that you will find.'

'I can't wait until I have my arms around her,' I exclaimed.

'Just be patient,' he counselled me. 'It won't be long. The sun is already setting, and night will be here before you know it. We are going to dine in the piscina, and you are to join us.'

The desire to see my mother was not the only reason for my eagerness to penetrate the retreat. In reality, I was more eager to taste of the feminine charms of the beauties I pictured to myself enclosed there.

'So I have finally made it,' I congratulated myself. 'The moment to which I have looked forward so long has come. The long dreary days I spent are going to be more than made up for, if what the Prior says is true.'

When the bell tolled eight o'clock, I returned to the Prior's rooms where I found him with five or six monks, all sharing the same intent as I. Silently we left in single file and walked to those ancient chapels which serve as ramparts to the piscina. Without the benefit of a candle, we descended into a pitch black cellar. In this underground chamber, we made our way with the help of a rope fixed to the wall until we reached a staircase illuminated by a lantern.

Opening the door at the top of the stairs, the Prior

led us into a sumptuously furnished chamber in which were several couches specially designed for the combats of Venus. On the table, we noticed the preparations for a veritable feast.

The room was empty, but when the Prior rang a little bell, our nuns appeared, six in all. I found them delightful and charming. Each promptly threw herself in the arms of a monk, leaving me the sole witness of their transports. I was not a little hurt at their apparent indifference to a new monk, but it would not be long before I had my turn, as I was to find out.

The banquet was superb with the tastiest dishes and wines. Each guest had at his side one of the lovely nuns, and as they drank, ate, laughed, joked and kissed, they discussed fucking with the same casualness they would talk about the weather.

Feeling alone, I had little appetite. Although I naturally wanted to see my mother, I was more anxious for a skirmish with one of the sisters. I looked for the one who could have possibly brought me into the world, but they all seemed so youthful and fresh that it could not be any of those present. Although the six were most attentive to the reverend fathers, they began to cast coquettish glances at me from time to time which changed my original impressions of them. And my prick, now in a state of prime eagerness, yearned for all of them.

My discomfiture was a source of amusement for the whole party. After all had heartily filled their bellies, the Prior announced that it was time to think of fucking. At that, the eyes of the nuns began to glisten. Since I was the newcomer, I was given the honour of beginning the dance.

'Father Saturnin,' the Prior addressed me, 'we have to see what you are capable of with your neighbour, Sister Gabrielle.'

No sooner had he spoken than I started to make her acquaintanceship by exchanging passionate kisses. As we were thus engaged, her hand descended to the slit of my trousers. Although she was not the youngest of the six, she held enough allure for me to be more than contented with my lot. She was a big, voluptuous blonde, whose beauty was marred only by a little too much *embonpoint*. Her skin was a dazzling white and she had a ravishing face with big, blue eyes that were sparkling with delight. Add to all that a breathtaking bosom that was as proud and firm as a young girl's. I could not keep my eyes from those superb globes, and when I found the courage to take them and weigh them in my hands, I was in sheer bliss.

Gabrielle enthusiastically bent to her task of exciting me.

'King of my heart, come and present me with your virginity,' she ordered. 'Lose it in the very spot where you found life.'

Her words made me tremble. Without being a prude, I had acquired some prejudices that would not permit me to do with Gabrielle what I had done with Toinette and Madame Dinville. I was eager to fuck, but the scruple of incest stopped me at the edge of the precipice.

'Heavens!' exclaimed Gabrielle as she rose from her chair. 'Is it possible that this is my son? How could I have given birth to a coward like him? Is he actually afraid of fucking his own mother?'

'My dear Gabrielle,' I replied kissing her on the

cheek. 'Be satisfied with the filial love I have for you. I can imagine no greater delight than that of possessing you, but please respect a prejudice that I am just unable to overcome.'

The avowal of a virtue is respected and admired by the most corrupt and libertine hearts. My reluctance was approved by the monks who agreed that they were wrong in trying to spring such a surprise on me. Only one attempted to dissuade me from my decision.'

'You poor fool,' he told me. 'So you are frightened of doing such a simple thing. Let us talk sensibly. Tell me just what fucking is. You know that it is merely the union of a man and a woman. Is it or is it not permitted by nature? I don't have to wait for your answer, for you realise that the two sexes have an irresistible attraction for each other. It is nature's intention that this mutual urge be satisfied.

'Didn't the Lord command the mother and father of us all to increase and multiply? How did God intend that it should be done? Was Adam to do it all by himself? Adam made with Eve daughters whom he later fucked. Eve had sons with whom she did what her husband was doing with their sisters. Let's get to the Flood. The only family left on earth was Noah's. It goes without saying that the brothers had to copulate with their sisters, the sons with their mother, and the father with his daughters if they were to repopulate the world. And how about Lot and his daughters? In other words, indiscriminate fucking is a divine decree.

'Even Saint Paul counselled fucking, but he called it marriage. When you get down to it, what is the difference? Men and women wed for the sole purpose of fucking. I could go on indefinitely, but I suddenly feel a great need to follow the advice of Saint Paul.'

There was general laughter at the witticism of the monk who was now standing, and, with his prick in his hand, threatening all the slits in the room.

'Just a moment,' broke in one of the sisters whose name was Madelon. 'I just have had the most marvellous idea how we can punish Saturnin for his obstinacy.'

Everybody clamoured to know what it was.

'Well,' she demurely hesitated before continuing. 'He'll lie on one of the couches, Gabrielle will recline on his back, and in that position, our eloquent father will exploit Saturnin's mother.'

There was general hilarity at this whimsical proposal. Laughing myself, I said I would consent only if I could fuck the pleasing Madelon at the same time the father was having my mother on my back.

'Well, I'm agreeable,' Madelone said merrily. 'I have never enjoyed myself in such a position, and the idea intrigues me.'

And I was congratulated for my powers of erotic imagination.

Just picture to yourself the figure we cut. The monk did not give my mother a job without her returning it threefold, and her derriere, dropping on my buttocks, served to shove my prick deeper into Madelon's cunt. This copulative ricochet was immensely diverting for the spectators, but we performers were so busy at our task that we could not join in the merriment.

I could have obtained revenge on Madelon by letting the weight of three bodies fall on her, for she was at the bottom of our four-tiered group, but I liked her too well to play such a dirty trick on her. Besides, she was so conscientious at lending herself to my movements. I made the heaviness on her as light as possible, but when a moment of rapture seized me, I sank down on her with my load. Instead of causing her pain, the weight seemed to enhance her voluptuousness. When I sensed the pair on top of me reach their orgasm, I remained immobile from vicarious lust. At my rigidity, Madelon gave one last upward lunge which produced the same result for the two of us. It seemed that we four, our bodies now one, were swimming in the same lake of bliss.

The praises we made of the enjoyments to be had from making love in such a fashion made the watching sisters' and monks' mouths water, and soon the whole gathering was rapturously fucking in our position – one we dubbed the quatrain, to differentiate it from the *partie carée*, or four forming a square. The greatest discoveries are the result of chance.

Delighted at the improvisation I had come up with, Gabrielle confessed that she had almost as much pleasure as if she had done it directly with me. Then addressing the gathering, she said she was going to tell me before everybody something about herself and her son.

'My boy,' she commenced by addressing me, 'you cannot boast of a long line of illustrious ancestors. I am the daughter of a housekeeper who worked in this monastery and a monk whose identity I never discovered.

'When I was sixteen years old, I discovered love. One young monk gave me such sweet instruction that out of gratitude, I repaid his kindness the only way I knew how, and soon the other fathers were giving me the benefit of their lessons. It goes without saying that I paid them in the same manner. I was quits with all of them when the Prior suggested that I live in a place where I would have the freedom to return their favours as often as I liked. Up to then, I could do it only on the sly, such as behind the altar, in the organ loft, in the confessional, and, at times, in their cells. The thought of being able to indulge myself at will was indeed tempting, and I accepted their offer to come to the piscina.

'The very first day I came here, I was dressed like a young girl about to be confirmed. The thought of the happiness I was going to enjoy gave my face an expression that delighted the fathers. They all wanted to pay me their homage, and each vied with the others to be the first to have me. I was of the opinion that my multiple nuptials could end in a fiasco if I did not do something. Consequently, I suggested that their turn would be determined by lot.

'"My fathers," I addressed them, "your numbers do not frighten me, but my powers may not meet your expectations. Since you are twenty and I am one, the struggle will be unequal. To solve the predicament, I suggest that we all get down to the buff."

'I set the example by divesting myself of every stitch of my garments. It was a matter of seconds until the sisters and monks were in the same state as I. My eyes eagerly devoured the twenty upright pricks, erect, thick and hard as rods of steel. I wished that my cunt were big enough to accommodate them all at once. If only that were possible. I would have gladly accepted them all at the same time.

'"Well," I continued, "It's about time to start. I'll lie

down on this couch with my legs as wide as I can. Then each of you fathers will come in turn as determined by the lottery with your prick in your hand and fuck me in order, one after the other."

'I think it was you, Prior,' she said, addressing him, 'who made Saturnin, for of the twenty who had me, it was you who gave me the sharpest pleasure.' Turning to me, she remarked: 'You have this advantage over other men. They can tell you the date of their birth, but not that of their conception.'

Oh, the delights of the piscina! I savoured them to the full. I was the life of the parties we had there every night, and in no time at all I had fucked every one of the recluses except my mother.

At times, during the necessary pauses, I wondered aloud how such attractive women were willing to spend the rest of their lives in a retreat such as the piscina, which was a form of prison. They laughed at my puzzlement.

'You don't seem to understand our temperaments,' one of the prettiest of the nuns explained to me. 'Where else can we satisfy our fiery desires as well as here? There is the bordel, of course, but there, more often than not, you have to give yourself to the most awful men.' She wrinkled her little nose with disgust. 'You see, we have all the men we need here, and they are all gentlemen, courteous and kind. Five or six times is usual to exhaust a man, but women like us require double that many times. So when our first partner has to leave the field of battle vanquished, there is always another ready to take his place. Isn't that alone worth the price of loss of liberty? What woman with fire in her veins wouldn't envy us for the freedom we have to indulge our caprices? Women on the outside who give in to their desires always have to fear scandal and talk. Marriage, you say!' Here she gave a little snort. 'Just imagine the boredom of having the same man for all of your days. The piscina for us is a seraglio where we exchange partners to our hearts' content, and there are always newcomers, like you for instance. Could a womam wish for anything more? Ah, Father Saturnin, rid yourself of the notion that we are unhappy here in our voluntary bondage!'

I had never expected such sound reasoning from a girl whom I had considered merely a vessel of pleasure. And I had to admit to myself that she was completely right.

Man is not born for lasting pleasure. Having everything my heart could desire, I became nervous and irritable. In fucking, I was like Alexander in ambition. I wanted to fuck the whole world, and if I succeeded in that, I would have sought new worlds for new cunts to conquer.

For more than six months, I was the admitted champion in our amorous combats, but after that, I fucked with the same ennui that I used to masturbate. Soon, I was with the six sisters like a husband is with his wife. My mental lassitude now affected my potency and desire. It was soon noticed, and the sisters reproached me for lethargy, but I shrugged off their playful scoldings. My visits to the piscina became more and more seldom. The Prior urged the sisters to exert themselves to revive me, and they spared no efforts in the task.

Not only did they employ all their natural charms, but also all the refinements that the most lascivious imaginations could dream up. Gathered in a circle around me, they offered to my eyes the most lubricious sights. One would be negligently resting on the bed, half revealing an enticing bosom and letting me see alabaster thighs promising the most delightful cunt in the world. Another would assume an attitude of readiness for combat, letting me know by her sighs and convulsive motions how she was burning with desire. Others would assume different postures, some lifting their skirts and agitating their cunts, some spreading their slits wide open so I could see deep into their interiors, and one even went so far as to make me lie on the floor between two chairs on which she rested herself so that her cunt was directly over my face and then she worked on it with a dildo. Madelon, who had stripped herself completely bare, was vigorously fucking with an equally nude monk next to me so that I could follow every movement of their prick and cunt.

Sometimes they took off all my clothes and placed me on a bench. One sister then would get astride my chest so that my forehead was concealed in the hair of her cunt, a second would be on my stomach, and a third on my thighs trying to introduce my prick into her slit. Two others were at my sides so that I had a cunt in each hand. And then another, possessed of the loveliest bosom of all the sisters, pressed my face between her luscious breasts. All of them were stark naked and discharging so that my hands, stomach, legs, chest, prick, and face were inundated. I was literally drowning in fuck, but mine refused to mingle with theirs. The attempt was as vain as the others had been. From then on, I was considered a lost soul.

Such was my condition when, walking alone in the

garden with my gloomy reflections, I came across Father Simeon, a wise and scholarly priest, who had grown white-haired in the labours of Venus and the table. He came up to me and put his arms around me affectionately.

'My son,' he said, 'I can see that your grief is deep, but don't allow yourself to despair. In my long experience, I have found ways to revive the desire for pleasure, that voluptuous ardour characterising a good monk. You are in a bad way, that is obvious, and for severe ailments, desperate remedies are required.

'Cruel nature has granted us only limited powers, although it must be admitted that it treats us monks as favoured sons. But excessive dissipation, even in a monk, can produce the same result as in an ordinary man, and it is this dissipation which is the cause of your sickness and your disgust with sex. What you need to restore your jaded appetite is a succulent dish, and I know of nothing better than a devout woman.'

I could not conceal my surprise.

'I am quite serious,' he told me, 'and what I am telling you is not a paradox. You are still young, and you do not know devout women as I do. You have no idea, they have infallible resources to relight extinguished flames. They are able to arouse the ardour of the most jaded man. I know it from my own experience. I have fucked them, and more than one, I assure you.'

I looked at him unbelievingly, for he was considered a broken old man with ice water in his veins. He could barely walk, his testicles were empty, and his prick had disappeared. That was his reputation. And since his novitiate, he was renowned for his celibacy.

'Yes, my son,' he continued. 'You are still in that happy age when you can enjoy unlimited pleasures. Take advantage of it as I did. At my age, I have more important things to think about, namely, eternal life. Nevertheless, I do not refuse to give my advice to those who have need of it. I repeat that the only cure for your lethargy is a devout and the only way to get one is to obtain permission to hear confessions. I'll take care of that for you.'

Although I had my doubts, I thanked him for his advice and his offer to enable me to be a father confessor.

'That's not all,' he went on. 'Before you start your new calling, you'll need someone to guide your steps at first. I'll be happy to play that role, but before I continue, let's sit on this bench, where we'll be more comfortable.'

We sat down, and the good father, coughing to regain his voice, went on with his talk.

'You probably don't realise that this happy mania known as confession goes back to our ancestors, that is the first priests and monks at the beginning of Christianity. The practice is the most precious heritage they have left us. I have always entertained the greatest admiration for their genius. At first, priests did not know comfort and ease and monks depended on a few charitable crumbs to fill their empty bellies. With the advent of the confession, all that unhappy condition changed. Riches rained down on our heads, and we now lead happy, contented lives.

'You will soon learn the advantages of being a confessor. The people will bless you and the women will adore you. God, whose mercy they beg through your intercession, is less their deity than you are. One piece of advice I have to give you is to fleece those dowagers, those old bigots who come to confession not so much to make their peace with God as to see a handsome young priest.

'Be merciful with the young girls, for seldom are they able to make donations other than token ones. But they have something more precious to offer, and that is their maidenhead. Skill is required to steal this charming gem. Concentrate on these young devouts, for they are the only ones able to cure you. In spite of your understandable eagerness for recovery, watch your step. Don't openly express your desires. A woman can take a hint. Her heart more or less tells her your desires before you have uttered a word. But a young girl is different. Although her conquest is more difficult, the victory is sweeter.

'With all of them, you'll find a natural penchant for the joys of love. To handle this inclination is an art. The shy lass who appears before you with a demure dress, a humble attitude, and lowered eyes has coals smouldering within her that are ready to burst into flame at the first gust of love. If you are tender and adroit, your triumph is sure.

'With some, you have to paint the erotic delights in such vivid colours that they cannot resist.

'Perhaps you will object that it is difficult to succeed in such an art, but all that is needed is a little practise. Their inborn desires always win out over their modesty. And have no fear of their blabbing. As a man of God, they hold you in too great awe. The usual way is to casually put your hand on their breasts, regard them with longing eyes, and go up their skirt. If they have any scruples, dispel them by saying you know many ways to avoid the danger of pregnancy.'

Father Simeon's discourse so heated my imagination that I kept after him and the Prior until I obtained what I so ardently desired.

Now I was mediator between sinners and the Father of mercy. I pictured to myself the pleasure I was going to have hearing the confession of a timid young girl who would soon yield to her latent passions. I went to the confessional box to take up my post.

I had heard of a young priest, who, on finding his first penitent an ugly old woman, returned to his cell and stayed there the remainder of the day. I did not follow his example, fortunately, when a similar hag presented herself to me.

I suffered a torrent of twaddle and consoled her so successfully with hypocritical moral advice that she would have willingly granted me evidence of her gratitude. Fortunately, the grille was a barrier. I recalled Father Simeon's advice – fleece the old ones – and I obtained a generous contribution. She was a chatterbox and skilfully I led her to talk about her family. She cursed her husband and inveighed against her son, another ne'er-do-well, who was unfaithful to his wife as her spouse was to her. All her praise was reserved for her daughter, who was her only consolation. She was a model of devoutness, of angelic purity, who, in order to remain uncontaminated by the filth of the world, left her room only to come to church. Her sole pleasure consisted of prayer.

'Ah!' I exclaimed in a sanctimonious voice, 'how happy you must be to see yourself incarnated in such a daughter. But does this saintly creature come to our church? How happy I would be to meet such an example of virtue.'

'She's here every day,' the old woman informed me. 'You can't miss her, for she is a striking beauty. But I should not mention that because it cannot be of any interest to one like you who is of the saints.'

'We admire all the works of the Lord, including the beauty of women,' I assured her.

Encouraged by my curiosity, the old lady began to depict her virtuous daughter, whom I now recognised as the ravishing brunette who never missed Mass.

'Father Simeon,' I said to myself, 'that must be one of the devouts you were telling me about. I hope she comes to me so that I can learn if your prophecy is correct.'

I perhaps could have scared off the mother if in our initial talk I had tried to persuade her to have her child come to me for confession. I decided to postpone the suggestion until the next time, and to win her good graces, I gave her a general absolution, both for the past and for the present. I would have absolved her for future transgressions, if she had wanted. It would not have cost anything. As she left the box, I urged her to come often for the holy water.

It seems that I hear you crying: 'Go on, Dom Bougre, you are on the right track. You'll soon be cured.'

Yes, dear reader, the sanctity I had assumed was commencing to work. Praise the Lord for his beneficence. I was starting to have erections of sufficient vigour to lead me to hope that I would soon be my old self.

The next day, I did not fail to attend services, and

one can readily imagine why. There I saw my brunette praying to God with all her heart.

'There she is,' I thought with deep satisfaction. 'There is that paragon of virtue. Oh, what a delight it will be to munch on a morsel like that. What a rapture to give the first amorous lesson to someone like her. I am cured, for I have an erection like a Carmelite's.'

My devout was regarding me. Had her mother spoken about me to her? Quickly now. Let's put out the fires that her look lit in me.

I could not help myself. Her ecstatic gaze excited me almost to a fury, and my hand went to my prick which was as hard as rock. My pleasure when I discharged was almost as great as if I had been in her.

One day, I had been away from the monastery for some time, and when I returned, the porter, on opening the gate, informed me that a young lady had been waiting for me for several hours and insisted on speaking to me. I hurried to the reception room, where I found, to my utter amazement, the devout object of my adoration.

As soon as she espied me, she rushed to me and threw herself at my feet.

'Have pity on me, Father,' she pleaded as tears streamed down her cheeks. Her sobs prevented her from continuing.

'What is wrong, my child?' I asked as soothingly as I could as I helped her to her feet. 'You can confide in me. The Lord is merciful, and He sees your sorrow. Open your heart to me as His deputy.'

She tried to speak, but her sobs did not let her. Then she fell in a faint in my arms. What an idiot I would have been if I had followed my first impulse and gone to seek assistance! I had already taken a few steps with that in mind, but on second thought, I halted.

'Where are you going?' she unexpectedly asked. 'Are you waiting for a more favourable opportunity?'

Approaching my devout, I undid her bodice and regarded the most enticing bosom imaginable. The satiny globes with their pink tips were like the pillars to the gates of Paradise. In jubilation and ecstasy, I pressed my cheeks to their firm contours and eagerly took the points in my mouth. Our mouths met and our breaths blended.

Beside myself with desire, I retained my reason sufficiently to hasten to the street door which I opened and closed as if taking leave of someone, and then returned to my jewel. I clasped her in my arms with ecstatic tremors. Barely could I contain myself at the sight of her beauties.

'Dear God, second me in my efforts,' I cried as I reached my room with the beloved burden in my arms.

She was as light as a feather. Putting her on my bed, I locked the door, and lit a candle. In the dim illumination, I saw that she had swooned again. After completely removing her blouse to regard the enchanting hemispheres in their full beauty, I lifted her skirt and spread wide her legs. My mind was a combination of lust and delight. Holding myself back, I examined her charms and soulfully admired them. What a voluptuous spectacle! Love and grace were to be found on all parts of her body: whiteness, *embonpoint*, firmness, delicacy – all were there, and all were a delight to the eye. The snow of her skin strewn with little streaks of blue veins, the black fleece finer than velvet, and the vermilion which set off with exquisite nuances the enticing cunt, threw me into a veritable rapture. Picture to yourself all the beauties of the Greek goddesses, combine them, and they would not compare to what met my eyes.

But to admire them without enjoying them was unthinkable. I furiously put my mouth and hands on all that met my sight. As soon as I did so, my devout showed some signs of life by sighing and taking hold of my hand. When I kissed her again, she tried to free herself by shoving me away. Surprised and terrified at finding herself on my bed, she cast disturbed looks around the room and seemed to be trying to discover where she was. She attempted to say something, but it seemed that she had lost the power of speech. I was burning with such a passion that I could not release her. She made violent efforts to get out of my arms, but I held her more tightly and turned her on her back. Making a powerful effort to rise, she scratched and bit my face and pounded me with her little fists. By now, we were both perspiring copiously.

Nothing, however, could stop me. I pressed my chest against her bosom, my stomach against hers, and trying to keep her quiet under me with the weight of my body, I permitted her to do with her hands all that her fury and rage dictated. Oblivious to her blows, I slowly opened her stubborn clenched thighs. Momentarily despairing at reaching my goal, I redoubled my efforts, and I was successful. The thighs were spread wide and between them I inserted my prick which had popped out of my trousers as if released by a spring. With a mighty shove, it was in. At that sensation, all the anger of my devout vanished. She fervently put her arms around me, kissed me, closed her eyes, and fell back in a sort of faint. I no longer knew what I was doing, but nothing could stop me. I jabbed and shoved, and attaining my goal, I flooded the recesses of her cunt with a boiling torrent. She responded to my discharge with an equally copious inundation. Then we relaxed, savouring mutually what we had just enjoyed.

My companion was the first to return to her senses, and her first reaction was to resume the game. Her cunt was a fiery furnace in which my prick eagerly desired to become seared.

'I am dying,' she panted. 'I am suffocating.'

With that, she suddenly stiffened, wiggled her derriere to which I responded with two, and we again discharged.

We continued until nature made us stop. As is the case, our powers were not up to our desires. We had to pause. Taking advantage of the respite, I hastened to the kitchen to take the meal that was destined for a patient in the hospital, a repast that was to restore his vitality. I said I was the patient and took the food.

Returning to my room, I found my devout in regret and despair. Comforting her with renewed caresses, we shared the nourishing repast. Afterwards, I gave her the delights I was supposed to have only on the recluses of the piscina. In other words, I broke the rules of my order.

After the meal, we both thought we were too tired to continue. We returned to bed, still nude, but when I casually put my hand on her cunt, the source and tomb of the delights I had just enjoyed, all thought of sleep vanished. In turn, she touched my masculinity, admiring its size as well as the fullness of my testicles.

'You have reconciled me to a pleasure I had made up my mind to hate,' she told me.

Instead of answering, I made haste to give her new raptures before she could return to her former resolution. Eagerly she welcomed my advances with a vivacity that would have snatched me from the arms of death himself. Her backsides rose and fell like the ocean's waves in a tempest. Our bodies were like two iron bars just out of the fiery forge. So tightly did we hold each other that we could scarcely breathe. We felt that the slightest pause would annihilate our bliss. The bed was shaking and creaking ominously. A sweet intoxication soon crowned our exertions, and I fell asleep on top of her with my prick still in her cunt.

Dawn found us in the same position as when slumber had overtaken us. When we awoke, however, we found to our surprise that the sheets and even the mattress were drenched with fresh juices of love.

We could not wait to renew our sports. Sleep had restored my forces, so I was confident I could acquit myself like a true monk. I cannot tell you how many times I did it. I was so busy fucking that I lost count.

It is now time to tell how the devout had come into my arms.

After we were through, I saw that she had a worried, melancholy expression which touched me. Tenderly, I begged her to tell me what was wrong, and I promised her I would do anything to remove the cause of her sadness.

'Will I lose your heart, dear Saturnin,' she asked me slowly, 'if I tell you that you are not the first who has enabled me to taste the delights of love? Yes, it is that fear that is bothering me.'

'Of course not,' I replied in relief. 'Don't give it another thought. Even if you have fornicated with every man on earth, you would be the same adorable desirable creature. The pleasures you have granted others, did they diminish the delights you have just given me?'

'You have given me back life,' she said as she threw herself in my arms.

## *The Story of the Devout*

'My misery has its source in my heart, in an insurmountable inclination nature has given me for pleasure. Love is my divinity, and it is the only thing I live for. My cruel mother got it in her head that the church should be my vocation. Too timid to expostulate with her words, I could only protest with a burst of tears. They had no effect on her cruel heart. I had to enter the nunnery, where I took the veil. The moment of my living death was approaching and I shuddered at the vow I was going to have to make. The horror of a prison-like convent and the despair of being eternally deprived of the greatest good in life caused an ailment that would have put an end to all my pains. At the last moment, my mother, reproaching herself for her severity, relented in her determination in her plans for me. She was living as a paying guest in the convent where she wanted me to take the nun's habit.

'Seeing my state, she left the retreat and took me with her. We returned to normal life and my mother was soon in search of a fifth husband.

'Knowing my mother as I did, I realised it would be dangerous for me to enter into competition with her. If any suitor appeared, I was positive that he would not hesitate to choose me over my mother, and that was what I was afraid of. Consequently, I decided to become a devout instead of a nun, for I knew I could have my pleasures under such a cover! I built a reputation of virtuousness for myself in order to indulge in my vices more easily. However, this reputation was sullied by an unfortunate happening with a young man at the grille.'

At this point of her story, I recalled what Suzon had told me about Sister Monique, her aversion to the convent, her passion for love, the scene she had with Verland, the stay of her mother at the convent, and I mentally compared Sister Monique with the pretty thing I had with me. Recalling that Monique, according to Suzon, had a rather long clitoris, I turned my devout on her back and carefully examined her cunt. I found what I was looking for – a vermilion clitoris slightly longer than average. No longer doubting that it was she, I embraced her with a new fervour.

'Dearest Monique,' I cried, 'is it you that good fortune has sent to me?'

Freeing herself from my arms and regarding me with a troubled look, she demanded how I knew the name she had assumed in the convent.

'A girl whose loss has caused me many tears,' I replied, 'and to whom you revealed all your secrets.'

'Suzon!' she exclaimed. 'The traitress.'

'Yes,' I agreed. 'That's she. But I'm the only one to whom she has told your story, and she only did so because I begged her so hard. I beseech you to forgive her.'

'So you're the brother of Suzon,' she said. 'Well, I can't complain because she told me everything that she did with you.'

Sighing at the pitiful lot of our poor Suzon, Monique picked up the thread of her discourse.

'Since Suzon left nothing out, including my skirmish with Verland, I may as well tell you the full story. Although he was banned from the retreat, he did not forget me. And when he saw me in church, all his desire for me was revived. On my part, I felt strange stirrings within me. I blushed when I discovered how handsome he had become, and I felt his eyes fixed on me. Quickly, he perceived my inner confusion. When I left the church, I took a little-frequented street down which he followed me as I expected he would.

'When he caught up with me, he said in a voice trembling with emotion: "Monique, can a man who did something wrong to you at our first meeting now pay his respects? I have repented of that ever since."

'I took pity on him and said that I considered it merely the act of an overly impetuous youth.

'"You do not know all of my faults," he went on. "Your kindness has just forgiven me for one crime. I now have need more than ever of your goodness since I am guilty of another offence."

'Falling silent after these words, he stood there with his head hanging down. I said that I did not have the faintest idea of what he was talking about.'

'"I have fallen madly in love with you," he declared, kissing my hand which I did not have the strength to snatch away.

'I let him know by my silence that I did not find this new crime unforgivable. Reluctant to show my feelings too openly at this first meeting, I left him, absolutely charmed and delighted by his avowal.

'I was sure that if Verland was sincere, he would

easily find ways to give me further assurances. He let me go, and as I went, I heard some sighs that I answered with those in my heart.

'We met again, at which time he asked me for permission to request my mother for my hand in marriage. I gladly consented, but she refused him, a decision that only enhanced my love for him. Verland, of course, was crushed. You have no idea of the reason for my mother's turning down my lover. She had become my rival for his affections. She betrayed herself by her continual praise of his charm and handsomeness. I was furious both with my mother and with myself. My love made me capable of doing anything. Although my mother suspected nothing, I saw Verland every day, for life without him was unthinkable. But would you believe that at that time, I had enough self-control not to yield to his insistences and to turn down his suggestion for the only method to bring my mother to her senses. Finally, touched by his tears, urged by my own love, and conquered by my own inclinations, I agreed to an elopement, and we discussed the day, the hour, and the means.

'The intensity of my love permitted me to picture only the pleasures that I would have with my lover. The gloomiest cave would have been a paradise if only I were with him. The momentous day arrived when we were to flee together. Suddenly, an invisible arm held me back. My passion had strewn with flowers the path to the precipice from which I was to make my leap. But when I was at the edge, and I saw how deep it was, I stepped back in horror. I did my best to overcome my lack of courage, and my tears were copious at my cowardice. The hour was approaching and I had to make up my mind. What should I do? I was in such desperate straits that I could not think straight.

'Suddenly, a ray of light illuminated my brain; I saw the way to be with my lover and exact a sweet vengeance on my mother at the same time.

'I made the signal to Verland on which we had agreed in case I could not carry out my end. We met again the following day in the church where he approached me without saying a word, but the expression was eloquent. It frightened me.

'"Do you love me?" I asked him.

'"How can you even ask that?" he replied. His despair prevented him from saying more.

'"Verland," I continued. "I see the grief in your eyes. My heart is also torn. Find fault with me. Complain of my lack of courage. When I ask if you love me, it is not that I doubt your love, but I am afraid that you are unwilling to give me the sole evidence of it. Stop!" I commanded him when he tried to interrupt. "You want to reproach me, but if you do, you will be unjust towards me. I repeat that I have not the slightest doubt about your feelings for me, and please do not think that my love for you has altered. But what use is it to burn with a flame that a cruel mother refuses to let us extinguish? Ah, my Verland, doesn't the scarlet of my face tell you the means I wish to employ?"

'"Dear Monique," he replied, putting his hand tenderly to my mouth. "Does your love finally make you feel the necessity of a thing that I have asked you for so many times without success?"

'"Yes, yes. Your love will no longer have cause for complaint. No longer can I conceal from you the urge of my desires which are now at their peak. But before we enjoy our bliss, I expect only one word from your mouth."

'"Tell me what you want me to say," he cried impatiently. "What do you want me to do?"

'"Marry my mother," I told him simply.

'He looked as if he had been struck by a thunderbolt, so great was his amazement.

'"Marry your mother?" he repeated automatically, looking at me with bewildered eyes. "Monique, what are you saying?"

'"I'm just proposing that you do a simple thing that will overcome our difficulties," I replied, impatient at his incomprehension. "What I am proposing has cost me a torrent of tears, and you greet it with coldness and indifference. I now regret the profound love I had conceived for you. What am I to think of a man who is as cowardly as you?"

'"Monique," he said piteously. "How can you wish me to do such a despicable thing as that?"

'"You ungrateful idiot!" I retorted. "If I am able to overcome the horror of the thought of seeing you in the arms of my rival for the sole purpose of deceiving her, you can quiet her now and then. My proposal is made just so that we can enjoy each other, to have the pleasure of seeing you always, to have the bliss of always feeling your caresses. I am risking my reputation and I offer you for your happiness what I hold most dear. I don't give a damn about the tortures of jealousy, which I am stifling in my heart. But you are shaking like a leaf. Is it that I am stronger than you? Perhaps you don't have as much love for me as I have for you."

'"You're right," he replied with determination.

"I'm ashamed of my irresolution. Remorse is not for hearts as impassioned as ours."

'Delighted at his courage, I would have willingly granted him the marks of my affection if it had not been for the spot we were in, a place where we could have easily been surprised.

'The nuptials took place and the pleasure I showed caused my mother to overwhelm me with tender embraces and kisses. I returned them with ones less sincere. My soul was drunkenly anticipating both revenge and the pleasures of love.

'Verland appeared. He was utterly irresistible. Countless new charms animated all his movements. His slightest smile sent me into bliss and his most casual words made my heart pound madly. It was an agony to watch him and not take him in my arms. During the general hubbub, he was able to come close to me and whisper: "I have done everything for love. Will it do anything for me?" I answered him with a fiery glance that he immediately understood.

'We made our escape without being noticed. I entered my bedroom with him on my heels. After throwing himself on the bed, he pulled me down on him. I could not speak. Words fail me, and I am unable to describe to you the ineffable pleasures I had with Verland. Only, you, my dear Father, only you have been so far. "Oh, mother!" I cried during our transports, "how dearly your injustice to me is going to cost you!"

'My lover was a prodigy. For more than an hour we continued without a pause. Like Antheus who had only to touch the ground to regain his strength in his struggle with Hercules, my lover merely needed to touch my flesh to feel his forces returning.

'The others were looking for us for some time. There were even knocks at my door, at which we had to separate for fear of discovery. Verland slipped out into the garden where he pretended to be sleeping on the grass. The hilarity was general, because it was thought he was exhausted from the marital labours with my mother.

'Realising that I would be looked for, I took the key out of the door so the curious could peek in. They saw me on my knees fervently praying before a crucifix. Their respect for my piety increased. Recovering from the effects of my amorous exertions, I returned to the gathering without anyone suspecting what I had been up to.

'As soon as I conceived the project of marrying my mother to my lover, I made every effort to bring about ways that he and I could meet without being surprised. To effect this, I feigned an increase in my piety and insisted that I should never be disturbed during my devotions. Soon the entire household was accustomed to not knock at my door if they did not see the key on the outside. For his part, Verland got my mother to believe that he was not as arduous and vigorous as she had thought, and under the pretext of having to take care of some business affairs, he slipped off into my room.

'Our joys, children of constraint and secrecy, did not diminish after a year of mutually exchanged bliss. It was so ecstatic that I thought that all the men in the world together could not have added to my raptures. But, one time, I found out how wrong I was.

'One day, I met a young girl I had known before in

the town. We greeted each other and I asked what she was doing. She replied she was looking for a job, and I engaged her as a chamber-maid.

'Well, my dear Father, I won't conceal anything from you. I have to tell you that this so-called chamber-maid was none other than Martin, about whom your sister must have made mention while telling you my story.

'I had not seen him since our separation. He was still goodlooking. In the eyes of the world, he was merely a pretty girl but to me he was a male of inestimable worth.

'I did not hide from Martin my liaison with Verland. Only too delighted to enjoy me again, he was not averse at all to sharing my favours with another. For my part, I was pleased at his docility and enraptured with his virility. Playing no favourites, I divided my gifts: Verland was given the day and Martin the night. Thus the days began for me with a serene deliciousness and the nights were ended in pure voluptuousness. Never has a woman enjoyed such continued transports as I. But the characteristic of pleasure is that it is of short duration, and its loss is one of the prices that must be paid for its possession.

'As I told you, Martin was able to pass for an attractive lass with his girl's dress. But that faithless Verland, damn him! Well, I shouldn't say faithless for I was being guilty of the same sin. Verland found my chamber-maid more and more attractive, and soon my days were empty. Compensated by the nocturnal pleasures, I noticed the indifference Verland showed me during the daylight hours. My hands endlessly tried to arouse him to his former ardour, but my two young men met more and more. But Verland was sly and he made me believe the reason he gave for his indifference. When I attempted to scold him, a smile, a kiss, or caress was sufficient to dispel my nagging doubts. A day of repose, he assured me, was necessary to restore his vigour, and his absences made me believe that such was so. I agreed to them, and Martin satisfactorily took his place.

'Yesterday, oh miserable day which I shall always remember with loathing, was supposed to be Verland's day off. In my room, with Cupid as our only witness, I was stretched out on my bed, my bosom bare and my legs wide open, waiting for Martin to regain his strength. In the nude, he was caressing my breasts and squeezing his thighs against mine. While his eyes and touches attempted to revive his desires, Verland unexpectedly entered the chamber and caught us in that position. Before we had time to disengage ourselves, he had closed the door behind him and come up to us.

'"Monique," he said to me, "I don't blame you for your pleasures, but you must share them with me. I'm in love with Javote (that was the name that Martin had taken), and I think I have enough forces to satisfy both of you."

'At that moment, he tried to kiss Martin. Dragging him from my arms, he put his hand... and he didn't find what he expected. Without releasing Martin, he gave me an indignant look. He didn't dare to take out his anger on me, but his fury fell on the innocent cause. His love turned into rage, and he began to beat Martin mercilessly with his fists.

'Throwing myself between, I kissed Verland and

cried: "Stop! He is just a youth, and if you really love me, you will spare him. Have pity for his weakness and my tears."

'Verland ceased his pummelling, but Martin, who had now come to his senses, became furious in his turn. Grasping Verland's sword, he made a lunge at him. At the sight of that, I fled and came here.'

As she finished, she burst into a flood of tears.

'Alas, what is to become of me?' she sobbed.

'Stop your tears,' I comforted her. If it is the loss of your pleasures that is worrying you, more intense ones will more than make up for them.'

Realising that it was impossible to keep her much longer in my room for fear of discovery, I felt the wisest course was to take her to the piscina. Without going into details, I assured her that the pleasures reserved for her there would, in comparison, make her past ones pale. Such a retreat was ideal for a woman with a temperament like hers.

'Dear friend,' she said, embracing me, 'please do not abandon me. Tell me that I can stay with you. Your decision will determine my fate. If I lose you, I shall be miserable for the rest of my days.'

I assured her that we would never part, and, at her timid request, I said I would find out what had happened to her two lovers. I left, promising to return as quickly as I could.

Asking everyone who might have knowledge of the affair, I learned nothing. Apparently, the quarrel had ceased with Monique's flight and the two combatants considered it wise to hush up the matter. When I came back with the news for my devout, a servant ran up to me and gave me a letter and a little purse with some money in it.

I opened the letter and read the following:

'You have been found out. We suspected you and we opened the door to your room. There we discovered the treasure you were unwilling to share with you brother monks. We took her and put her in the piscina. Flee! You know the horrors our order is capable of. Flee for your life! Brother André.'

A clap of thunder over my head could not have stunned me more than the perusal of this missive. I felt that all was lost. Where could I take refuge? How could I save myself from their vengeance? Suddenly, in my consternation, the thought of Ambroise's house came to mind. It would be the safest asylum. I resolved to go there.

It was not without pangs of grief that I left the place that had been my repose, my happiness, and my pleasure. I bewailed the loss of Monique, but I consoled myself with the thought of the delights she was going to enjoy in the piscina.

When I arrived at Ambroise's, I only found Toinette to whom I told my woes. Touched by my account, she helped me the best she could. She gave me one of her husband's suits, and I decided to leave the next day for Paris, where I was confident I could find compensation for all that I had lost. For the sake of safety, I walked only at night, and after several days, I reached the capital of France.

Now I felt I could defy the vengeance of the monks. The money Father André and Toinette had given me would keep me for some time. My intention was to find a job as a teacher in a private home until fortune offered me something more suitable. Although I had some acquaintances in Paris who could have helped me, it was too risky to turn to them.

Even though I had decided to give up the pleasures of the flesh, a pretty little thing accosted me on the street one day and I immediately forgot my good intentions. She led me by the hand to a shabby building, in which we ascended a narrow winding staircase. The door was opened by an ancient witch who told me to wait for a moment in the room. In the meantime, my guide had disappeared. Although I had never been in one, I realised that I was in a brothel. A sudden anxiety and fear took possession of me when a coarse, plump woman approached me. Placing some money in her hand, I pushed her rudely away. She was indignant.

Then I heard a voice that was not unfamiliar to me. It penetrated to my heart. I began to tremble all over. I could not believe my ears. The door opened and there was... Suzon! Although the years had changed her features, I recognised her right away. Wordlessly, I fell into her arms and tears welled in my eyes.

'My dear sister,' I finally asked in an uncertain voice, 'don't you recognise your brother?'

After scanning my face, she fainted.

The hag tried to offer assistance, but I pushed her away. Pressing my lips on Suzon's mouth and wetting her face with my tears, I restored her to life.

'Leave me, Saturnin,' she cried. 'Leave a miserable wretch like myself.'

'My dear sister,' I exclaimed, 'does the sight of your Saturnin inspire you with such horror? Do you refuse his kisses and embraces?'

Touched by my reproaches, she showed her joy.

Happiness reappeared on her cheeks. She ordered the old woman to bring us something to eat and drink. I gave her some money. I would have given her all I had for was I not rich with the possession of Suzon?

While waiting for the repast, I kept holding Suzon in my arms. We did not yet have the strength to ask each other how it came about that we found ourselves so far away from home. Our eyes were the interpreters of our souls. Our hearts were so overflowing that our tongues were tied. We opened our mouths, but no words came out.

'Suzon,' I finally said, breaking the silence. 'How is it that you are in such a vile place as this?'

'You see before you one who has suffered all the vicissitudes of fortune,' she sadly answered. 'I see that you are impatient to hear about my miseries. Now that I am with you, I feel no embarrassment at telling you how I came to lead this life of shame. You are partially responsible, but I readily forgive you.

'I have always loved you. Do you remember that happy time when you told me so simply of your growing passion? How I adored you when I told you about Monique and all our secrets. My intention was to arouse you and instruct you, and I wanted to see what affect my discourse would have on you. I was a witness to your gambols with Madame Dinville, and the caresses you lavished on her were like stabs in my heart. When I took you into my room, I was consumed by a fire that you were no longer able to extinguish. It was then my misfortunes began.

'You don't know the reason for that horrible scene in my room. It was Abbot Fillot, that scoundrel of scoundrels. He had an urge for me that he intended to satisfy at any cost. During the night he had hidden himself in the space between the wall and my bed, and he took advantage of your flight to take your place. Since I had fainted from fright, he was able to do what he wanted with me. Revived by the pleasure I was experiencing, I was under the opinion that it was my dear Saturnin who was giving it to me. I overwhelmed with delight a monster whom I overwhelmed with curses when I recognised who it was. He tried to calm me with his caresses, but I shoved him away in horror. Then he threatened to tell Madame Dinville what I had done with him. Thus I had to give my all to a creature I detested, and fate snatched from my arms the one I adored.

'It was not long before I began to experience the bitter fruits of the incident. I concealed my shame as long as I could, but I would have betrayed myself by too obstinate a silence. After having repulsed his further advances, he consoled himself in the embraces of Madame Dinville. When concealment was no longer possible, I had to go to him and reveal my condition. Feigning sympathy, he offered to take me with him to Paris where he said he would do everything to help me. All I wanted was a place where I could rid myself of my burden, and I hoped that afterwards, he would assist me in getting a position with some lady. I allowed myself to be persuaded by his glowing promises and came with him here.

'But the shaking of the carriage had upset my calculations, and I brought into the world a league from Paris the hateful token of a villain's passion. Since I was disguised as a monk, everybody laughed at the miracle. My travelling companion immediately decamped, leaving me to my misery and woes. A compassionate woman took pity on me by taking me to the charity hospital in Paris. Although I had been saved from death, I was penniless. When I thought all was over with me, I met a girl who helped me by teaching me her trade, the one I am leading now. Although my life has been miserable, I have no complaints because I have found you. But how about you? Did you leave the monastery? And why are you in Paris?'

'A misfortune similar to yours is the reason for my being here,' I replied, 'a tragedy caused by your best friend.'

'My best friend?' she repeated with a puzzled look. 'Do I have any left? Oh, that must be Sister Monique.'

'You hit the nail on the head,' I said. 'But it will take some time to tell you the whole story, so let's eat first.'

The meal I shared with Suzon was the most delicious I had ever eaten in my life. But my desire to be alone with her and her eagerness to learn of my adventures prompted us to leave the table quickly. We retired to a room, where, on the bed with her body pressed to mine, I told her all that had happened since I left Ambroise's.

'Then I am not your sister,' she cried when I had finished.

'Don't have any regrets,' I consoled her. 'Even though you are not my sister, you are still my adored Suzon, the idol of my heart. Let's forget the unhappy past and consider the beginning of our life this day when we found each other again.'

At these words, I ardently kissed her breasts and my hand was between her thighs as I was about to turn her on her back.

'Stop!' she commanded, escaping from my embrace.

'Stop?' I cried, utterly amased. 'How can you possibly say that? How can you turn down the offers of my passion for you!'

'Stifle those desires,' she sadly said. 'And I'll set the example.'

'Suzon, you must no longer have any love for me if you say that. There is nothing to stop us from making each other happy.'

'Nothing, you say?' she sighed. 'How wrong you are.'

At that, tears streamed down her cheeks. I urged her to tell me the sorrow that caused them.

'Would you want to share with me the cruel price of my dissolute life? And even if you did, could I be so unfeeling as to let you?'

'Do you think I would let such a feeble argument influence me?' I exclaimed. 'I would gladly die together with my dear Suzon.'

Promptly I had her on her back and proved to her that I had no fears.

'Ah, Saturnin, you are a lost soul,' she wept.

'If I'm lost, let it be in your arms.'

Dear reader, I leave to your imagination the transports I enjoyed. I more than recaptured the lost delights.

Day appeared before we noticed that night had disappeared. Not once had I left Suzon's arms. I had forgotten all my griefs. In fact, I had forgotten the entire universe.

'We'll never leave each other, my dear brother,' she told me. 'Where will you find a more tender mistress, and I a more passionate lover?'

I swore to her that I would never leave her side, but we were going to be separated soon, never to see each other again. There was a storm hovering over our heads, but we were so dazzled with each other that we did not notice it.

'Save yourself, Suzon,' a panic-stricken girl panted as she rushed into our room. 'Hurry. Use the hidden staircase.'

Astonished, we got up, but it was too late. A burly soldier burst into the chamber. Suzon, with a screech of fright, threw herself in my arms. In spite of my efforts to hold her, he managed to drag her from me. God! The sight enraged me; fury lent me strength; and despair rendered me invincible. The andiron I instinctively grabbed became a lethal weapon in my hands. With a powerful blow, the would-be ravisher of Suzon lay at my feet. I was grabbed, and although I made valiant efforts to defend myself, I had to succumb. When they tied me up, they left me with hardly a stitch of clothing on.

'Good-bye Suzon!' I cried, trying to stretch my arms to her. 'Good-bye, my dear sister.'

I was shoved down the steps so harshly that the bumps on my head soon caused me to lose consciousness.

Should I finish here the account of my misfortunes? If there is any compassion in your soul, dear reader, you will consent to hear the end of my woes. Haven't I shed enough tears? I am safe in harbour, but still I regret the dangers of a shipwreck. Continue to read in order to learn the frightful results of libertinism. You will be lucky if you don't have to pay for them more dearly than I did.

When I came to my senses, I found myself in a shabby bed in a hospital. When I asked where I was, I was told the hospital was the Bicetre. Heavens! Bicetre. I was petrified with terror and burning with fever. I had been cured only to find I had a much more virulent ailment than broken bones – syphilis. Without a murmur, I accepted this new chastisement from heaven.

'Suzon,' I said to myself, 'I would not complain of my lot, if you were not suffering from the same disaster.'

My ailment gradually became so serious that desperate remedies were required. In order to save me, I was told that I would have to undergo a slight operation. When informed of its nature, I fell into such a deep faint that it was feared my last moment had come. If only it had! When it was over, the operation, I put my hand where the pain had been.

'I'm no longer a man!' I screamed so loudly that it was heard in every extremity of the establishment.

Now my only wish was for death. I had lost the ability to enjoy life. I could only think with horror at what I had become. Father Saturnin, once the delight of women, was nothing. Fate, a cruel fate, had deprived him of his most precious possession. I was nothing but a eunuch.

Death did not heed my appeals. I gradually regained my health, and the head doctor said that I was now free to leave the hospital.

'Free?' I asked him in surprise. 'Free for what? But may I ask as to the fate of a young woman who must have been brought here the same day as I?'

'She was luckier than you,' he replied brusquely. 'She died during her treatment.'

'She is dead,' I muttered to myself in a daze, crushed by this last stroke. 'So Suzon is dead and I am still alive.'

I would have put an end to myself at that very moment if I had not been stopped. Then I was shown the door.

Shabbily dressed and with scarcely a sou in my pocket, I decided to abandon myself to fate. Let come what will. Taking the road leading out of Paris, I spotted the walls of a Carthusian monastery where a profound silence reigned.

'Lucky mortals,'' I cried to myself, 'who live in this retreat, protected from the storms of fortune, your pure and innocent hearts have no conception of the horrors that tear mine.'

The thought of their felicity inspired in me the yearning to become one of them.

Throwing myself at the feet of the Father Superior, I told him the story of my miseries.

'My son,' he said benevolently as he put his arms around me, 'this is the port for you after so many wreck. Live here with us and try to be happy.'

For some time I stayed there without being given anything to do, but soon I was being employed. Gradually, I rose to the position of porter by which title I am now known.

It is here that my heart has hardened in the hatred it has conceived for the world. Here I await death without either fearing or desiring it, and I hope that when I depart this vale of tears called life, there will be etched in letters of gold on my tomb the following:

*Hic situs est DOM-BOUGRE,*

fututus, futuit.

FINIS

# Part II

## Preface

*Monsieur Satan:*

*During my adolescence, you were my instructor. It is from you that I learned all the tricks that served me so well during my early years. I have followed your dictates faithfully, as you know, and in return, I have exerted myself night and day to expand your empire and increase the number of your subjects.*

*But, Monsieur Satan, things have changed. You must be getting old, for you stay down in hell. Even the monks are unable to persuade you to come out. Your younger devils, poor fellows, don't have as much knowledge as our apprentice pimps. The reports they bring you are false because the women cheat and fool them.*

*I am discharging now my debt to you by dedicating this book to you. In it you will learn what is going on in the court and the doings of women, financiers and devouts. You will read about some escapades in which you would have been delighted to participate.*

*May the tableaux I am about to present to you revive your sense of ribaldry, and I hope that everyone who reads this work will have an erection.*

*My most respectful regards,*
*Your Diabolic Highness,*

*CON-DESIROS [Cunt Lover]*

Up to now, my friend, I have been a bad lot. I have pursued beautiful women, and I have been hard to please. But now that virtue has returned to my heart, I see the error of my ways. From now on, I am going to fuck only for money. I shall be a stud to middle-aged women and instruct them in amatory games at so much a month.

Already I think I see a clod of a woman on the verge of finishing her forties offering me the flabby thickness of her ample body. Fortunately, there are patches of pristine freshness still to be found on her dumpiness. Her ruddy sagging tits are in agreement with her piggish eyes in expressing something other than modesty. She rubs my palm, for the financieress, like her senile husband, rubs everything to make it move. I have the decency to blush.

Ah, somehow that pleases me. My eyes sparkle. My virginity is stifling me, for you will recall that I still have that precious jewel which I am most anxious to rid myself of. I am given much more than I expected. With alacrity I start to show my gratitude.

Damn it! I can't get an erection. It is because of the woes that overwhelm me. My creditors are snapping at my heels. . . .

When my hand wanders, she becomes animated. How gentle I am, but, at the same time, cunning! The tempo becomes a spirited throb. My voice is an *adagio* with a lively *presto sostenuto*. Ah, take a look at how milady's bottom is bouncing up and down. Her bosom is heaving, her windpipe wheezes, her cunt dribbles, she is beside herself and she wants to carry me along with her in her rapturous wave.

Oh, please, take it easy. I am in such pain. She

makes me an offer, but how can I accept money from a woman whom I esteem so highly? When she doubles the ante, I weep. The gold appears. Gold!!!! ... A miracle! No sooner do I spot it than I get a hard-on and fuck her.

After this easy victory, I pay my respects to Madame Honesta, the last of her line. Her home is redolent of rectitude and respectability. Everything bespeaks abstinence including her face, the features of which are not exactly such as to inspire tender sentiments. Her cheeks are pinched and her figure slightly on the scrawny side. In all honesty, I am unable to praise her bust, although a gauze scarf permits me a glimpse of what there is of it. One could have wished for a better turned leg, although it does taper into a dainty foot.

Her talk concerns her nerves and headaches and a husband she never sees except at meals. Are you going to say that a woman like her would never pay anything? Don't be fooled. Of course she will, because she is vain and prides herself on her generosity.

At first we observe the conventions by exchanging witticisms and gossip and making epigrams and *bons mots*. Madam is right when she comments that it is a very agreeable morning.

A bonnet is delivered. Dear God! It must have been designed by the Graces themselves. The deity of style fixed the blossoms to it, and all the zephyrs are playing in the plumes that cover it. How this plum colour perfectly matches the English green! But who is it from?

You can easily guess that I am the guilty one. The culprit blushes. I pout and sulk as I betray myself.

Victoire, Madame's maid whom I have won over with a few kisses and coins, pleads my cause during my absence.

'Ah, Madame, if you only could hear how he raves about you. He's such a kind gentleman and far better than that chevalier who is always at your heels. I know that he would never cause you a day's grief. His man told me that he doesn't toy with women's hearts like so many men nowadays.'

'But do you think that I am. . . ?' Madam stutters.

'What an utterly stunning bonnet! It becomes you perfectly. Why, you don't look a day over twenty when you have it on.'

'Don't be a little fool. Don't you know that I am thirty, and even a little more?'

('More' indeed. That has been common knowledge for over ten years now.)

In the afternoon, I return and find her alone. I apologize for my intrusion. Freely granting me pardon, she becomes tender and I passionate. Then we . . . . (Damn it! The woman is in such a hurry that I am in danger of losing what I paid out for the hat.) But I was smart enough to have told my flunky to come and remind me that I have an appointment with the Minister. With an audible sigh of regret, I kiss the hand that trembles in mine and take my leave.

While this is going on, I strike up an acquaintanceship with one of those women who, jaded with life, seeks pleasure at any cost. She approaches me because, with her honour, her reputation, her high moral standard. . . . Bosh! Those have all gone the way of her youth. The bargain is quickly struck. She pays me and I am in her. But I refuse to discharge, and she knows it. She pesters the life out of me.

Ah, beloved money! I sense your august presence. I am stubborn and we languish in a stalemate for two solid weeks. Finally, I modestly give her to understand that while I hold her in the deepest affection, I have certain obligations. . . . Is that all that's the matter? . . . She gives me a princely sum. . . . My gratitude knows no bounds. I rush into the arms of my benevolent Messalina and experience, not exactly pleasure, but the satisfaction of knowing that I am not an ingrate.

Tired of her? What do you expect? When you have crammed the hen, it doesn't lay any more eggs. The fees become less frequent, and I frequently fall asleep. – *What? You go to sleep?* – Yes, during the night, and what is more, in the morning, too. The beloved morning which gives life to hope and throws its light on amorous combats. When she complains, I get angry. She sputters about misbehaviour and ingratitude, but I show her that she is wrong, for I leave her.

Plutus, come and inspire me! A god does appear in answer to my prayer, but he does not have the happy attributes. It is the deity of good sense, the busy-bee Mercury. After consoling me, he sends me to Monsier Doucet. I am sure that you don't know this gentlemen, so listen.

A figure that seems taller because of a long cassock and cloak, a face beginning to show the ravages of time, a ruddy plumpness, the eyes of a lynx and a jaunty wig. His open honest visage on which wit has left its imprint beams with complacency. The only time he smiles is when he wishes to reveal two rows of perfect white teeth. Such is the most fashionable confessor in Paris. Throngs of the female devout wait in his reception room and the consultations never cease.

His favourites are those spinsters and widows entombed in a perfect quietism of conscience but whose hinges swing all the more easily because of that. The man of God conceals under his sanctimonious demeanour an ardent soul and several admirable talents. You correctly surmise that it is my intention to reach these women.

I worm my way into the good man's confidence by letting him know that I am almost as much of a hypocrite as he. He puts me to the test, which I pass with flying colours, and introduces me to Madam ****.

Her home is a mausoleum of saintliness. The luxury is solid and unostentatious. But – a young man like me with a lady of impeccable reputation and virtue? Right you are. My visits become more frequent and our familiarity increases.

One day, as we are leaving church where she had dragged me to hear a sermon, I start making comments on the other women who were present. Note how garrulous she becomes.

'What did you think of Madame Y****.'
'Good heavens! Her feet are like barges.'
'But she is pretty.'
'She could be if she knew how to apply cosmetics. But she would never have any fresh complexion.'

(You can imagine how her colour heightens at these words.)

'I think that the Countess's dress was a little daring for church.'

'She made herself a laughing stock by showing her bust the way she did. What a pitiful bosom. There's only one lady I know who has the right to display such nudities, for they would be at least beautiful ones.'

(Note the pleased glance she gives me. A second punishes me for my temerity, and I become properly timid and abashed.)

'What did you think of the sermon?'

'To tell the truth, I didn't pay much attention to it. My mind was elsewhere.'

'The moral was excellent.'

'I agree, but it was presented in such a cold way. A pretty mouth is always much more eloquent. For example, your words always make such a deep impression on me. They lift me up and encourage me to mend my ways. Alas, you make me love virtue because . . . I love you.'

(My friend, you should see me as I stand before her, quivering and thunderstruck, at my own boldness, I beg her forgiveness. The more she grants it, the more I exaggerate the gravity of my offence.)

My madonna pulls herself together before I do, but I can see that she is still deeply moved. Trying to cover her nervousness, she says that she is going to read me a tract on God's love. Seated opposite her, I run a fiery eye over her meagre body. I turn her statements around, and soon I am reciting Rousseau to her.

This is my opportunity. The chapel becomes a boudoir. I am victorious.

But money! When am I going to get some money? To the devil with it for the moment, and I sent her to paradise with my speculative ejaculation. What bliss she revels in! What delightful nonsense she babbles! How soft and pliant she is!

'Ah, dear Holy Mary! Sweet Jesus!' she sighs. 'My dear friend, did you feel what I did?'

I assure her absent-mindedly that I did, but my thoughts are turned to the damned question of money. I hope you don't think I am stupid enough to have come out on the short end.

I consult with my mentor and I tell him everything. He is discreet, for he would lose too much if he were not. He listens and then tells me he is going to help me. That goes without saying, for he wants his commission.

During the three days. I am absent, my pious friend's only solace is her dildo. The holy man arrives.

'That poor young fellow,' he begins with a mournful shake of the head. 'He has gone back to his evil ways. Abandoned women are dragging him down.'

The news is like a dagger stroke in her heart.

'What a pity, Father. There is good in him.'

'Yes, and it is not his fault. Within him burns the flame of virtue. And he is honest. He confided in me that he has debts of honour which hang over him like the sword of Damocles. If he cannot meet them, I am afraid of what he might do to himself. He said, too, that his greatest regret would be leaving Madame.'

At these words, she demurely lowers her eyes.

The priest pursues his advantage.

'Not only that, but he sighed that although you had his heart wholly, he would have to flee you. Then he pulled his hair, rolled his eyes, and cursed his unlucky star. That is what he said and did, Madame, and there were tears in his eyes. Well, too bad. Let's talk about something else, since there is nothing we can do.'

'But . . . but, how much do his debts amount to?'

'Three hundred louis.'

Now you can be sure that a woman who has tasted of my lovemaking, who is sure of my discretion, who does not find me a lout, and who wants some colour in her drab life, will send me the sum as soon as she can. Don't you agree?

I see that you are pursing your lips in disapproval.

*But that is detestable. Real love is generous and untainted by money. You are nothing but a scoundrel.*

Come now! Don't play the role of a hypocrite. She is thirty-six and I am twenty-four. Although she is still good, I am better. She spends money and I spend my virility. She gets good value, and don't I deserve some compensation?

Moreover, I persuade her to give up her shapeless clothing and straitlaced ways. I launch her into society, which she takes to like a duck to water. She owes me much.

*But would it not have been better to leave her in her obscurity? You'll lose her, or somebody will take her away from you.*

No matter. I have other plans. Her money is gone, her jewellery sold, and my passing fancy over. But she decides to be faithful to me, and I know she does so just to irritate me. I'll have to behave badly to her. Here is what I have made up my mind to tell her.

'Madame, I shall never forget your kindness, and

my gratitude is nearly costing me my life. The worry I have about your reputation is destroying the happiness I find with you. I have to cease these compromising visits. I realize with heavy heart that with this decision I have signed my own death warrant.'

In the end, her piteous grimaces succeed in weakening my resolve. When she sees that I relent, and my Dulcinea's tears of grief, suddenly hope shines in her eyes. My departure is interupted by halts on every sofa and couch in the house, and I make my escape only at her last ecstatic swoon.

Well, she has made a name for me. No longer do I have to beat my own drum. I just let her sing my praises. In the social barnyard, I am the cock of the roost. You can see that I keep my head about me.

Madame is the intimate friend of the Presidente, a wealthy widow I have had my eye on for some time. She will hear all about me from my rejected mistress, whom I convince to keep up the friendship since it will enable us to see each other now and then. She is so happy that I am not abandoning her just for some Madame So-and-So's beautiful eyes.

Everything goes just as I planned. But now the time has come when I have to make them turn against each other. Discord, heed my voice! There is a little tiff, feelings cool, and the two inseparables hardly ever see each other anymore. The Presidente demands that I side with her, but I lay down some conditions. What a woman won't do for revenge! She surrenders to me just to get back at her old friend.

Although the Presidente is thirty-five, she is well enough preserved to be able to pass for twenty-eight. She could have been a lady-in-waiting if the small talk did not bore her so. She is polite with women, charming with men, and unassuming in public. It is obvious that she is a woman of breeding.

I have never known in a woman such a fiery and sustained passion that changes its colours like a chameleon. Her caresses are all the more seductive because they are sincere. More than once I have been tempted to fall in love with her.

Like most women, she is not without her faults. For one thing, she has a very high opinion of herself. Her decisions are oracular and her views immutable laws. Imperious is the word to describe her. It is true, however, that she does not make it too apparent. More often than not it happens that you are following her dictates when you think you are acting of your own accord.

It is not long before I am lionized by her friends who guess the nature of our relationship. She trusts me implicitly and nothing is right unless I say so. We spend six whole weeks together before I remember that she wants to be privy to all my affairs.

One day, I appear in her boudoir with a downcast mien.

'What's wrong darling. You don't seem your cheerful self?'

(I try to squeeze out a smile.)

'How could I possibly be out of sorts when I am with you?' I bravely say.

She questions me, but I persist in my silence. Even the gaiety at dinner does not drive away the scowl from my face. When we are alone again, I refuse her suggestion of a gambol in bed and take my leave at midnight.

What more do you want, you will ask. Well, I'll tell you.

My lackey, who is as sharp as they come, had the brilliant idea of fucking the maid to pass the time while waiting for me. That evening his appearance is as gloomy as mine. When his sweetheart urges him to tell her what is bothering him, just as mine is doing, he is not so reticent and blabs everything.

'Last night, he dined at Duchess Z's where, in spite of my good intentions, he sat in on a game of faro. His luck was unbelievably bad, and he lost everything he had. He even had to pawn the precious diamond the Presidente gave him. But that was not enough to pay all that he owed, and, as a result, he is absolutely penniless.'

Then he recounts his own woes, for the character is just about as cunning as I am. He took a hand in a game with the other servants, and now all his possessions are in the shop with the three balls above the entrance.

Poor Adelaide, who really loves the rogue, takes out of a drawer forty ecus, her entire little fortune, largely accumulated from the gratuities I had given her. He pockets them without a qualm.

I notice the whisperings between mistress and maid and the stealthy comings and goings. Everything has been told to Madame.

She has my bandit confirm the story and then presses a purse containing five hundred louis into his hand.

*Fifteen hundred francs?*

In gold, I tell you. It is to pay my debts with a little left over.

When I leave, I find my accomplice already in the coach, and we triumphantly bear home the loot.

*You can't be that low.*

Of course, I can. And why not?

At seven the next morning, I put on casual dress and hurry to the Presidente. Her eyes sparkle with pleasure when she sees the diamond back on my finger. I try to make her speak. (You remember that my flunky must not breathe a word to me under pain of death.) She lies to me with the most charming grace. But she recognizes from the vivacity of my caresses which are enhanced by gratitude that I am not her dupe. After I am somewhat recovered from my transports, I speak of good deeds. She orders me to be silent. If someone has rendered me a service, I would take away all the pleasure from the benefactor by expression of thanks. My voice wavers.

*What a cad you are! You are not touched by so much love and generosity?*

Of course I am. To show my gratitude (and to get rid of her at the same time), I marry her off to one of my friends who makes her the happiest woman in Paris. From lovers, we become friends, and I flee, not to new laurels, but to new purses.

Disgusted with ideal love and the methodical passion of the devout and the Presidente, I sadly languish for some time until chance leads my steps to Madame Saint-Just. She is the notorious procuress for elegant orgies at the Rue Tiquetonne. I inform her that I am free and that I am hurting in the purse. She hands me the list of what is available. I scan it.

'Baroness de Conbaille [Yawning Cunt] . . . That's a beautiful name. Who is she?'

'A little provincial come to Paris to squander the fifty or sixty thousand francs she had been saving for the last ten years.'

'Is there much left?'

'No.'

'Let's skip her and go on to the next. Madame de Culsouple [Supple Ass]. How much does she pay?'

'Twenty louis a time.'

'In advance?'

'Never. But she's nothing for you. She's too wide.'

'Madame de Fontendiable.'

'Now there is something. An American and rich as Croesus. If you satisfy her, there's nothing she won't do for you.'

'Well, when can you present me?'

'Tomorrow if you wish.'

'Here?'

'No, at her residence.'

The name has a diabolic sound which piques my curiosity. As I return the list, Saint-Just speaks to me with a mysterious air.

'My friend, you have had many younger women, and what did you get out of them? Nothing to speak of. Now listen to the voice of experience. I have here in my house a real treasure. An old woman worth her weight in gold, and with one like her, you run no risk of infection.'

'The devil fuck you.'

'I only wish he would. He's better than nothing. But I am talking about something special. Let me handle it and we'll pluck her together.'

'All right. I'll trust your judgment.'

In the meantime, I appear at my American's the

next evening at seven. There I find a vulgar and tasteless luxury along with bales of coffee, sacks of sugar, scales, bills and a pervading fishy odour resembling a not unfamiliar smell.

I am slightly uneasy at the gruff sound of a man's voice in the next room. Her husband? The door opens. Who can it be? It is my goddess! But, damn it, what a woman!

Picture to yourself a colossus of six feet with fuzzy black hair fringing a narrow forehead. Bushy eyebrows set off a certain hardness in her ardent eyes. Her mouth is a cavern. A sort of moustache rises towards a nose stained with Spanish tobacco. Her arms and feet are like a man's and her voice like a klaxon.

'Fuck!' she says to Saint-Just. 'Where did you dig up this pretty lad. He's very young and not my size at all. Well, as the saying goes, little man big prick.'

To get better acquainted, she gives me a bear hug that nearly cracks my ribs.

'Good heavens, how shy he is.'

'He's new at this.'

'We'll take care of that. But did you lose your tongue?'

'Madame, the respect . . .'

(I am still trying to catch my breath.)

'To hell with your respect. Good-bye, Saint-Just. I'll keep the little fucker here. We'll have dinner and a romp in bed.'

When we are alone, my lovely flounces down on a sofa, and without wasting time on preliminaries, I pounce on her. In a twinkling, she is ready to be pillaged. I discover a tawny bosom hard as marble, a superb body, a dome-shaped *mons Veneris*, and a fetching wig. As I caress these charms, she snorts like a bull. Like a mare in heat, her derriere beats the call and her cunt. . . .

My God! I am overcome by a holy frenzy. Seizing her with a vigorous arm, I hold her fast for a moment and then dash on her. It's a miracle. My beloved is tight. With two determined thrusts, I am into her up to my testicles. I bite her and she claws me. Now blood is flowing. Sometimes I am on top, sometimes below. The couch creaks, breaks and collapses, but I am still firmly in the saddle. My strokes redouble in velocity and intensity.

'Keep going, my friend. You're doing fine. Fuck harder. Oh, what bliss. Damn it! Don't pull out. Now it's coming. Get in deeper! Deeper, I say.'

Confound it! She's wiggling her behind so convulsively that I am dislodged, but I hurry to regain. My prick is burning. Grabbing her by the chignon, I return to my former position in triumph.

'Ah, I am dying,' she sighs.

'You slut, if you don't let me discharge, I'll strangle you,' I threaten her.

She is panting more heavily and her eyelashes are fluttering as she begs for mercy.

'No quarter.'

My testicles are in a rage. She falls into a swoon. I pay no attention and withdraw only when we simultaneously emit a flood of fuck and blood.

I think it is about time to put back on her underpants. When we are restored to our senses, my bested opponent gallantly congratulates me. She goes to the bidet. While she is away, I try to put the couch together again.

'What in the world are you doing?' she asks when she returns. 'Don't trouble yourself. My servants are used to that. I have a cabinet-maker who checks it every morning.'

Of course, our conversation is not sentimental. Do you think she can be bothered with such nonsense? We go through her house and to her vault which is chock-full of gold bars. Treasures from the four corners of the globe are assembled here. Finally, we come to a room where she opens a little casket.

'Here, take this wallet.'

'I pretend to be reluctant.'

'Go ahead, you simpleton. Anybody who can fuck like you deserves to be rewarded.'

First ascertaining that it contains five hundred louis in bank notes, I put it in my pocket. It is a generous gesture on her part.

We sit down to a late supper, and I find that I am famished. With her own hands, she serves me morsels, ham stuffed with truffles, mushrooms à la Marseillaise, and for dessert, pastilles so hot that tears came to my eyes. All this is topped with fiery, stimulating liqueurs. From the table, we hasten to her bed where a scene unparalleled in the annals of love takes place.

We make a rendezvous for the next day. I am prompt. Madame is not feeling well. Oh, it is nothing. She is just very hot, and she asks me to open the windows wide, even though it is a bitterly cold January day. Pneumonia carries her off in three days.

Oh woe! I am going to say a *De profundis* for her at Saint-Just's.

After having dried her tears and calmed her nerves, she tells me that my princess had been one of her best clients. In turn, I assure her how deeply shocked I am by this regrettable incident. I add that I have been thinking matters over, and on reflection, since I have always honoured old age, I have come to enlist in the service of the widow she had mentioned.

We take our leave and within eight days I have the honour of being introduced to Madame Methuselah. Since I had been informed that she was extremely wealthy, I am not surprised at the magnificence of the residence and the luxury of the furnishings. I mentally compute how much she might be worth.

I am expected. Before my arrival, I took steps to restore my vitality and charm. In an apparent attempt to repair hers, my hag is still at her toilette. I wait in the lavender and white salon with mirrors and lascivious pictures on the walls. A heady aroma pervades the chamber. Already my imagination is become heated and my heart starts to beat faster. It seems as if fire is coursing through my veins.

The door opens and a young woman presents herself to my eyes. She is simply dressed, which sets off her incredible beauty. This is Julia, the niece of my future patroness. She apologizes for her aunt's tardiness and has come to keep me company if I do not mind.

I gallantly accept her kind offer, but she politely refuses to sit next to me on the divan. My glance follows her as she flutters around the room. I feel love being born in my heart. When Julia becomes aware of my amorous regard, the conversation languishes. But our souls speak.

'Mademoiselle surely must be the comfort of her aunt.'

'I do hope so, for she has been very kind to me.'

'Among the many people who surround her, you must have many anxious suitors.'

Julie's only reply is a deep-felt sigh.

My face turns as red as a beet.

'Monsieur, if you only knew what a worthless lot those admirers are.'

'What!' I exclaim. 'You haven't found one who merits your attention?'

Her voice falters.

'Excuse me. I was going to do something I shouldn't.'

'Mademoiselle, I would welcome it.'

At a sudden noise, Julia's only answer is a significant look.

The aunt has completed her coiffure and makes her appearance.

My friends, picture to yourselves a little girl about sixty years old. Her figure is an upside-down oval. A fiery red wig covers what is left of her hair. Blood-veined eyes regard me in a squint. The lips are tinted a ghastly carmine. From a cavern of a yellow-toothed mouth are squeaked words of welcome.

I notice strings of pearls in the *decolleté* of her black velvet gown. They fall in wave after wave and end where there might have been a bosom forty years ago.

Such is my first impression. It is fortunate that I have not seen or smelt her before.

'My dear boy, I'm so sorry that I had to leave you so long with my niece whom you must have found terribly boring,' she simpers. (Julia disappears.) 'Not many people know that she is my relative.'

'I can't believe it,' I answer in mock surprise.

'Yes, that's so. Her mother was quite a bit older than I.' She clutches my hand and says with a smirk: 'The things Saint-Just has told me about you!'

'She always exaggerates,' I modestly disclaim. 'But I am grateful to her for this opportunity to pay you my respects.'

'Listen, my dear. Let's dispense with ceremony. Relax and I promise you won't regret it. I'm having some people for dinner tonight and I expect you to be one of the party.

My deferential bow of assent is answered by a wet kiss full on the mouth.

(She stinks like a sewer.)

'For the sake of appearances, I want you to pretend that you're my niece's suitor. Pay a lot of attention to her.'

(Heavens, how I would like to make love to that delicious morsel.)

'When the others are gone, you and I can be by ourselves,' she continues.

'So my agony is to be postponed. We pass into the main salon where a numerous company is gathered. While Julia and her aunt are seating the guests, I begin to reflect.)

Love! Love! Again you come to deceive me, lead me astray, break my heart. Cruel deity! Have I not been your victim long enough? Or do you wish to get revenge on me? What role are you going to impose on me? Her beauty and charm will be my torment. She is so desirable, alas! In return for all the incense

I have been burned at your altar, I beg you to spare me. Hear my prayer. A new passion is setting me ablaze. Julia, the lovely Julia, will have my heart and transports while her hideous aunt will have from me only a tribute that she will pay dearly for.

Because everyone is intent on gambling, silence reigns in the room. Julia, at the far end of the salon, is reading a book. In a moment, I am at her side. She is nervous and I am timid.

'Ah, Monsieur, so you have been assigned your place.'

'If you could see in my heart, Mademoiselle, you would learn how dear it is to me.'

'I don't know what you can see in me. I think you are just making fun of me. Besides, it ill behoves you to pay me compliments.'

'So you forbid me? Now, I see. You believe that I am just another of your aunt's employees. I can no longer stand your disdain.'

I stand up as if to go.

'My God, Monsieur, what are you going to do?' she asks in a frightened voice. 'If you leave, my aunt will get suspicious.'

'Mademoiselle, you are right. I am your aunt's lover, but what is wrong with that if it is the only way to be near you? I have been head over heels in love with you for six months now. Have you not noticed how I have followed you everywhere?'

'The poor thing is deeply touched. Her bosom heaves. God! What an admirable and adorable bosom!)

'So you don't answer, Julia. We don't have much time. Quick. Your decision will decide my fate. Do I have to undergo at the same time the favours of your aunt and your contempt?'

'I said the word *favours* in such a mournful tone that the girl could not conceal a little smile.)

'Well, I believe you,' she says. 'Why should you lie to me? I'm so unhappy here, and all I need is for you to make me more so.'

I shall not detail the rest of the conversation except to relate that it was agreed that I would be the aunt's lover and that, affecting indifference for each other, we would meet secretly whenever possible.

We dine. After the meal, the guests start to leave. At midnight, I am alone with my dear aunt who immediately commences to give me an idea of the horrors I shall have to suffer. I grimace at her hands fumbling on my body and face. She goes to her room to get ready for bed while I prepare to join her. Finally, the lover's hour, the fatal hour, sounds. I answer the call, and when I arrive I look everywhere for you know what. I find nothing. Guess where it is hidden. The fat purse is between two candles on Madame's night-table.

My goddess wearing a nightcap is suddenly as desirable as Venus. What charms she possesses! When she smiles at me, I notice that she is no longer able to bite. I finally mount the altar.

*Did you have an erection?*

Alas, I had to work one up or lose both Julia and the purse. And I desperately needed the latter.

With my hands and feet, I traverse the senile attractions of my Dulcinea. The bosom. There isn't any. Long emaciated arms. A dejected Venus mount. A flabby cunt, whose natural smell is not concealed by the perfume. Closing my eyes and using my imagination, I succeed in stiffening my prick. I get on my old nag and put it in her. She wraps her skinny legs around my neck as I get to the bottom of her. Stretching her neck as I get to the bottom of her. Stretching her neck, she offers me a slimy tongue that I avoid just in time.

Finally, I begin the canter. The old mare is sweating in the harness, but she is returning jab for jab. Her arms go slack and her eyes are rolling. Damn it! I slip out. I am furious. Now I am back in. Things are going smoothly.

'Ah, my friend. My darling. My dearest. I think I am dying. It has been such a long time. Oh, here I am . . . co . . . ming.'

The devil take me. Her convulsions last a full five minutes. She is enjoying herself as a thirty-year-old would. It takes a long time for her to pull herself together. She is absolutely exhausted. I am drenched.

While drying myself, I come across a double wig. It is my hag's that had come off in the scuffle. My beloved is a pitiful sight. She must realize it, for she has a shamefaced look.

'Come, my love, I would like to start all over.'

With that, I spring on her again and acquit myself creditably. Thank God she has taken off her false teeth. Otherwise, she would have chewed me to pieces.

After this second romp, she rings. Mademoiselle Macao comes to repair the disorder of Madame's nightdress and the bed. As I put back on my clothes, the good old woman is praising me to the skies.

'Twice, my dear, just imagine. He did it twice.

That fellow is a prodigy. The others were nothing in comparison to him. Just put your hand in here and feel. I am flooded with his sperm.'

It is four o'clock in the morning and I go to the bed to take my leave. After embracing me, she gives me two purses instead of one. She says that they contain two hundred louis, although she normally pays only one.

'No, Madam,' I tell her nobly, 'if I have been happier than the others, I do not expect double compensation. I accept the token of your kindness, but I do not wish to remove the possibility of coming here often and satisfying your desires in a way which seems to give you pleasure.'

She could have taken me at my word, and I don't like to spoil these old bitches. But she is delighted with my response, for she removes from her finger a magnificent ring worth easily two thousand ecus and slips it on my forefinger. Then I part with the permission to come any time I wish and the injunction to appear still in love with Julia in order to conceal our affair. I put up an objection to the latter proposal, but she insists. I yield with poor grace, which pleases her greatly.

Do I find sleep when I return home? No, Julia, your image disturbs me. I see you. I am prey to all sorts of desires. I let out deep sighs. I hear you moaning and accusing me of having betrayed you. Oh, this horrible thirst for money! What makes me squander my essence just for its sake? And it falls on barren ground.

But I am compensated, aren't I. Where would I ever find a more adorable creature than Julia. Dear girl, let love paint me in your dreams and transform the charm of revery into a sweet reality.

Gold! Damn it! Gold. It is the sinews of war. Let the flame of love set fire to my courage and restore my pristine strength which made fall so many virgins under a bloody knife. And you, Priapus, patron deity of fuckers, I invoke your aid. Let me be seized by a lubricious intoxication after I am through with my hag, who I hope splits when I am in her. It would be a disaster worthy of you.

You can imagine that the morning does not pass without my calling on my beloved. Faithful Macao, who admits me, gives me advice on how I can please Madame. I sacrifice to her a pebble of my gold to win a mountain of it. My hag welcomes me cordially. But what a surprise! There is an unaccustomed freshness in her face. The wrinkles are gone. There is colour in her cheeks. If only she had teeth, breasts and hair, she would be eminently fuckable. My hand is frolicsome. My mischievous smile animates her. She orders me to keep my hands where they belong, then she is serious and tells me she has household matters to attend to.

Mademoiselle Macao is Julia's governess. She is understanding. This woman who, in her youth, frequented places where everything is equal, has a sympathy for innocence. She even taught Julia a hand game very popular among Frenchmen.

Now that she is my confidante because of my little donation, she takes me to Julia who is at her toilette.

I don't know why but I become as timid as a rabbit. Her loveliness is stunning. Long ash-brown hair, clear black eyes, and features I would have liked less had they been more regular. We are alone. I kneel down on one knee before her and passionately kiss her hand. Damn it! What has got into me that I am so shy? Julia must be angry. Her modesty must feel repugnant to my caresses. But no. She seems pleased to receive them. She permits the petty larcenies I commit on the peignoir veiling those enchanting globes. I can't keep my eyes off them.

The days pass peacefully by. I gradually make progress with Julia. The aunt overwhelms me with gifts which, I must say, I earn. Then one Saturday, I appear for dinner. My dear aunt announces that she cannot join us, since she has to go out. She will be back only about eight or eight-thirty. It is some charitable function which she never misses. I throw a tantrum. I was so looking forward to being with her. The good woman tries to appease me.

'Don't be so angry, darling. I don't want to leave you, but I have to. But you won't be alone. Julia will keep you company, won't you? She will entertain you on the harpsichord.'

'Yes, Aunt, if you say so,' she answers with a blush.

I frown. Mademoiselle Macao is ordered not to let me escape. The hag departs, leaving Julia and me alone together.

The gods above from whom comes this celestial fire which lifts us above ordinary mortals witnessed my bliss. Dear friend, if you want to penetrate into the mysteries of Paphos, read on as you masturbate.

Everything favours my ardour. The beauty of the day, whose rays were softened by a diaphanous drape, add new charms to the objects in the room. It is spring and Julia is innocent, a condition I am determined to change. In glowing colours, I paint the joys of lasciviousness while making protestations of eternal love.

I can see that she is as animated as I. When I touch her, I am positive of it. I get bolder. Already her mouth is prey to mine which is pressed hard to her lips. Her glorious breasts are becoming irritated at the ribbons confining them. Hateful bonds, begone. The tears which are streaming from her eyes I dry with my kisses. Her breathing is laboured. The fires of our hearts and souls become one mighty blaze.

I continue. Julia's arm seems to be pulling me toward her rather than repelling me. Her will to resist is vanishing. Her eyes have a dreamy quality and her eyelids flutter. The treasures I discover and explore!

'Stop!' tender Julia cries in a fading voice. 'How dare you take advantage of me this way? I think I am dying.'

The words expire on the lips of rose. The hour has sounded in Cythera. Eros has waved his torch in the air. Flying on his wings, I battle, and the skies open. I have conquered. Oh, Venus, come to my succour.

Let there be no reproaches for my actions. Julia certainly will not scold me. She wants me to master her and give her pleasure. She expires only to be reborn to taste anew the joys. But a miracle has occurred. Our sofa has come to life. A variety of movements combined with the greatest skill causes a thousand kinds of flowers of voluptuousness to blossom in her heart. Finally, exhausted from the raptures and the caresses, we cease. (And I send away the demon who had lent me his assistance in such an unexpected way.) I no longer recognize the sofa.

When Julie gives me credit for what she has enjoyed, I do not disabuse her of the notion.

I don't stay much longer. My clothes are rumpled. Also, my hag would have a miserly offering.

Without going into boring details, our liaison lasted three months. Julie loved me madly and unthinkingly, so much so that we are discovered. I am given my walking papers and Julie, snatched from my loving arms, is placed in a convent. The Marquise de Vit-au-Conas [prick in cunt] takes charge of the latter affair, and that is how I happen to come to know her.

Interesting herself in me, she asks more information about my affair with Julia. I paint her an accurate picture. Since she is a woman, too, how can she be severe for a crime which is nothing but homage to beauty? She is a friend of pleasure. She learns of my double employ, which, to her, is a good measure of my worth.

'My God!' she says with awe. 'You could have killed yourself.'

Casting modesty to the winds, I tell her that my constitution, far from being enfeebled, is strengthened and requires a job at least as arduous. Her eyes open wide while mine wander. They finally meet. She is no novice, and we soon come to a tacit understanding.

Her service requires her to be often at Versailles, where I go often, also. But at court one is so at loose ends. Her husband is with his regiment and I offer to fill the gap.

During the first days of our liaison, I go one evening to her suite to spend a little time with her while awaiting the King's bedtime. Among the men in the Marquise's circle, I notice a Knight of Malta, a very thin pale man with a haughty air. The grumpy look on the Marquise's face convinced me that he was my predecessor and is about to be given his leave. To help in getting rid of him, I attack him with mockery. But he defends himself poorly.

When I go out he follows me. After the *coucher*, he asks me to accompany him to the park, saying that he wishes to tell me something in confidence. It is a fine night and we stroll until we reach a solitary deserted grove. Suddenly, his hand is at his sword. I grab it and take it away from him and throw it twenty paces away with the greatest composure. He gets angry, but I just laugh at him.

'My dear Chevalier,' I tell him. 'I think I can guess your motives. You were on friendly terms with the Marquise, but now she is throwing you over. It is your opinion that I am your successor, and you are not wrong. You would like to slit your throat along with mine, and I am very grateful for this token of your friendship. However, I'll tell you quite honestly that I shall not fight until I learn if she is worth the trouble. Let's wait until you have had time for reflection and I have been in bed with her. If you still want to after that, we'll amuse ourselves.'

I hasten to retrieve his rapier which I politely hand to him. Then I bid him good evening and go back to my apartment and bed.

The Chevalier comes to me the next day and admits that he was in the wrong. We cordially embrace. Then I repair to the Marquise, who does not look at me unfavourably because of the adventure she has heard about.

The days go by. The Marquise is coquette, playing with my desires perhaps with the thought of awakening true love. We are in the season of little excursions and we see each other fleetingly. I am irritated for time is weighing heavy on my hands. After several earnest entreaties, I obtain a rendezvous for the following day. I can see from the significant look in her eye that it will be all that I want it to be. I appear at the appointed hour. The King is hunting and everybody is outside. The chateau is like a desert. But there are enough people in the Marquise's apartment. Just she. We are alone and our desires gradually increase. On my word, I don't think I've ever had a more delightful companion.

It is noon and the atmosphere in the room is sensuously warm. Occasionally rays of sun appear through the drapes. The chamber is redolent of perfumes and voluptuousness. Picture to yourself on a heap of cushions a tall woman with a fine figure adorned with ravishing contours. Several sashes carelessly tied hold together the flimsy gauze that veils her delightful body. Her bosom is flawless and her eyes are eloquent. The rest of her charms also bespeak invitation.

The preliminaries commence. Without asking her permission. I remove the offending bits of cloth. With two twists of my hands, I have the Marquise in position. I make a rush on her.

My God! I am barely able to hold it back in time. There must be a hex on me. That was a narrow escape.

We assume postures which are mutually agreeable. The Marquise is vivacious without being soft, for hers is a fiery temperament. She truly believes that she is in love with the man in her arms, and once her desires are contented, her heart opens up. Ten years at court can shape a woman. She is skilled in intrigue and dissimulation and seduction.

When strength returns to her, she grabs me with impudence that would have made me blush if one still blushes today. I hold myself back.

'Come,' she says. 'You're just a child. When I first came to live in this country, I was revolted by everything. I was just out of the convent, young and rather pretty. I was bashful and awkward as could be. But women shaped me and men have found me desirable. I won on both sides.'

I live with her as if I am in my own home. We sleep together, and since she finds me extremely virile, she is desirous of keeping me. But the money is not coming, and how does one get it from a woman of the court who is still young and attractive?

The devil provides it.

One day in a delirium, we perform every position described by Aretino in his bible of sex and when we are through, the Marquise takes a fancy for my backside. She insists on doing something with it. I refuse.

'My dear friend,' she begins, 'did you ever see a parrot try to defend its tail against a cunning cat? Well, I'm like that cat.'

'But, Madame, it is a maidenhead.'

'Well, I'll pay a hundred louis for it.'

'Not for all the money in the world. Two hundred. Oh, go ahead.' (I am dying of shame.) Here I am buggered.

The Marquise looks very proud of herself at her

heroic feat. I, with a grimace on my face, am holding my poor wounded behind. But she is so gay that it is infectious and I join her in the mood as she covers me with kisses and caresses.

'Damn it, you nearly killed me, but I forgive you.'

We seal the reconciliation in a way that there is not the slightest rancour remaining.

Good King Dagobert was right when he said that the best of friends have to part. Our liaison lasts six solid weeks. Moreover, I profited mightily from heteroclitoric tastes. It cost her piles of gold.

'Darling,' she tells me one day, 'I can see that we no longer love each other. But I have always liked you, and I hope you will remain my good friend. Nevertheless, let us prevent disgust. You will never want for women. You are young, and I don't want you to waste any precious time. I'll be your guide. For one thing, I'll tell you candidly that the women of the court, and that includes myself, are dangerous beyond words. Nothing is lacking for them to make themselves attractive. Men find in us the manners of good society and the vices of bad. And all these vices are based on one thing, treachery.

'We are flirtish in appearance and depraved in character. Pleasure for us still has its attractions, but we enjoy it out of habit. A new lover is sure to please us. When my husband comes home in the winter, I overwhelm him with my favours, but after twenty-four hours, the illusion of love vanishes. The blindfolds fall from our eyes; we recognize what we really are; and we separate.

'Sentiment is regarded by us as a chimera. We speak of it often and calmly and with interest precisely because we have never been touched by it. You should do well here with your staying powers, your willingness to oblige, and, above all, your talent in the art of lovemaking. I know at least twenty women who would ruin themselves for you, since you would be able to revive their jaded appetites.

'Here modesty is a wry face, decency hypocrisy. Good qualities become corrupt and virtues are tinted with the colours of vice. But fashion and manners cover them. Spirit is appreciated only for the jargon that accompanies it. In other words, fortune depends on us and we are as blind as it is.

'Assume outwardly a bold expression, even impertinent, in a tete-a-tete. Be fast with your affairs and get to the goal quickly. But in public, change your manner. Be as courtly and courteous as you can with the female object of your desires. It is not that we fear indiscretions. We are only afraid of revelations if they are not to our advantage.'

The Marquise stops. Her sofa is not far. There we make our last impassioned adieux. When I leave, I obtain her permission to renew our acquaintanceship from time to time with the stipulation that I not be impaled from the rear again.

A few days later, I run into Madame de Confroid, whom I have had before and who I heard had come into some money. She is petite with a rather nice figure, but there is nothing striking about her face. Although her love grotto is as cold as an icy cavern, she does have a remarkable and extraordinary talent for sucking pricks.

I have never come across any woman even remotely approaching her skill in this art. In my time, I have permitted myself to be fellated by members of the third sex who certainly are no amateurs, but Confroid puts the best of them to shame.

At her coquettish glance, I follow her home where we get into bed. There she sucks me continually for two hours without taking the organ out of her mouth. While she drains me, she masturbates and I fondle her pointed breasts, which is about all I can do.

That is the only way she can get pleasure – sucking a man and playing with herself at the same time. It takes her at least an hour at this activity before she can come to a climax.

I have had normal intercourse with her in every conceivable position without producing any reaction. Once I brought two of my friends with me and we had her simultaneously in all three orifices, but when it was over, she was still as motionless as a rock.

There is nobody like her to get my prick standing up. First she grazes it with her delicate fingers, and then she breathes on it. Her lips wander over my stomach and groin. She nuzzles her nose in my pubic hair, gets close to my sex, teases it with her blowing, and finally gives it a fugitive kiss. She is driving me out of my mind.

When she sees how my prick is throbbing, she knows the precise spot where I am most sensitive. She can judge perfectly the rise of my seminal fluid, for she stops just when I am ready to explode.

After letting it calm down for several moments, her mouth grazes the gland again. She gives it little darts with her tongue. Then her mouth is wide open to take each of my testicles in turn.

Then she quickly turns her attention back to my

virility, running her tongue up and down it, and bestowing little kisses on it. I am trembling through and through and I feel the sperm rising like the mercury in a thermometer on a hot day.

The vixen senses it. She swallows the tip of my prick for just a moment before spitting it out. A second later I would have come. My prick is in agony from this abortive frustrating pleasure, but it is an agony that I could endure forever.

All this time she is masturbating, violently. Furiously her busy fingers open the lips of her cunt as wide as possible. She squashes her clitoris that springs up red and hard and then scratches it with her fingernails.

Because the gland has quietened down, Confroid renews her oral caresses, inserting it in her mouth down to the very bottom of her throat. Again she rejects it just before the supreme moment to pay attention to her own pleasure. Finally, she is becoming aroused.

This succession of suctions sends delicious shivers running up and down my spine. They are a series of voluptuous vibrations which make me shudder like a palsy sufferer. I hear the rattles in my throat.

This time, I think she has made up her mind. The gland is all the way in her mouth. The tip is touching her tonsils while her tongue is all over it.

I can't stand it any more . . . Now . . . I'm coming.

But again the same confounded frustration. With her extraordinary prescience, she ceases her activities a fraction of a second before my ejaculation.

I remain in that suspended state for I don't know how long. I twitch exquisitely with my nerves taut from the interrupted voluptuousness. It lasts interminably.

During one of the pauses, Confroid masturbates even more vigorously. She passes her thigh on my breast so that the cunt with the busy finger in it is only a few inches from my eyes.

She once told me that she had been playing with herself since she was four years old and has been doing it three or four hours every day since then.

While she is thus engaged with herself, I feel the urge to return the homage she plays my sexuality, but she does not let me, saying it would ruin her pleasure. I content myself by stroking her bottom and sticking my finger in her rear aperture.

Waves of passion rush through my nerves, muscles and veins. My entire body is on fire. I fidget and quiver like a woman in heat. I think my organ is going to expire from the raptures.

Suddenly, my whole being is concentrated in a wild torrent rushing across my stomach and through my prick like an unleashed wild river. It is a marvellous fireworks exploding in a thousand spangles that her mouth avidly gulps down.

I am dead from the bliss, but Confroid's persistent suction revives me. She has drunk all my sperm down to the last drop. She is still sucking me. My God! How she sucks me! It is pure ecstasy. I no longer know where I am, perhaps in a sort of coma. The rapture of my prick is my sole sensation. It penetrates my entire being. My mind is a mire of voluptuousness.

I must have a prick capable of eternal pleasure.

Of course, I do not get limp. Fifteen minutes later,

I discharge again, this time even more copiously. Now it is beginning to hurt, but the pain is so delightful.

Indefatigably, Confroid continues to suck while she thrusts her fingers in her cunt more enthusiastically than ever. I see her wrist and fingers dance in a mad twirl. Her irritated hardened clitoris is a purplish blue.

Again I ejaculate. Two times, three times. And each sensation is more rapturous and more grievous. She never ceases her implacable sucking. I clench my teeth in order not to scream.

I no longer have any control over myself. Again I spurt. Writhing in delirious spasms, I think I am going out of my mind. Now pleasure and pain are inextricably blended, and I no longer know if I ejaculate or not. Finally, I am out of sperm.

Confroid is now near the zenith. Her body throbs, her bosom heaves, and her thighs open and close spasmodically.

Now is the time. Brutally I insert one hand in her cunt and other in her rear – three fingers in the vagina and two in the anus.

She gives a convulsive jolt. Finally releasing my lifeless sex, she gives a yelp like a mortally wounded animal. Her body becomes taut, arches, relaxes . . . and collapses. Her screech of rapture is muted and prolonged.

Confroid has reached the climax.

When I take my leave of her, she, knowing my insatiable thirst and need for money, gives me a purse containing a hundred louis.

Here I am free again. I make my way into the various court circles where I cast curious and piercing eyes on the women who are a part of them. Less and less do I keep in mind what the Marquise told me. The season of balls arrives, and I am mad about dancing. But since I am not a blueblood, I am not permitted to take part in the terpsichorean revelries. Nonetheless, being able to watch has its compensations. I have obtained the permission to pay my respects to a spirited and good-hearted princess. I think her just right to inspire a lasting relationship but too intelligent to tie herself down that way. At her age and with her beauty, she would be stupid to do so.

What would Eros say? Has he put his arrows away or is he going to let them all fly on a single heart? Heavens! She is desirable! Perhaps it is possible if I play my cards right.

Now, I am with some gentlemen who express their opinions of the dancers.

'Who is that wild little thing? Her hair is all ruffled, and look at the condition of her gown! But I find her the most seductive creature on the floor. She's absolutely stunning,' I cry.

'That's the Duches of ***,' answers the Count de Rhedon. 'Don't you know her? I'll introduce you. She likes music and I think you'll get along with her.'

The next day, taking the Count at his word, I call on him and we depart.

At six o'clock in the evening, the Duchess is still in her negligee. Long tresses escape from a net on her head. To kiss the Count, curtsy to me, ask me twenty questions, and take me to practise the *pas de deux de Roland* is a matter of only a moment. I am clumsy with the first steps. A lascivious movement makes me bold, gets me all hot and causes me a.... How delicious an erection is while doing a *pas de deux*! The Count loudly applauds. She cries that I dance like a god and makes me promise to come often and try out new steps with her. The Count leaves and I remain. She arranges her hair in such a way that I can barely stifle my laughter. When she asks my advice, I arrange it in a coiffure that delights her. She dresses and leaves, and I, too, withdraw.

'She doesn't have the time to be naughty,' I say to myself, as I make my way to bed. Her roguish face torments me all night.

I get up and hurry to the Duchess's at ten o'clock in the morning. She is just getting out of her bath and is as fresh as a rose. A dressing-gown covers from head to toe, but in spite of that, I feel tingles running up and down my spine. After chocolate is served, she leaps up and trips to the clavichord. Her tiny hands run over the keys faster than the eye can see. She has a thin but charming voice. From the expression on her face as she sings, I perceive that she is susceptible.

We play a duet. When I touch her, I soften her in spite of herself. She loses her head and her heart tightens. I hear an almost inaudible sigh. Her voice dies, her hands stop their movement, and her breast rises and falls. My inflamed eye misses not a detail.

All of a sudden, she slaps me on the face, begs my pardon, throws herself face down on the sofa, and then gets up with a great burst of laughter.

Luckily for me, she regains her calm. As we dance, again I happily notice that she seems to be interested in me, for she affectionately praises me. Before I leave, she implores my forgiveness and asks me to impose on her any penitence I might wish. So here I am, an executioner, before this little hypocritical face. I seize one of her hands which I cover with kisses. The other gives me a gentle tap which a bolder kiss makes amends for on the spot.

The following day, I fly there on wings of love. She had asked me to bring some new songs which I have under my arm. She is still in bed. A maid opens the drapes when I appear. Next to her bed an armchair has been placed. I prefer to lean against a console, however.

Where are your brushes, Fragonard, so that I could paint this exquisite child?

A peasant's bonnet half covers her head. Her features have no proportion, but her black eyes are superb. Add to this an irresistible mouth, a retroussé nose, a narrow forehead but piquantly fringed, to or three tiny beauty spots, a peaches-and-cream complexion, and carmine lips that the purest vermilion would not equal.

After an exchange of polite chitchat, I show her the notes. She begs me to sing. I am just getting in voice when suddenly a lifted sheet reveals to me a breast of lilies and roses. My voice quavers, but I continue as best I can. Now appear an arm that must have been fashioned by Love himself, an enchantingly rounded thigh, a well-turned leg, and a dainty foot. I am so intoxicated that I no longer know what I am singing. I am trembling throughout my body.

'Keep on!' she commands in a voice of authority I would not have believed she was capable of.

I start over. My blood is boiling, my nerves are jangling, my heart is beating madly, and my face is covered with perspiration. The little witch is watching me with a malicious smile. One last bound and she is uncovered entirely. Damn! My eyes are bloodshot. Throwing aside the music, I undo the buttons that are constraining me and hurl myself into her arms. She answers my yells and bites in kind, and I leave her only after four vigorous, victorious assaults.

The Duchess has fainted, and when she does not come to, I get a little worried. Consequently, I employ a remedy that has never failed me. My tongue is incredibly voluble. I apply my mouth to the rosebud that surmounts a delightful globe. An involuntary shudder of her body reassures me.

'Dear God! You found it!' she exlaims as she throws her arms around my neck in an ecstasy.

'What did I find?' I ask in some astonishment.

'The passion everybody said I did not have,' she exalts.

Now we are face to face and I assure you that the Duchess is not one of those prudes afraid of a man completely in the buff. As she sensuously wiggles, I discover new charms. A more beautifully formed body cannot be conceived. Fleshy without being plump, slender without skinniness, and a litheness of the thighs which need naught but a little exercise. Her buttocks are bouncing in the air like a performer on a trampoline.

I do like to fuck, but since the Lord in his wisdom did not see fit to grant us the gift of perpetual motion, we have to start sooner or later, for this game exhausts rather than tires.

Now, my duchess has only one jargon, the few words of which she repeats endlessly in a monotonous voice. They become boring uttered in a singsong voice. How I would like to hear from that purple-rimmed mouth those silly little words that a woman, drunk with voluptuousness, delivers so eloquently. The right expression can render a single caress ever so much more exciting. Now, as one philosopher remarked, ennui yawns with us on the breasts of our beauties. Love vanishes, the swarm of pleasures flies away, and one sleeps the sleep of the dead.

Those are the degradations I have been suffering for two weeks with the Duchess. Our beginnings are so delicious and the endings are so disgusting. Satiety finally wins out.

I am at that point one evening when I am entering my doorway. My servant hands me a jewel-case and a note, which I immediately read:

'An instant rendered me your mistress. Another instant has changed everything. Nevertheless, Monsieur, I am very grateful to you, and I ask you to keep this little case. It contains the image of a woman who once seemed lovely to you and who regrets not having been able to prolong your bliss with her.'

I immediately recognize from which hand this note came. It would have been impossible for the Duchess to have written it. I answer her forthwith:

'Madame, your kindnesses have the right to touch me if your heart has deigned to perceive the littleness of my worth. In our affair, I have exerted an energy which seemed to please you. I am neither spiteful nor bitter. It is enough for me to have had the honours of triumph without even thinking of retreat. For eight days, I have been waiting for your orders, and the proof of my respect for you is not having foreseen them. Your portrait will be for me the token of the esteem you accord to my *talents*. I do hope, Madame, that my successor will bring you more *beneficial gauges*. Both of you will have a very tender obligation toward me, especially when he realizes the price he will have to pay.'

My follower, an intelligent and charming man, was able to last but a few days. After him came a prince, whom she liked for his wit and gallantry, but she had to satisfy herself with his flunkie, the daily bread of a duchess.

Once my reply was finished, I open the case in which I find the Duchess *en deshabille* along with some jewels which were of some value. I take the miniature in my hands. Dare I confess what I did? I make another sacrifice to that pretty robot. The libation pours out over her impish face.

I repair to the residence of Vit-au-Conas, with whom I spent my liberty. Besides, we are good friends. But from the manner in which she receives me, one would think that we were strangers. Soon she warms up and is ready for my tale of woe, about which she had heard something from the Count of Rhedon. She is amused by the catastrophe which I am relating to her when Madame de Sombreval and another woman of equal rank are announced. The latter is attractive and witty and I ask permission to call on her. It is granted.

The visit over, dear Vit-au-Conas says to me: 'So I am going to lose you again, my dear friend. I see that she has designs on you. You are a godsend for her. Act wisely. And dont' forget to push your advantage. Push, push!'

'Ah, Madame, you know that I never fail to do that. Look.' (I make the gesture.)

With my Marquise wishing me good luck, we part, and I rush home to prepare myself for the attack.

Dressed like a dandy and as radiant as a peacock, I hurry to Madame \*\*\*. The gathering is numerous. After the preliminary exchange, I examine the assembly. Eight or ten fops pirouetting around, the fawners of the mistress of the house who lean over her and are attentive to her every word, a dozen or so rather coarse women with insolent looks. I am standing with a monsignor, whose income from a bishopric and two abbeys, thought to be a hundred thousand francs, gives him the right to preach virtue to the ladies of easy virtue in Paris and the noble-women at court.

'Do you see that big baroness?' he asks me. 'The one with the flushed face and the porcine eyes with the bristly eyebrows. She is insatiable. Anything that comes her way – coachmen, lackeys, what have you – is her meat. She changes lovers often. Last week alone, she put two in the hospital. She got herself a husband once for lack of anything better, but the poor fellow is now incurably insane.'

'Who is that tall pale blonde?'

'Don't you know the Countess of Minandon?'

'No, but she's tearing her fan to pieces.'

'She's a conceited bitch whom you had better watch out for. Six months ago, she was kind enough to give me gonorrhoea. My prick is still burning. That's what happens when you get out of your diocese.'

He chuckles when I smile at his pleasantry, diocese meaning condom.

'Who is that whispering in her ear?'

'She's the chamber pot for the King's guards. Don't have anything to do with her, either, unless you want to run the risk of syphilis.'

I was going to put more inquiries to him, when someone addresses me and our dialogue is over. The conversation becomes general.

The music hour has come, when Madame *** abruptly addresses me.

'Monsieur, this is your speciality. I know how much you love music.'

'Madame, I am not a musician. All I can do is listen.'

'Well, then,' interrupts the Marquis de Fier-en-Fat, 'you can listen to me. I was born to music. I have a touch all of my own. I am not boasting since it is merely a natural gift. Which devil has bragged about his ears? Now I don't like Gluck. You can't even dance to him. Piccini has no sense of harmony.'

'Monsieur does not like *Iphigenie*?'

'No. It gives me gooseflesh. Now, give me *The Deserter*. That really has an overture. Le Floquet really knows how to compose an opera.'

Madame *** smiles at our little contretemps. When the recital is finished, I prepare to leave, but she holds me back a moment to tell me she would like to see me tomorrow at her toilette.

I have forgotten to describe her. Madame *** is thirty-eight and she makes no attempt to conceal her age. She has a pale complexion and almost transparent skin. Her face is oval-shaped. Her lovely eyes express her thoughts without simpering. A wide mouth. She is rather tall, but the regularity of her curves make one unaware of her height. One thing wrong is her bosom which is small and beginning to sag. It still retains some of its firmness. Although her arms and hands are lean, she has a dainty foot. Even the King has commented on the clearness of her voice. In court circles, she is highly thought of.

Do you have a problem? Her advice is always good. Is a young nobleman looking for a wife? She finds the right girl for him. She knows everything, has experienced everything, guessed everything. She advances her favourites and watches over her protégés. She holds audiences, has a secretary, an office, a treasurer, and there is nothing that goes on which she does not have her finger in.

My God! I'll make my fortune with a woman like that. I am expecting favours. Soon I'll be able to distribute them.

I arrive at the appointed time and am received as an expected caller. While she is at her toilette, we exchange gallantries.

The maids disappear and we are alone. Damn it! I feel this bashfulness again. When Madame sits on the divan, I crouch at her feet. I am very fond of sofas.

'To tell the truth, I think I have made a most extraordinary invitation,' she tells me.

'As for myself, I don't see anything unusual about it.'

'I didn't think you would take liberties this quickly.'

'I think we can come to an understanding, Madame.'

'Whatever are you saying?'

'Simply this. I adore you and my fondest hope is that I do not displease you,' I fervently exclaim.

'I have some plans for you, my dear friend.'

'My only happiness will be to carry them out.'

'You have spirit and fire.'

'Ah, Madame, how could one lack them when one is with you? You would electrify nature.'

She is electrified. Her brow flushes, her eyes sparkle, and her hand trembles. Love, love, come you little bugger.

'That is a pretty dress you're wearing.'

'Since you seem to like the colour, I'll keep on wearing it.'

'What pretty ribbons. They're in the latest fashion.'

'What in the world are you doing?' (I'm untying the ribbons.) 'What would my servants say if they saw you?'

'Madame! We are losing time, time that could be better employed.'

'Suppose somebody came in?'

'So much the worse for the curious.'

My hands wander over her lips and my mouth rests on a breast that heaves under the licking of my tongue.

'Ah . . . Ah . . . You little demon.' Her voice fades. 'I can't resist any longer.'

The hour has come to take my city. I press, squeeze, shove and penetrate. With the second jab, I am in to the bottom. She is around my body like a boa constrictor. Not a movement is wasted.

'Ah, my friend,' she moans 'Not even the Duke can equal you. The Prince would have succumbed by now. The Ambassador never made me discharge so abundantly.'

I wonder if she is going to pass the whole court in review. When we are convinced that there is nothing more to do, we take up our conversation again. Now Madame *** leaves off that haughty air that she affected. I am the fortunate lover to whom she grants all the prerogatives.

Since I can further my career better by inflating her pride, I let her talk about herself. Also, it is in my interest to penetrate into her secrets and intrigues. Never do I lose from sight my ultimate goal – money. The knowledge I glean will help me in my manoeuvres. I realize that my first coup has genuinely dazzled my adorable one. But ambitious women are impervious to real sensuousness, for vanity and cunning absorb all their faculties. Constantly obsessed by envy and hatred, she is poisoned to such an extent that love is impossible. I can only look forward to frigid raptures. I know that I cannot captivate her by playing on her senses, but I can with her vaingloriousness. Also, I know that in sexual matters her views are limited. My plan, therefore, is to subject her to me, to master her, to make use of her fortune, or to get rid of her if she serves no purpose.

As a rule, all I need is a fortnight to gain my ends. By that time, I have been able to twist Madame *** around my finger. She adopts my ideas in the belief that they are her own. I know her thoughts without her knowing mine. That is not all. She has business affairs which I intend to run. All I have to do is suggest it, and she turns them over to me. I make deals, sign contracts, and pay myself a salary without any objection on her part. My only guide is my conscience.

I am too intelligent not to remain in the background. Madame *** is still in titular charge and also takes the brunt of my mistakes. That is the sign of a crafty man. Before telling the final catastrophe, I want to mention two or three incidents that are somewhat out of the ordinary.

The world-famous Abbot Ricaneau had been asking for donations for some time. He has a good income, but the good Abbot, possessed of the virtue of proliferation, regularly produces four infants a year. Being not without a conscience, he pays the salary of the wet-nurse before enriching the collection of the foundling home. Someone suggested our office. He comes to see me, and I thought his request reasonable. But I demand a detailed report, which he brings the following day. With a smirk, he tries to bribe me with a purse whose thinness makes me knit my brows.

'Monsieur,' I tell him. 'I assume that these are just for the incidental expenses such as the gratuities to the porter, nurses and secretary.'

The Abbot does not dare contradict me. I look at the report carefully and discover several difficulties. He begs my help to overcome them.

'You have to make up your mind,' I say. 'You want an abbey with an income of twelve thousand livres. Since you are one of my friends, you can have it for a mere thousand.'

He expostulates. 'What!'

'A mere trifle, and I am disappointed in you.'

When I go out the door, he follows me like a dog, screaming and yelling. But I outshout him, threatening to tell one and all about his scandalous offer. I mutter something about *lettres de cachet*. At that, he makes his escape, leaving me with the purse, which I find held a miserable hundred louis.

A few days later, a very attractive woman is ushered into my office. Her request is a lieutenancy for her husband, who had served in the army for twenty years and had suffered several wounds in battle.

Do you think that I spoke with the voice of generosity? Well, you are not mistaken. I make several gestures to her signifying my benevolence. At first, she is very shy, but I soon win her over. Then we are chatting like old friends. In less than an hour we are one flesh.

*Did you fuck her?*

No, I turned her over to someone else. God, what a fool you are! She was one of the best I ever had. For a woman from the provinces, she showed real talent.

*At least you got some money out of it.*

That goes without saying. I have her write her husband to deposit ten thousand livres to my account. In exchange, I give her a gold ring some scoundrel presented me with that morning to enlist my help in getting him knighted. It was worth about twenty-five louis. You see how generous I am. It was more than the interest on her investment.

Our business is going famously. Under my skilful management, dross turns to gold. Madame \*\*\* adores me. Of course, she sleeps with everyone, but I am her favourite because I hold the purse-strings. At times, I feel pangs of conscience, but she soon cures them.

Now here is what happened. There was a lovely young woman, very wealthy, who had only one lover.

*And who was he?*

Her husband. There are still some eccentrics who believe that their wives should only sleep with them. She naturally thought he was out of his mind and had him locked up. She came to me to help in arranging the formalities. We saw to it that he had an income of six hundred francs a year and that he would be dressed decently. Madame *** and I fixed a fee of ten thousand ecus, which was a bargain. Eight days later, officials took the lunatic, shaved his hair, and led him off to the asylum.

We thought that the matter was finished. The wretch was supposed to have rotted away or at least have become insane. But he had the devil in the flesh, for nothing of the sort happened. A certain magistrate happened to visit the asylum where our inmate told him his story. The official was sympathetic and believed him. He informed the minister, who immediately preferred charges against Madame ***. She was found guilty, heavily fined, and went to bury herself in her estates in the country.

My dear friend, do you think that I was going to hang myself? Of course not. I just went to count my money. I found I had twenty thousand ecus plus quite a bit of jewellery. But I was sorry about the fate of the poor woman. I could have got much more through her. I wondered if I should pay my debts. Oh, I decided not to worry about that. Why should I give those usurers anything? They've always sucked me dry before. They could wait for my will or marriage. In short, I made up my mind to seek new fields.

There was a fete in which the town and the court participated. I cast my eye on the assembly and the alluring faces therein. Oh Satan, get thee behind me.

Already I felt my face lighting up and my pocketbook being emptied. With great fanfare appeared Madame Cul-Gratulous, who because of her position, felt she had to attend the festivities. That was the only reason, for she would never go to public places to seek her pleasures.

Remembering me, she invited me into her box. It certainly was not her figure which tempted me. Her head, neck, torso and derriere were all one piece. Dowdily dressed. Fat arms with varicose veins. Thick thighs and bowlegs. Squint eyes out of focus. A moustache stained with tobacco. Her head was topped with a tousled wig. She was adorned with diamonds, ribbons and fluff. That will give you an idea of the physical appearance of the Countess.

*What about her morals?*

Fuck. Let's not talk so loud. You realize that she is a grande dame. Every time she walks by, her servants kowtow. She terrorizes her husband, her father, and even her grandfather. But she does not have overly high aspirations, for fear she fall too far. For the rest, she is malicious, peevish, shameless, vulgar and opinionated. She thinks that she is the soul of generosity when she hands out her coins.

*But what do you think you are going to do with a monster like that?*

What am I going to do with her? That's a fine question. I am going to plunder her and swallow her up while I fuck her.

The spectacle finished late, and she invited me to have dinner with her in a tone that was almost an order. I pretended that I was overwhelmed by the honour.

The meal was formal and consequently dismal. One ate little and spoke less. As we began to file out, a valet whispered to me that Madame wished to speak to me before my departure. He added that I was destined to spend the night with her.

Mademoiselle Branlinos, the Countess's personal maid, greeted me at the bathroom where she said she had orders to prepare me.

'Heavens, I never expected such cordiality, Mademoiselle, but do with me that you will.'

We entered the bathroom, but I was hesitant about appearing completely nude before Mademoiselle Branlinos, who was helping me off with my clothes. She was a delightful thing, not more than twenty.

'Hurry up, Monsieur, I have to get you ready.'

Ripping off her clothes and the last of mine, I fucked her on the rug of the bathroom. She was not displeased and I was amused by the game. But we had to think of my bath. We both got into the tub, Branlinos mentioning that I had dirtied her. She also said that she would form the third of the trio for the evening.

When we were thoroughly washed, dried and anointed, she nimbly escaped my grasp, fearing, she said, another pollution. Five minutes later, she came to fetch me.

I entered the bedroom. The Countess was already in her couch. She extended me a hand which I kissed with as much ardour as if she had been pretty. I sat on one side of her and Branlinos on the other. Although Madame was a little more human, decorum still prevailed.

'My dear,' she said to Branlinos, 'see if he has an erection.'

As soon as the petite touched it, it sprang up like a soldier standing at attention.

'Oh, Madame,' she cried. 'It's as hard as an iron rod.'

At that, Madame Gratulos turned around and presented me – guess what?

*What?*

You certainly are stupid.

*I'm sorry, but I don't have the faintest idea.*

Her derriere.

*Her derriere?*

Yes, her backside, an enormous mound of sagging flabby flesh.

I immediately went soft at the sight, but Branlinos resurrected me. When she opened the entrance to the abyss, I gritted my teeth and began to do my duty like a man. I was in the midst of doing what I doubted I could do while Branlinos was masturbating the old cow. During my fucking, I was sweating through every pore. The moment of discharge was nearing. Did you ever hear the sound of a squeaky gate with rusty hinges being opened? That was exactly how my lovely released her load.

When the ordeal was over, she had the kindness to give me a wet kiss. Damn it! I preferred the other aperture because it did not smell so bad.

After an interlude during which we conversed, I had to perform the same ritual. Never have I felt more ridiculous. Nevertheless, I acquitted myself valiantly.

'Would you like to fuck Branlinos?' my future patroness suddenly asked me.

I jumped at the proposal. Suddenly, I felt myself being rummaged. Her finger was all the way in the most shameful part of me. So that was why she let me fuck the little one, so that the pill wouldn't be too bitter to swallow. Cul-Gratulos left off only when I was groggy with fatigue. Dawn was breaking when I withdrew. I was made to promise to keep the goings-on a secret, and I have faithfully kept my word.

The following days were marked by the same adventures. The gold she showered on me was sufficient compensation. But if it had not been for Branlinos, an erection would have been out of the question.

When my term was finished, she left to take the waters at Vichy, loading me with farewell gifts with her haughty air, and I went back to Paris.

Back in Babylon which has the most corruption of any city in the world simply because it has the most people, I wore myself out paying calls on every coquette and scoundrel in Paris. For more than two weeks nothing eventful happened. I was bored to tears, I gambled and lost. I saw that my sustenance would be gone if I continued, and so I considered flight to avoid the temptation of the tables It was a momentous decision which I carefully weighed.

Already the sun was gilding the crops and the Graces were retreating to the copses. And all the women were flying to the countryside. Their example decided me and I followed them. You can be sure that like a busy bee I sucked only the juiciest blossoms. Nevertheless, it was tedious.

You know as well as I those enchanted palaces that

line the shores of the peaceful Seine. I went there and found nothing.

Finally, I went to the Marne where rise walls built by our forefathers. Their imposing aspect seems to proclaim that kings reside there. But no. It is merely the abode of the brides of Our Saviour, the convent of ***, whose abbess is the aunt of one of my acquaintances. She has been told that I am likeable and I am welcomed with open arms. You have no idea of the excitement I cause when I arrive. The pretty little nun coquettishly adjusts her wimple when she sees me. All rush to the visiting room.

When Madame Abbess appears, all vanish out of respect. What a voluptuous figure she has. I could almost eat her.

She has just reached her fifth lustrum. To the flower of youthfulness is joined the blossom of perfect health. A glittering face with eyes blacker than jet, a rose-bordered mouth, and teeth of ivory that she permits me to admire. There is something of the flirt about her which her garb cannot conceal.

When she notes the lust in my eyes, she says to me teasingly: 'Are you another Abelard?'

I don't know what to say. But I know that I am going to fuck my Abbess or know the reason why. The compliments we exchange are prettily turned on her part and gallant on mine. Soon we are chatting as if we had known each other for years. My God! Now I have an erection that is killing me. It is the result of gazing too intently at those seductive breasts.

I shall not speak of the parties that were given in my honour or the recitals. There could be heard my sonorous male voice blending with the titters of the timid novices. A satyr is loose among captive nymphs, in effect. In vain do they try to flee, but there is something about me that stops their steps. As they totter, the squeals they emit are not those of fear.

What a wonderful thing to find yourself in a seraglio of twenty little nuns who vie with one another in loveliness. Their eyes reveal a tender languor. Several of the innocents have twitches they have never before experienced. How sweet they look. Let's fuck. Let's fuck. Oh, my prick, show what you are capable of. Hail Venus! Hail Priapus!

Contemplating such matters, I toss about in my bed. I am unable to sleep because of my excitement.

The next day, Madame the Abbess is slightly indisposed and keeps to her bed. I receive permission to pay my respects in her apartment.

What has come over me? She is as lovely as an angel. I forget why I have come. She extends her hand to me as she asks about my health. With passion I kiss that hand. She gives a sigh. Another sigh is my response. We are alone. Her half-closed eyes, her fluttering eyelashes, the distension of her stomach, and the palpitation of an alabaster bosom still covered by an inopportune veil embolden me. 'Julia! Julia!' Such are the first sparks of our fires. I kneel at the side of the bed with my burning lips on the hand that I did not relinquish. She makes no attempt to snatch it away. Heavens! She has fainted. She is dying. I summon her servants with screams of terror. Salts, waters, scents!

'That's one of Madame's dizzy spells,' cries one of the maids.

But it is not her final attack. After a quarter of an

hour, she returns to her senses, pale as a sheet. Her pallor, however, is that of a woman in love. Several tears have dampened her beseeching eyes. Finally, we are by ourselves again.

'I apologize for these attacks which nearly kill me. The doctors cannot seem to diagnose them.'

I note the colour returning to her cheeks. Her pulse becomes normal. My heart is pounding as I approach her. Several disarranged pillows offer me a pretext. As I advance my hand to straighten them and hold her up – oh wonder of wonders! – her opulent bosom is offered to my view. The sight intoxicates me. I press my amorous mouth against her amorous mouth. My tongue gives her quivers of voluptuousness. Gradually, I make my way to the sanctuary. A finger penetrates it. It gives a twitch, one which excites her still more. What ineffable bliss!

'Sweet Jesus!' she moans. 'I can't stand this wonderful feeling. I think I am expiring.'

The sensations are too much, too new. Unable to withstand the shock, I sink back in a faint. She is worried to such an extent that she rings for her maid. When I come to, I find myself in their arms. Their efforts to revive me are so successful that the petite maid, on seeing the condition I am in, deems it wise to retire. The Abbess and I reiterate a thousand times our vows to love each other eternally, and after each oath, we seal it with the appropriate ceremony.

I am nourished with the strongest broths and foods. I spend the day as I did the morning, and the night is just as joyful. The following days, diversions without number are prepared for me – hunting, fishing and games. Such thoughtfulness strengthens my ties to the

Abbess even more firmly. She is lascivious without being coarse. She takes my advice and my lessons inflame her. Her lovely svelte and flexible body and her shapely legs enlace me, melt into my body. Only in my arms does she enjoy repose.

I would have been true to her, but the flesh is weak. Young hearts are pining for me, and should I let them wither and fade away? No, I am too compassionate.

I establish a schedule – my nights are with the Abbess and my days are occupied otherwise. The dormitories and cells are all open to me, and I take advantage of it. The first one I fuck is discreet.

*Discreet? You must be joking.*

I am not. It is with the maid who restored me. And that's the truth. She was in charge of my meals. One day, I was so excited by the chase that I return late. She is not expecting me. I enter her cell. Guess what meets my eyes.

She is sprawled out in a big armchair with her robe lifted up to her navel and her legs spread wide apart. With a great deal of enthusiasm she is manipulating – a dildo!

I shut the door quickly. Precipitately, she drops her petticoat and leaves the spear in the wound. With a deep blush, she stands up and starts to walk away with her thighs squeezed closely together. The devil inspires me. Taking her under the arms, I free Priapus who soon finds refuge deep in the centre of the comfortable chamber. She makes a feeble protest.

'My dear, I caught you in the act. And I am going to finish what you started. Don't worry. I won't betray you.'

I lay her on the couch, where I perform the sweet task twice.

'God bless you,' she sighs when it is over.

One day, the Abbess beckoned me and led me to a cell. Putting her finger to her lips, she pointed to a peephole and motioned me to have a look through it. I did as I was bid and saw Sister Stephanie in the adjoining cubicle.

Dear Sister Stephanie – such a romantic name. Young, rosy cheeked and ash blonde, she reminded me of a bouquet of flowers with her gentle charming voice and her veiled look which seemed to conceal so many tender secrets.

And the cell. It was a weird world, a bizarre enclosure whose walls were not limed with white but with blue, a sky blue that was almost ethereal. The ceiling, too, was painted with the same azure while the floor was of carefully waxed white planks. The bed looked comfortable.

What was out of place in the nun's cell was a Christ nailed to an oversized cross bracketed to the wall, but the figure was not that of the emaciated Saviour that is so familiar. He was a robust male with powerful pectoral muscles. Moreover, the body was made of a material with an astonishing resemblance to human flesh. I saw Stephanie touch it and her finger sank in.

As for the face of the Christ, the expression was one of ecstasy, a profane rapture that had absolutely nothing to do with religious exaltation. It was a handsome face, masculine and virile. The nostrils and lips were sensual, and there was a glitter in the eyes.

The door opened and in stepped Angela, one of

the more delicious of the novices, who was warmly welcomed with a kiss.

'What lovely hair you have,' Stephanie remarked.

'And how about yours, Sister Stephanie?'

'I am rather vain about it.'

'But I thought when you took your vows, you had to have your head shaved.'

'Yes, you do. But if you get on the good side of the Mother Superior, she gives you permission to let it grow and fix it any way you like. It goes without saying that you can't let it show. Certain nuns would understand these special marks of favour.'

'Show me your hair,' Angela demanded.

Without any hesitation, the woman removed her wimple, and a cascade of tresses tumbled down over her shoulders. Silky curls, elegant waves fell on the white starched collar that formed a part of her costume.

After a gasp of unfeigned admiration, Angela asked permission to brush it.

The girl sat down facing the sister and began to brush the hair with measured strokes. Suddenly, Stephanie kissed Angela's lips with her moist mouth. At first, the girl shrank back but then surrendered her lips and tongue. In a trice her body was embraced. I could see that her sex was being ignited. The sensation must have become even more unbearable when Stephanie caressed the yearning breasts through the blouse. Then, baring them, she took the nipples in her mouth and sucked them slowly and avidly.

'I think I have wet myself,' Angela murmured.

Finally, Sister Stephanie disrobed, exhibiting her nude body with arrogance and hauteur. She possessed opulent round breasts, a thick fleece, smooth thighs, and delicious buttocks.

With deft nimble hands, she quickly divested the girl of her clothing, pushed her back on the bed and began to fondle her ardently.

I could see that Angela had lost touch with reality and I surmised that this was the first time she was experiencing true voluptuousness. Her twitches soon became violent convulsions.

She sank back in a faint from the force of the sensations. But she recovered under the tingling caresses that the sister was bestowing between her open thighs with her agile darting tongue. Then I heard the enamoured sighs, the squeals of joy, and the prolonged moans of pleasure which announced the arrival of the supreme sensation.

They fell back in exhaustion, but I kept my eye glued to the aperture. After a few moments, Stephanie rose and left the bed. I followed her with my eyes as she went to the Christ, pressed herself to it, embraced his muscular thighs, and licked his face. Now she stepped back and began undoing the loin cloth. When it dropped down to the floor, I observed to my astonishment that crucifixion did not necessarily cause loss of virility. And what virility! It was a long member which swayed and vibrated, a foully attractive object the like of which I had never seen. Although it was monstrous, I found it strangely attractive, and I could recognize that this organ nestled between hairy bloated sacks could promise a woman certain raptures.

Stunned with amazement, I watched Sister Stephanie slowly impale herself on the colossus. As she let herself slowly down it, she shuddered and gave little groans. Now she slowly jabbed herself with it in a regular cadence. The cheeks of her buttocks were tightly closed to augment the sensation.

Now the nun began an almost motionless dance which ended with a loud shout followed by a long obscene rattle.

Let's pass over in silence several rather ordinary incidents. I fucked Sister Lapine, Sister Magdelon, Mother Bonaventure, etc. The dormitory, the garden, the dispensary and the chapel are all the theatres of my exploits. But let's discuss the novices.

They are five, and among them, Sisters Agatha, Rose and Agnes stand out. They are the most adorable creatures imaginable. The first two are inseparable and play with each other for lack of anything better to do. Agnes is in love with me, but she hides her feelings and weeps to herself. One day, I find the means to share her room with her.

'What's wrong with you, Agnes?' I demand of her.

'I really don't know.'

'For the last week, something has come over you. You are completely different. You used to laugh and be so much fun, but now you just look out into space and sigh. Tell me what's wrong. Or don't you trust me, who loves you so much?'

She flushes. 'You do love me? If only that were so.'

'Have I offended you?' I ask, taking her hand.

'Please leave me. I don't feel well.'

She rises.

'I see that you are afraid of me. Perhaps I am hateful to you. I think it is about time for me to leave.'

'You're not going?' she cries.

Poor child. She's mine. No further effort is needed. I shall soon have her.

The head of the novices provides me with a good opportunity a few days later. You will recall that she is a good friend. The choir is supposed to sing a motet, but the music-master does not come, and so she confides Agnes to me for the rehearsal.

As soon as the good sister closes the door on us, I resume my attack: 'Lovely Agnes, are you always so cruel?'

She lowers her eyes.

'How unhappy I am. Only God knows how much.'

She raises her hands to heaven.

'Agnes, you have made tears come to my eyes.'

'What do you think about me. I have been crying my heart out.'

Her tears fall fast and heavy.

'Let us console each other. If we don't, I shall die.'

'No,' she sobs. 'You cannot die. It is I who shall have to.'

I take her and put her on my knees with her head against my face.

'Agnes, it is only you whom I love. Tell me that you love me. too.'

'You wicked man, how can you have any doubt about that?'

Her mouth grazes my lips. The girl does not recognize the significance of the outbursts of her heart. Her hour is come. I cover her with kisses. I transfer into her heart the fire that is devouring me. I make her drunk with caresses and kisses. When I remove the last of the veils, I am stunned by the treasures that are revealed. Modesty no longer holds me back. She no longer knows what she is doing. Like a flash of lightning, I strip her bare. The scream that Agnes lets escape is the signal of my victory.

You are probably thinking, fool that you are, that she makes a painful face and puts on airs and that she is despising me as her rapist. On the contrary, she thanks me from the bottom of her heart, the poor child. It is true that I merit the praise, for the fortress is damnably difficult to take.

Afterwards we begin work on her part in the motet. When the Mother Superior returns, Agnes is singing with the voice of an angel. As for myself, I am scorched and scalded. But twelve hours of repose heal my scars.

*What a way to spend your time.*

What do you mean, you fault-finder?

*I'm scolding you because you are wasting your time without getting any money.*

Oh, I forgot to tell you that the Abbess was the soul of generosity. No woman has ever been so bountiful. Now that your fears are calmed, let me continue with the account of my exploits.

Sisters Agatha and Rose are deserving of my homage. The elder cannot be more than eighteen. The former, possessed of an irrepressible spirit, has the devil in her flesh. Rose is more thoughtful but gay at the same time. These two girls are united by a mutual understanding. The Abbess, whose jewels they are, told me in confidence that more than once she allowed them in her bed to appease their desires. The excesses they gave themselves up to! When I give them dancing instruction, we do all sorts of silly things.

'Sisters,' I say one day, 'would you be good enough to show me the games you play with each other.'

'What games?' demands Agatha as Rose blushes.

'If I knew, I wouldn't be asking you.'

'Well, Rose, I think he means hide-and-seek.' She begins to giggle.

'There's nothing hidden,' I tell them sternly. 'I saw everything.'

'What?' asks Rose in consternation. 'You saw? Agatha, we are lost.'

Both begin to weep.

'Dry your tears,' I order them. 'I promise I won't say a word.'

That reassures them somewhat. Besides, what they have done is considered in a convent only a little sin.

'But how were you able to spy on us?' Agatha timidly asks me.

'I really didn't see you. A little genie told me what you were doing.'

'A genie?' she exclaims.

'A genie?' echoes Rose.

'Yes, a genie who comes to me every day.' I can barely stifle my roars of laughter. 'I'll introduce you to him on the condition that you teach me your game and that you listen to what he has to say.'

'What? Does he speak, and how?'

'We talk to each other in sign language. I'll explain later.'

'Let's see.'

'Yes, let's see,' chimes in Rose.

'Easy,' I warn them. 'Wait until I summon him. In the meantime, perhaps you would like to show me your game. . . .'

(I had my reasons, but never has my jinni been so recalcitrant. I did my best to spur him to action, but nothing occurred. Finally, the imp arrived. Here is what happened. I produce the Monsignor, which makes Agatha's eyes pop. She springs towards it.)

'Oh, Rose, I have it in my hand. Look at how beautifully it is fashioned. But it doesn't have any nose!'

'Help me to hold it lest it fly away.'

Rose clutches it.

'How quickly it came.' She tries to unhinge it.

'Young ladies, just a moment. Don't you see that it is just a little snail. It's in its shell.'

'That's so,' Rose says. 'Look at it in its cushion.'

'I've never seen a snail like this one,' Agatha comments.

'It's probably from China.'

'Where are its feelers?'

I am dying of fear lest I should be emancipated in their tender hands.

'I think he wishes to speak,' I tell them.

'We would like to hear him,' they reply.

'I have to warn you that if you get him angry, he will go away and never return. Now, mum's the word.

I grasp Agatha and throw her on the bed. She is a brave little thing, not uttering a word. In a moment, I have her skirt up to her waist. Wild with curiosity, Rose flutters around.

'Agatha, is he speaking?'

'Oh, yes. I have never heard such eloquence. I don't think I can stand it any more.'

'What is he saying?'

It goes without saying that she has other things to

do than reply. The little she-devil wiggles so divinely that I am about to begin all over again, when Rose, unable to contain herself any longer, grabs me. The overheated perspiring genie emerges from the carnage and begins to work on Agatha's companion. Although she is not as vivacious, she is almost mad with voluptuousness. But she has that rare quality I have always appreciated in a woman – the door of the sanctuary closes after the sacrifice without leaving me time to go limp. By now, neither of them is plying me with questions. They are in a state of utter ecstasy. As for myself, I take keen enjoyment in their confusion. We no longer speak of the game. They realize that they have been fooled, but they hold me no grudge.

I am at the peak of bliss, although somewhat fatigued. Every time I consider giving up the game, the devil comes out of his hiding-place and spurs me to new efforts.

Life becomes heaven and hell. You remember that three goddesses fought for one apple. Well, imagine what it is like when twenty little eager nuns compete for one man.

My friend, you have no idea of a female republic whose doge is the Abbess. The majority of the girls have been enrolled in the celestial militia against their wills. Although they are the wives of an ethereal being, they still have corporeal desires. The result is a charnel revolt, a conflict between the senses and reason, between the Creator and the creature. All that stimulates the passions, irritates desires and inflames imagination. That is why the girls get spasms and nervous attacks. They can't be praying all the time.

The normal object of their adoration is the confessor. If there are two, they share the fold, each hating the other cordially. If there is only one, the lambs fight amongst themselves for his favours.

'What! Over an old monk?'

'Yes. Over an old monk. They would do anything for him, for at least he is of flesh rather than wood or metal.'

Consequently, in these abodes of peace and innocence, one enjoys all the comforts of hell.

If only you knew the ruses the girls employ to sneak their lovers over the walls. I could tell you of the horrors of the despotism the vicious old women wield over their charges. There take place orgies worthy of being described by Aretino. When they are married, they have been initiated into every vice imaginable.

The murmurs of discontent are becoming louder. The governing body holds a session. Fault is found with the Abbess who demands that her tastes and pleasures be respected. The reverend mothers are all ears as they eavesdrop. The little innocents are trembling with fear. The way they all look at me leads me to believe that I'll be the scapegoat. For fear of losing me, the Abbess stoutly defends me. The complaints are brought to the attention of the Bishop and thick-witted priest, who announces that he is coming in person to restore order in a house into which Belial has insinuated himself. I am ready to face him, but my dear Abbess persuades me that if I stay, she will be ruined. Loaded with sugar and gold, I make my departure. There is scarcely a dry eye when I leave.

I stop in Paris just long enough to deposit my loot and then proceed to Picardy to finish the season. I do not stop in the provincial capitals where the vices are the same as in the capital with the difference being that they are cruder and more ridiculous.

The friend I am staying with has a rather large estate where the hunting is excellent. The mansion is venerable and imposing. His wife is lovely and he holds his years well. But they are Philemon and Baucis. It is not that she is devout. No, she likes a joke, and she gladly receives gallant advances for she knows how to take them. When I am with her, I feel nothing but admiration and respect.

Monsieur and Madame d'Obricourt live amicably together with her husband entertaining no suspicions. Nevertheless, Madame has a lover with whom she mocks her spouse. A rash act destroys the complacency of Monsieur. While everybody is out hunting, I am alone in the house with Madame. She goes to her boudoir to write some letters while I remain in the salon reading a book. Suddenly, with a missive in her hand, she goes out. Her husband, unexpectedly returned, enters at the same moment.

'Ah, Monsieur,' she says. 'What is wrong with you? You are as pale as a ghost.'

He turns his face to the mirror. Unfortunately for her, I am reflected in my entirety and he sees her slipping me the letter which I do my best to hide. He is seized by an attack of jealousy. Before I can gather my wits about me, I am facing a rifle. 'The letter or your life.'

'You're out of your mind,' I retort. 'Even if I have one, it is obviously not intended for you and you have no right to it.'

'I do not need your advice,' he tells me coldly. 'The letter, or you'll have a bullet in your body.'

I have no choice. I get up, give him the envelope, and shove Madame into the study for she was stupid enough not to have budged.

The perusal of the letter gives the husband more information than he would have liked to have. He realizes that he is a cuckold. Under his phlegmatic exterior, he is a man of violent emotions. The other guests who have come back from the chase do not notice anything wrong. Monsieur uses the same terms of affection when talking with his wife. I cannot get over it.

I have always been suspicious of concealed anger, and I am not wrong this time. Finally, one morning, he finds her in her bedroom with some other women, wives of friends, and beats her within an inch of her life. Unaccustomed to such treatment, she leaves to go to her mother-in-law who has a weakness for her. The old woman is a Jansenist who has little liking for her son because he does not share her views on the after-life.

Madame is aware of this, and on the basis of this knowledge, she lays her plans.

'Mama, I have come to throw myself in your arms,' she says. 'For more than a year now, I have been suffering the tortures of the damned. And it is all because I am a Jansenist, and he has no use for them. He has been mistreating me terribly. He got his hands on a letter I wrote to a priest who was giving me instruction in this belief. And then he accused me of having an illicit affair with this man of God. Now he has been beating me. These ladies are my witnesses. I don't know where to turn except to you.'

Tears stream down her cheeks as the ladies nod their heads to back up her story.

'What a scoundrel and blackguard!' exclaims the mother-in-law. 'My daughter, you will stay with me and I'll take charge of things. If he is rash enough to try to do anything to you, I'll. . . .'

It is necessary to get the letter from her husband's hands. The old woman orders her son to send it to her immediately, or he will be disinherited within twenty-four hours. He knows his mother, and he is not about to forfeit an income of forty thousand livres. There is no choice but to obey. He sends it but with a note of explanation. It is in vain. The mother-in-law turns everything over to Madame, who throws the envelope and its contents into the fire.

The furious Obricourt calls me up as a witness. I say that I don't know anything. Yes, I had a letter, but I was ignorant of its contents. That is not the end of the matter. There is a separation. The old Jansenist dies, leaving her daughter-in-law an inheritance of twenty thousand livres a year.

Tired of shooting hares and bored with the company of the landed gentry, I take refuge on the banks of the Somme. There, an old chateau dating back to the twelfth century is now the home of owls and bats, or at least, it seems that way. But, in reality, it is the abode of an old cantankerous baron. Because of his geneaology, he does not have to have intelligence.

As the old song goes, the Baroness yearns to have someone clean her flues. The Baron, who cannot, does not wish anyone else to perform the task. It is to do this charitable work that I come. I heard that he is rich as Croesus, and in order to part him from some of his wealth, I am ready to suffer his boring conversation and coarse manners.

I am not given a cordial welcome. When he observes that his wife pays me little attention, he becomes warmer. I bring him numerous greetings from mutual friends in Paris, and while he is going through them, I observe the belle.

She is a piquant brunette with a tawny complexion. Her lovely black eyes sparkle lasciviously. Her teeth are like pearls set off in a frame of carmine lips. The bust is slightly too big for her delicate figure. She cannot be more than twenty. All in all, she is eminently fuckable, even though someone should give her some advice on how to dress.

At dinner, we happen to start talking about women. The Baron recounts to me all his woes, including his wrong marriage and lack of ability. I promise to do what I can with his wife to help him to get back his virility. (Naturally, it is my intention to fuck her.) At that, he gives me full liberty. I planned to leave the next day, but he makes me promise to stay for two weeks at least. He will see that I have company with other guests.

'Come now, my dear Baron, your company is sufficient for me. Whom do you think you are going to bring here? A couple of bores and prudes. You are the only charming person I have come across in these parts.'

'I think you can bring me back into contact with youth,' he admits.

The next day, I accompany the Baroness on her stroll. Her husband cannot be with us for he is suffering from a cold, but he almost forced me to get ready the Horns to be placed on his head. I don't lose any time. After a few vague preliminaries, I come to the point.

'I hope I shall not offend you, Madame, when I state that I did not come here without an ulterior motive. That motive was to be pleasing to you. I love you and I want you to love me. If you have any inclination for me, let us make arrangements. Get revenge on that tyrant of yours. I offer you consolation, assistance, delights, and a warm heart. Lovely Baroness, your reply will decide my lot. Your piteous condition should remove any indecision on your part. If I am unlucky enough not to find favour in your eyes, I'll leave.'

'What the devil! One is not that abrupt with a lady of breeding.'

'You're quite right.'

'You're incorrigible.'

We seal the bargain with several kisses, and she goes off to make arrangements so that she can spend the night with me.

How stupid it is to sleep with a woman when the man is on top. It is so monotonous. But she insists. I am petrified.

'The cure says that it is the only right way.'

But in two hours, she is climbing all over me. We finally separate, promising to meet again during the night.

The Baron does not suspect a thing, and she gives

me more money than I could expect from a provincial woman.

*But, where did she get it?*

Quite simple. Husbands in the country generally put their wives on an allowance. But my oldster is madly in love with his young wife and he gives her the key to his coffers. Without his knowledge, she removes two hundred louis which she presents to me. They are for my travel expenses. I then take my leave with the Baron horned and content. There are tears in the eyes of the Baroness as I get in my carriage.

My final rural excursion is at Salency where a bucolic festival is being held. The touching simplicity of the spectacle went to my heart. A young girl comes to bring me a rose. She is fresh and delicious and about sixteen. She gives herself to me freely. Never have I enjoyed such innocence. Not for anything in the world would I have paid for her favours. It has been so long since I have made love without financial transactions involved.

*So, you are on the banks of the Lignon?*

I gather that you are afraid of sheepfolds. What is wrong about relaxing in the arms of artlessness now and then? She was so enticing. And fresh. I still remember the naive way she mounted me. The heat from her mouth transmitted into mine is still there. Her eloquence was that of nature. We don't speak much. If only you could have inserted your hand into her bodice. Never would you have come across such delightful globes. They are firm and elastic at the same time. If only I could reveal to you her alabaster body. She had the contours of the Venus of Medici. Her skin was peaches and cream. Naturally, I have an erection. Her first scream is, 'How that hurts!' Her second is: 'How good it feels!' The way her adorable bottom wiggles and bounces is a delight to see. She does not yield but meets my attack courageously. Now she is returning thrust for thrust. When she discharges, every fibre of her body is affected. Her caresses become more animated. Her tongue darts lubriciously into my mouth. There is not a part of our bodies which does not serve as a venereal sanctuary. She is intent on her own pleasure, but she does not forget mine.

'You are the first one to make me feel what love really is,' she tells me one day. 'None of the boys here in the village is your equal.'

I blush modestly.

All things must come to an end and I leave this peaceful, innocent place. At the gates of Paris, I feel all of my old wickedness returning.

But one gets rusty in the country. There one talks all the time about morals, virtue, honesty and honour. Those people would have ruined me. I mentally count those whom I am going to turn into suckers. What money I am going to squeeze out of them! How the fuck is going to flow! But who are going to be my victims? I think I'll despoil our sisters at the Opera. I know I shall have both money and pleasure. After all, it will be merely retaliation. Let's pillage those who rob us and fuck those who fuck us.

Inspired by this noble sentiment, I hasten to the Opera. There have been many changes in the last three months and I have to get my bearings. I find myself in the dressing-room where all the nymphs nearly suffocate me with their kisses and embraces. I am grabbing breasts and bottoms.

'Where have you been? The story went that you were dead, devoured by wolves, castrated or converted, which is the same thing.'

I finally manage to disengage myself to go up to a charming ballerina.

'Hello, Mimi.'

'No. I am angry with you.'

'Come now. Let's make up. I would like to give you my virginity.'

'I don't want it. I'm in love with my patron.'

'What do you take me for? I am no novice.'

'I'm going to remain faithful to him.'

'Who's talking about infidelity? How about going to bed with me tomorrow?'

'Suppose he finds out?' she laughs.

'How silly can you get?'

'He's old and jealous.'

'All the more reason to cheat on him.'

'He is a very important nobleman.'

'Damn it, he'll be nothing but a poor fool. If you don't agree, I'll give my all to Rosette. What would you say to that?'

At that threat, she readily accedes to my demand. I then go to dine with a banker who has some twenty male guests of distinguished name and boring conversation. This company is augmented by fifteen young girls.

'Horrors! You are back in your evil ways. You promised to renounce these creatures.'

'I'm keeping my word. My intentions are purely

dishonest. All I'm going to do is extract some money and bleed them a little.'

'But your trade is dishonourable.'

'There is no such thing as a dishonourable calling when it provides a living. After all, those fellows owe their fortunes to some whore's cunt. And those strumpets, don't they owe us everything? Who forms them in the art of perfidy and treachery unless it is us courtiers? We debauch a girl and take her away from her parents. Then we enroll her in the music academy, after which she can lift her head high while leading a life of vice and sin. But her heart is still innocent. What a delight to corrupt it! It is one of our favourite diversions. When we have finished, we congratulate ourselves on the result. In fact, we are praised to the skies.

'But that's not all. I would like to corrode the last remaining germs of virtue and poison the blood stream. I want her to be a pitiless corsair with a greedy soul. She will never know what gratitude is. Moreover, beneath her enticing exterior will be concealed the blackest of hearts. I want to inject into her all of my wickedness and teach her to take full advantage of a victim when he is defenceless. Then she will be able to fly on her own wings, snatching young men from the arms of their sorrowing fathers and weeping mothers. She will be sufficiently astute to bring wealthy merchants to penury and persuade husbands to abandon loving wives. We shall laugh together at the havoc we have caused as we share the spoils.'

Picture to yourself a brilliantly illuminated chamber with the doors locked and the drapes drawn. The women get down to the buff. What a charming sight meets my eyes. One, plump and dimpled, offers me a dazzling bosom. Another, a stunning blonde, resembles the Venus of Titian. A third is an alluring delicate nymph. What do we do when the signal is given? Why, we all start masturbating, of course. It won't be the last time for me, I assure you. All of a sudden, the atmosphere becomes charged. Voluptuousness is reproduced in myriad forms. There is heard the murmur of sighs, the sound of groans, and the swish-swash of copulation. The couches are creaking, tears are falling, and spasms seize the bodies. All are drowning in deluges of sensuousness.

What a tableau! How to describe fifteen women discharging simultaneously?

Now the orgy begins with free-flowing champagne exhilarating the participants. The tribades become true bacchantes. There are two in the sixty-nine position busily arousing one another. Take a look at that group twisted in the most bizarre formation. One lass is stretched out on a sofa with six admirers. She has her tongue in the cunt of the first who, suspended above her head, drenches her face with fuck and then stimulates herself by rubbing her cunt on her opulent bustiness. Then she is had from behind by the clitoris of a particularly lusty miss. Another, her head ensconced between the rounded thighs, is eagerly tonguing her grotto. Finally, she is revived by a dildo in both apertures.

They look as if they have gone berserk. And they are all ladies of breeding.

I go to spend the night with Mimi whom I find in bed. She has been expecting me. I quickly undress and am beside her. At first, she is somewhat shy, but my caresses dissipate her bashfulness. I enjoy myself thoroughly. You know the deliciousness of fresh fruit. I barely have enough time to employ all the twenty positions I know best when I hear a scratching on the door.

'Your cat is locked up.'

'Oh, let it stay there,' she breathes.

'All right.'

After a gratifying night, I get up at eight in the morning, leaving my lovely to continue her slumber. When I unlock the door to the bathroom, I find there the Chevalier de *** with only his shirt on. He is half-frozen and looks forlorn.

'My friend, how happy I am to see you,' he squeaks as he embraces me. 'I think I am dead.'

'What happened to you?' I inquire.

'I was in bed with Mimi when we heard a noise. She said it was her patron and squealed that she would be lost if I were found with her. I hid under the bed, and then I made my way here. I started to ponder how I could make my escape since I had no clothing. He is an old man, but he does have servants. I heard him fuck her. At least twelve times. My God! He must have stuffed himself with some aphrodisiac.'

'That's impossible,' I interject. 'Even I can't do that.'

'I repeat. Twelve times. I counted them. Finally, he left, but I was locked in.'

'I think you're making this all up,' I laugh.

He protests that it is the gospel truth.

'I think he fucked her in the rear,' he adds.

'That's enough, Chevalier,' I tell him sternly. 'I'm not a buggerer.'

'Well, who's talking about you?'

'You.'

'I?'

'Yes, you, for it was I that you heard.'

I leave him with his mouth gaping.

Our liaison runs its course, but I need more than a good romp in bed. Mimi is well endowed with diamonds, furnishings and cash. She gets an income of a thousand ecus a month, not counting the gifts. That is about fifty thousand francs a year. And I don't get a sou out of it. What good are those diamonds? They are not in fashion. Should I borrow them and sell them? No, that is not feasible. There is a Count who had his suspicions about me. Perhaps I could pocket the jewels and deny that I took them. It is damnably difficult to be a rogue today, because so many people of quality have adopted this code. I suppose the best way is to be an honest man. I'll have her hold open house with magnificent dinners. She will pay. When the jewellery and money are gone . . .

When the plan is put into effect, the polite world gathers in the house that is now *ours*. All Paris buzzes about our dinners. We have the prettiest girls and couples with the most outlandish apparel. There is a Knight of Malta who has brought back from his caravans only the most depraved Asiatic tastes. Although he is well past sixty, his only pleasure is with the young. The nascent fleece on a *mons Veneris* shocks him. What does he think he can do? Even whips on his withered buttocks fail to restore him to life. All he does is slobber piteously at the entrance of the sanctuary which he cannot penetrate.

Take a look at the abbot next to him. Are you blushing for him? He has a prick like a mule's and is as unscrupulous as he looks. No matter, he will get his mitre. Regard the carbuncles on his forehead and the veins on his nose. He grabs Martin, who well realizes that mice have only one hole and lets himself be taken.

Turcaret is getting sentimental. But just wait until the candles are extinguished. There he is now on top of Quincy, in whose hand he has placed his engine.

'Why are you always so timid?' he whispers angrily.

'I suppose that Mademoiselle Rosette will lend me her intestines for a fee of a hundred guineas,' Milord *** remarks.

'Go ahead and take her. I hope you won't be disappointed.'

D'Orbigny is giving satifaction to Colomba with his hand. She looks so respectful.

'Listen, Hortense,' says the Count, who is going to Rome. He is somewhat tipsy for the trip. 'You've given me gonorrhoea, but I suppose that's the way it is. I'm not complaining about that, but you've infected my lackeys and valets. That's disastrous for me.'

She looks remorseful and gives him an excuse. Soon they are together again.

Mimi gives balls with the added attraction of gambling. Young people and old children lose their all. Mimi is not happy. Within two months, we have consumed the trinkets, cutlery, diamonds, money, and furnishings.

While this is going on, a master butcher offers to keep her. Since I do not want to stand in the way of my beloved's future, I discreetly withdraw to attach myself to Violette.

You know that pretty little thing with a body that must have been shaped by the Graces. Her amazing bust consists of two perfect hemispheres. In addition to these allures, she has the unequalled talent of deceiving her patron. One has to be careful with her.

Her present protector is a gouty banker quite unable to meet the needs of a healthy young woman. Moreover, he is ugly as the devil and all he talks about is money. But every time he comes to see her, he brings a present. In a short time, we are rolling in money. In order to avoid unpleasantness, I have Violette pass me off as her brother.

One day while the Croesus is dining with her, I enter with a downcast expression. He asks my name and my employment.

'Monsieur, I am a tapestry worker,' I tell him.

'Do you know how to read and write?'

'Oh, indeed, I do. I spent three years in school.'

'I have kindly sentiments for your sister, and if you behave yourself, I'll have some for you, too.'

He slips two louis in my hand.

'He's a handsome boy,' he says to Violette. 'He has your eyes.' He turns to me. 'Do you have a mistress?'

Bashfully, I lower my head and twist my hat in my hands.

Violette cannot stand her lover. He bores her to tears. I do my best to make up for it during the night, for Monsieur's chaste spouse does not let him out after dark. Two ways of fucking particularly delight my sweetheart, and since I invented them, I'll describe them.

After the first two times, because you have to be warmed up, you seize your lovely and place her slightly diagonally on top of you. Then you pass your left arm in the gap caused by her position. With your hand you massage the left breast. She will be fucked dog-fashion, that is clear, but her head, bent down on yours, will enable you to put your tongue in her mouth. Your right hand rests on her clitoris. Imagine all that going on at once – the mutual movement of the two hinges, the busy tongues, and the gnawing teeth. Even the most frigid women are driven out of their minds. I must say that Violette does honour to my discovery.

But my name will not pass on to posterity. Ungrateful mortals, you honour with laurels and panegyrics those who bore you. To the shame of France, there are no prizes for those who are master fuckers. Monks and priests without testicles are esteemed and given rich livings while I enjoy my prick with no praise except from my partner. In days of yore, Apollo played the lyre with his prick.

What I propose is an academy of fucking, which will be the glory of France. Each member, to be elected, must have invented a new position or variation. There will be awarded a prize to the most graceful method of fucking and a gold medal to the best one performing it. The judges will be a duchess, a stewardess, a ballerina from the Opera, and three whores. Then we shall see the flowering of priapism, a superior religious faith. Fucking instead of prayers will be the form of worship to that highest of deities.

Violette has the most beautiful hair in the world, and she has a mania for being fucked in her tresses.

*Being fucked in her hair?*

What's so surprising about that? You can fuck in armpits, eyes, and in ears. It is impossible with her bosom, for her breasts are too firm and far apart.

But here is what I do. The little Messalina stretches out with her legs spread. Putting my feet where I should have my head, I fuck her in the mouth. Then with my head between her thighs, I do *minette* to her. You would die laughing if you could see us.

Monsieur Duret continues to provide us with money, which I take care to see that all is spent. Our debauchery clubs give me a certain amount of amusement. It goes without saying that he does not take part in our meetings.

One fine morning, I go and ask a little hussy I know if I can lunch with her. The servants are never around and I get into her bedroom without any difficulty. A significant noise makes me realize that she is occupied. I am retiring when I hear her cries.

'That's enough, Reverend. Enough! You bugger of a monk, you'll kill me.'

'On my honour, I just want to finish my daily dozen.'

He is one of us. Picking up a julep, I wait until he has finished his litany. Then I open the curtain.

'Father,' I say very humbly. 'Wouldn't you like this cooling drink? You seem to be very hot. Heavens, what a prick! I have never seen anything to equal it.'

It's none other than Father Ambroise, in charge of a mission.

'Let's be friends,' I continue. 'Here, we'll have a drink together and you have nothing to worry about.'

Reassured, he continues his rutting.

'This is the result of our robes,' he tells me. 'I hate them. Beneath them we conceal pricks of iron and hearts of chicken, for fear of the frightful punishments that await us.'

'Punishment for having fucked a pretty woman?' I innocently inquire.

'No. Only if we are stupid enough to be caught. But we bring many benefits to many homes where the husbands are indifferent or incapable. As long as the peccadillo remains secret, we have nothing to fear, but if it comes out, we are sequestered.'

'You mean you are locked up?'

'Yes, I had to pass the sentence once myself when I caught a young padre with Madame Dumas. Since we live on charity, hypocrisy is our second nature. We practise a thousand frauds to support our indolence and vices. To tell you the truth, we are not worth a damn.'

'For your age, Father, you have come far,' I remark.

'That's true, but let me tell you why. I entered a seminary at the age of nineteen. There I thought the devil was lurking in every corner. The thought of his horns frightened me out of my wits. Since I have been here, I have put them on many heads. In the name of sacred obedience, I was buggered. Since I was big and well built, I became the favourite catamite of the order. At the same time, my prick attained the eminence which you now see. Because I was desirable both in front and back, I was presented to the archbishop who was visiting our cloister. After measuring me, he honoured me with the supreme mark of his favour by turning his rump to me. I entered the abyss which stank to the high heavens. As a reward, he gave me permission to become acquainted with cunts.

'Then he took me to Spain, a marvellous country where there are many blossoms to pluck. I prefer milk-white flesh, but a monk cannot be too choosy. I won't tell you how many beautiful girls we imprisoned as Jews and fucked as Christians. We gave them absolution with our pricks. Unfortunately, we had to burn at the stake about a dozen because we were not sure if they would tattle or not. Yes, discretion is the noblest of the virtues. Father Nicholas died a martyr's death — syphilis. I performed several services for Cardinal Carrero, who made me a vicar. But I soon tired of the life of a bugger. I was high enough in rank to indulge in my own tastes without any fear. I fucked, I fuck, and I shall fuck. That's the end of my story.'

We sprinkle holy water on him.

'Father, do your devouts pay you?' I wanted to know.

'Of course. I generally make about a hundred pistoles a month. I guide cunts as well as consciences.'

'What about confession?'

'A perfect occasion to instruct a pretty girl and tranquillize an overly respectable matron. You certainly are stupid for a man of the world. What sense is there studying Saint Augustine or Duns Scotus? Drinking and fucking are much more enjoyable. We titillate the old women and give pleasure to the young.'

'But, Father,' I object, 'what about the sanctity of the family?'

'That is where we shine most brightly. For a woman, no matter her age, to have only one man is sheer stupidity, and we point that out. We literally ruin families by knowing all their secrets. If there is a young girl I want to fuck and she is reluctant, I see to it that she is swallowed up in a convent where she can repent her excess of virtue. If a woman's fiancé does not surrender to me, I break up the intended marriage by spreading rumours that he is impious. I see to it that he is disinherited, and all that for the greater glory of God. I give comfort to the wife who wails the night through because of the impotence of her disgusting spouse, and when I am through with her, I see to it that she is disgraced and dishonoured. Let's have another drink. As they say, *in vino veritas*. But I warn you that you had better not betray the secrets of the church. You'll be sorry.'

'I, Father? But I am not dependent on you like the others.'

'You're not dependent? We'll see about that. I won't stand for being insulted.'

'Stop it, you villainous monk,' cries Alexandrine. 'You fuck like an angel, but you have the soul of a devil. I am disgusted and I don't want to talk to you any more.'

'You're biting the hand that feeds you, but go away. I am not hard now.'

He turns to me. 'Do you think we would attack you openly? Of course not. We would begin by going to your friends and praising you highly. But we would mention certain faults. The seeds of suspicion would be planted.'

'But I would not give you any hold on me.'

'It makes no difference. People love to gossip and believe the worst. There would be anonymous letters which would be avidly read. Your enemies, and everyone has some, will be delighted.'

'But I could defend myself,' I assert.

'I am sure of that. But as Machiavelli remarked, always slander, for at least a scar will always remain. It is infallible.'

'Indeed, Father, I never realized how crafty and clever you are.'

'We have to be to exist,' he modestly replies.

'I have almost a mind to take orders.'

'You could do worse. From talking with you, I think you have a definite talent for our calling.'

After this edifying conversation, I leave him with Alexandrine in bed again, and return to Violette. She tells me that Monsieur Duret has lost all his money. We don't have a sou. I tell her to sell her furniture to pay the debts, and I leave her in order not to disturb her while she is breaking up our household.

Since I love music, I take refuge with Gaymard. The bitch is ugly, but she has a good voice. Also, she fucks like a madwoman. Because of my reputation, we are able to cut short the preliminaries. I agree to six times a day. She dismisses her water-carrier, whom she has worn out, and allows her lackeys and hairdresser to have some peace. We decide on a common purse (with the understanding that I do not have to contribute anything to it). She gives recitals and receives guests who eat her out of house and home while despising her.

My life is spent with musicians of varying talents, but my ogress is starting to tire me. She swears like a trooper and has no manners. All she can do well is fuck. One final trick decides me to give her up. One evening after the theatre, I go to her house. She is going to dine in town as I am. But can one leave without having one's boots greased? I sit on a chair and when she gets on me, I fuck her. At the peak of pleasure, she pretends to lose her senses, which, in reality, she does not. I have a fine watch she has always wanted. She gets the idea of purloining it. She deftly lifts it and puts it in her pocket. I notice what she is doing. In turn, I manage to obtain possession of hers, which is extremely valuable. We are even.

The next day, she is very worried but I am completely at ease. I tease her a little.

'You are shameless,' I tell her. 'Here is your watch back. You can keep mine because you have profaned it. My sole vengeance will be to tell everyone about your kleptomania.'

While she is making all sorts of excuses, I bow and depart.

I decide to make Dorville my sultaness. Indeed, she is worthy of the honour. A nymph figure which is gently rounded, peaches-and-cream complexion, and big blue eyes which beg me to kill and then revive her. We sleep together in her house, and the first night is decisive and eloquent. I establish myself as master of the household.

This new arrangement pleases me very much. Every day there are new refinements in the art of love. One morning, I find her as she comes out of her bath. She is like Venus emerging from the waves. Adorned in nothing but her own beauty, her tresses flow down her back while her hand caresses a bosom of alabaster.

With a pleased smile, she contemplates her charms while reclining in a chair. As I witness this voluptuous spectacle, I become aware of a stiffening in my trousers. Flames race through my veins.

The rustle I make offers me another tableau. With a deep blush, she bends down and attempts to conceal her nudity with the locks of her hair. At that moment, her toy poodle leaps down and takes position before her grotto, yelping ferociously all the while. Laughing until my sides burst, I enter and console my beauty, and one does not have to be told how.

I suppose you think I have every reason to be happy. Well, I am not. Within this temple of beauty, Dorville encloses a capricious fury which is constant only in evil and foulness. She attracts lovers merely to devour them.

'I am irritated,' she tells me one day about some innocent she has plucked clean, 'that I left him eyes to weep with.'

She corrupts everything. Her perfidious tongue distorts the simplest things. Under a veil of ingenuous naïveté, she hides the most treacherous of souls. She is capable of any crime as long as she is sure she is not going to get caught.

*Well, why do you live with such a monster?*

I don't know. Perhaps because she is seductive. I thought she loved me. Well, I pay heavily for the mistake.

One of my friends, Count *** has been coming regularly to see Dorville and his presence does not constrain me. I did not think he had his eye on her. Gradually his usual good humour disappears to be replaced by gloom and moodiness. I feel sorry for him, and when I try to cheer him up, he repulses my advances with a coldness that presages a rupture. I take Dorville into my confidence and ask her help. She agrees. The traitress!

A few days later, she alarms me with her mournful appearance. Then I surprise her as she is shedding hot tears. I keep after her until she tells me what is bothering her.

'My dear, my heart is breaking. If I tell you why, you must give me your word that you will keep your temper.'

I promise.

'You thought that the Count was your friend,' she says. 'Well, he's nothing but a Judas.'

'You can't mean that,' I exclaim.

'Yes, he is a coward and traitor. He got on his knees and told me he loved me. I tried to dissuade him. I told him to think of his friendship with you. I reminded him of honour. He swore that his former friend was now his enemy. I can't repeat the terrible things he said about you. My heart was bleeding.'

Again she is racked by sobs. Her tears bathe my visage. Now her fumblings stoke the fires of voluptuousness and jealousy. I feel a new sense of indignation. My pride is aroused and I vow to avenge my honour. Under the guise of trying to appease me, she puts more fuel on the fire. I am seething within.

When the Count appears, I provoke him. Dorville prevents any explanation of my ill humour. The situation becomes so unbearable that the Count insults me. After I slap him, there is only one thing to do, and we do it. I get him with my first lunge and he is stretched out at my feet, his sword on the ground at his side. Forgetting our animosity, I kneel at his side and try to stanch the flow of blood gushing from his breast.

'There's nothing you can do,' he whispers. 'I am dying and I deserve it, for I tried to kill you. Dorville asked me to.'

'Dorville?' I am stunned.

'I wanted her so badly that I would have done anything for her. And this was her price. Please forgive me, and let me die still your friend.'

With a final attempt to embrace me, he expires.

Seized by a senseless fury, I make my way to Dorville's house with the sword still stained by my friend's blood.

'Well, I killed him,' I shriek. 'You wanted me to murder him and him to slay me. Well, you got part of your wish.'

I see an expression of serenity and even joy on her face. She even dares to stretch out her arms to me and congratulate me on my victory.

'You termagant, you had better tremble for your life. This hand which you have rendered criminal may punish you.'

At this threat, uttered in a menacing tone, she gets on her knees before me. Her cheeks take on an ashen colour and her bosom heaves convulsively. When I throw my rapier aside, her self-confidence returns.

'Yes, I arranged it,' she admits. 'I loathed him, but I led him on so I could get rid of him. So I turned him against you. I knew that you would be in no danger, for he is not much of a swordsman. He offended me a number of times before, and now I am revenged.'

I scarcely hear what she is saying. Wearily, I leave her and go home, where I immediately gain my bed.

For a long time, I am inconsolable. I avoid all human contact. Never can I get out of my mind the memory of my friend's last moments. I am so depressed that I long for the rest of the tomb.

In my house in another apartment lives a colonel's wife. She leads a retired existence. Because of my dissipated life, I have never come to know her well, only exchanging an occasional greeting with her. Becoming worried about my state of mind, my valet has the idea that the young woman can distract me. He tells her chambermaid about me and this is repeated to the Marquise. Her curiosity is piqued. When she learns the cause of my lassitude, she is genuinely touched. Every day she asks about me. When she comes to inquire about my health, I am so apathetic that I am unable to thank her.

One day, as I am going out of my house, we meet. I hasten to make amends for my lack of courtesy. We soon became bosom friends. For all practical purposes, I live in her apartment. Her understanding and comfort gradually assuage my grief. But I have to watch out for love. A companionship between a charming young woman of twenty-two and a man not advanced in years is bound to lead someplace. Moreover, sorrow is always susceptible to tenderness. The inevitable occurs.

She is attractive without wishing to appear so. She has a kind heart and a good head. But she is not happily married. Like many military men, her husband neglects the treasure he possesses to chase the frights that hang around encampments. Nevertheless, he is a brute who demands absolute fidelity from his wife.

What a difference there is between the caresses of a woman like the Marquise and the tarts one meets in polite circles. The latter may provide temporary diversion, but when it is over, there is a bad taste in the mouth.

The Marquise is in the flower of young womanhood. If she did not have such a perfectly proportioned figure, she would appear to be a giantess, for she is almost six feet tall. I have never seen such a ravishing bosom. There is a delightful irregularity about her features which I find irresistible.

She turns off the compliments that I contantly rain on her.

'My friend,' she tells me, 'if you keep on like this, I'll be as vain as a peacock.'

Perhaps because she is both chaste and pure, I have never known such heights of pleasure.

The battles I must fight to conquer her virtue! I keep telling her that love is no sin. Dare I admit it? For a long time, her sense of respectability is stronger than my desire. She senses the danger. She even writes her husband to come and be with her so that she will not yield to temptation, but he dismisses her pleas. For her pains, all she gets is indifference and insults.

I launch one last attack and I am successful. She no longer blushes when she is with me, and peace reigns in the house. Who can blame her for her defeat. For six months we live in paradise. We are sufficient unto ourselves. When the fires go out, they are immediately ignited again. Constantly we discover new charms in each other.

How long can bliss last? We are nothing but the playthings of destiny. It is not long before my Marquise is bearing the fruit of our love. Soon her condition can no longer be concealed. On his return to Paris, the husband soon finds out about our affair, which he immediately divulges to his cronies. The insults he hurls at us! I am ready to exact vengeance, but Euphrosia restrains my arm. Now the happiness is gone. She weeps all the time.

'Euphrosia,' I tell her one day, 'how I regret that I cannot lessen your grief. I suppose you hate me.'

'Hate you?' she protests. 'Nobody has ever been so dear to me. This poor child I am carrying will be born under unfortunate auspices, but at least it has tied more tightly the bonds that unite us. I have no regrets for what we have done. I am afraid that I have little to offer you now. I do hope that this infant will remind you of its mother.'

'What are you saying?' I cry in anguish. 'Is that how you show your love? Go ahead and die, my cowardly mistress, but before breathing your last, you'll have the cruel satisfaction of seeing the demise of your lover. So you're going to deprive your child of our tender cares and leave it a target of the darts of fate?'

Euphrosia interrupts me with her sobs. Her flood of tears seems to give her some relief from her grief.

'Darling, let's banish these funereal thoughts. Courage. Keep going for the sake of love. Haven't you told me a thousand times that you lived just for me?'

She promises to pull herself together.

A few days later, I have to go to Brittany on a short trip. But Euphrosia's pregnancy is becoming more pronounced. I have gloomy forebodings. Our farewells are shot with misgivings. We feel that it is the last time that we shall see each other. She faints when I get into my carriage.

I conclude my affairs quickly when I receive a letter from a friend: 'Return instantly. Don't lose a second.'

Dropping everything, I hasten back. A black wreath is hanging on Euphrosia's door. My God! She is no longer. I want to see her and kiss her one last time and then die with her. Ignoring the attempts of those who try to hold me back, I advance. They speak to me, but I do not hear them.

'Stop, young man,' a venerable gentleman orders me. He is coming out of my beloved's rooms. 'Have respect for this site of sorrow.'

I am moved by his severe but gentle tone, and I kneel before him.

'Whoever you are, please have pity on me. Permit me to see one last time my mistress. That is all I ask of you. Afterwards, I demand nothing but to die to be with her.'

'Get up!' he commands me courteously. 'You are hurrying me to the grave, you young idiot. What have I ever done to you? Until now, nothing has besmirched my white hair, and now you want to expose me to shame and disgrace. Your dastardly affair has cost me both my son and daughter. The one was my support and the other my happiness.'

'Are you her father? Heavens, take your revenge for

my having taken your daughter. I won't deny the love I had for her.'

'Although I have lost everything, I cannot blame you for my woes. I can't find it within me to hate you.' My sobs are my only reply. 'Now don't take it too hard. Euphrosia is still breathing.'

'I have to see her. Oh no, you are just saying that to get vengeance.'

With those words, I sink back senseless, not hearing a word, in an armchair. Euphrosia's father takes me by the hand.

'I am speaking the truth, but that does not mitigate the cruelty of our lots. I wish you to listen to the misfortunes which brought all of this about. A week after your departure, my son-in-law came to see his wife who was telling her brother about her love affair. When he heard about it, the Marquis became furious. My son tried to calm him down, but it was in vain. The Marquis threatened Euphrosia, even by trying to beat her. My son threw himself in front of his sister to protect her. When the Marquis refused to desist, my son drew his sword and wounded him. Then the Marquis pulled out a hidden pistol and fired. The bullet killed my grandchild. At the sight of the horrible happenings, Euphrosia fell into a dead faint, giving a stillbirth. For a time, the mother's life hung in the balance, but today she seems much better. But how will she escape her grief?'

Without making a movement, I drink in this horrible recital.

'So, she's alive, but I know that she detests me. On the other hand, she can't hate me. Let me be your son to make up for your sad loss. Gladly will I assume the duties. I promise that Euphrosia will live to love you.'

The old man is obviously moved. He sees a ray of hope.

'We are deluding ourselves,' he says. 'Euphrosia is coming back to life, but her life has been poisoned for ever. She refuses to talk to me and hides under the covers. She threatens to go to a convent.'

I do my best to dissuade her, but she is adamant. A few weeks later she pronounces the vows and takes the veil.

I am so depressed that I decide to go to a Trappist monastery, resolved to spend the rest of my days there.

But the gods are against me. A thunderstorm forces me to stop at Verneuil. I am soaking wet without a change of clothing. When I am in bed, I am in the depths of depression and contemplate suicide. Suddenly, cemeteries seem lovely places to me. I see the rows of crosses. The chimes from the church tower seem to presage my death. I desired death, but fate was not of the same mind.

Absorbed in my own reflections, I do not notice the pretty young maid. I snap myself out my revery, only to fall into another. The girl asks me what I would like to have for dinner. When I look at her blankly, she thinks, rightly, that I am slightly mad. Finally, I focus my attention and exchange repartee with her. We both laugh.

I order. Madeleine goes up to remake my bed. When she returns, she allows me to see a well-turned leg. The gods are smiling on me. But, I repeat to myself, I am destined for the grave. Well, why should not this delightful little creature benefit from me before I am buried? She'll be the last fuck of my life.

I throw her on the bed have her skirt up to her neck before she can utter a word of protest. She makes a sign of resistance, but what woman can complain after she has received the third thrust? She wiggles as if she has the Saint-Vitus dance. As usual, I would like to begin again, but she tells me that she still has to work. But we agree to meet again together that night. I give her a few louis for I shall have no further use of money.

We spend the night together. It is the last time for me. She is a little vexed at first, but after her fifth homage, there is not a whimper out of her. She is thrashing about as if she were out of her mind. As usual, I am ready to start all over, but she protests, saying that she is expected below. But she quickly returns.

A miracle occurs. The more I go in and out of that carmine-rimmed hole, the more calm I become. My resolve weakens, and I decide to put off my plan until the next night.

The next day at dinner, two men join me. Great is my astonishment when I see that they are my closest friends.

'What's wrong with you? You look like the last rose of summer,' exclaims Saint-Flour.

With that, they tease me mercilessly until I have to laugh along with them. Finally, I am persuaded to go back with them to Paris.

For a time, I am at a loss as to what to do. To add to my difficulties, I am deeply in debt, and my creditors with their hangdog looks are camped on my doorstep. Finally, I make a momentous decision – I am going to get married.

It is the end.

I am acquainted with an old woman who knows everybody. I go to her and tell her what I want.

'Do you want her pretty?' she inquires.

'That's unimportant,' I say airily.

'Do you want her to be rich?'

'As wealthy as possible.'

'Intelligent?'

'It would help.'

'I think I have the right party for you,' she declares. 'Do you know Madame de l'Hermitage?'

'No.'

'I'll introduce you. She's one of my best friends, and she has an eighteen-year old daughter. She has lots of money and a lovable character.'

My amiable duenna leaves immediately to make the overtures. Two days later, I go with her to meet my future mother-in-law. She has the figure of a skeleton and the bearing of an empress. She overwhelms me with compliments. As the two hags exchange idle talk, I examine the salon. Rich tapestries cover the wall. An enormous chandelier is suspended from the ceiling. In every corner and nook are antiques. All in all, it speaks of a wealth that tickles my cupidity.

My go-between and I leave. She tells me that I have made a favourable impression and that in all probability I will be invited to dinner to meet Mademoiselle Euterpe. What a name!

I receive the expected invitation and meet my promised. She must have been carved with a hatchet with a monkey as a model. She is the spitting image of her mother. When she smiles, she is even uglier. My God! Am I expected to marry that?

*So you're not going to take her as your wife?*

Well, she has forty thousand livres for an income, and all I possess is a fine prick which she'll hardly ever feel. My creditors are yapping at my heels, and I suppose I have to immolate myself.

After fifteen days, we exchange the marriage vows. An annuity of twenty thousand is settled on me. After the ceremony, my wife goes to the nuptial couch, where I find her huddled under the sheets. She is weeping her heart out.

'Madame,' I tell her, 'marriage is a hard road which can lead to happiness. The roses lining the way are not without thorns and it is up to me to pull them out as your husband. Our Lord has joined us to make us one. In order to complete His task, He has seen fit to equip the man with a peg.' (I put her hand on it, but she withdraws it in terror.) 'Now this has to find its hole, which is in you. Allow me, please, to look for it and then plug it.'

I take hold of my Christian who squeezes her thighs tightly together. When I start opening them with my knee, she punches me in the face with her fists. Finally, she raises her derriere and I am knocking at the door.

Now the gate is flung wide open. I rush in. She is scratching me like an enraged cat and yowling like a maniac. The sputtering mother comes bustling in, but she soon calms down.

'My son-in-law, I know how it is,' she says.

'I know better than you,' I retort.

'Don't worry. It was the same with me on my wedding night.'

'To hell with your whole family.'

'Don't say that. She's just a child. She'll come around. Win her over with gentleness.'

'Let the fucker who began her take her back. She's as big as a mare.'

'I suppose it is because you are incapable,' she remarks with a frown.

'What do you mean, I can't? No trouble at all. You could drive in there with a carriage.'

The old hag gets angry again. I ignore her and storm out of the room, leaving that cursed house forever.

The story gets around. The sarcasm will be the death of me. Where can I flee? Where can I hide?

That's not all. The following day, a man dressed in black asks to have a word with me. He shows me a document.

'Monsieur, you are mistaken,' I stammer.

'No.'

'From whom is that?' I ask.

'From Mademoiselle Euterpe de l'Hermitage, your lawful wife.'

'If you don't get out of here . . .'

He beats a hasty retreat when he sees my threatening fists.

The bitch makes a legal demand for me to treat her as a wife. If I don't, she insists on an annulment. I rush to my lawyer and we fight for three months in the courts. In the end, I am deprived of ten thousand livres income and declared the father of a child with whom the monster is pregnant.

In desperation, I abandon this miserable country where I have met with so many misfortunes. Never again shall I insert my prick into a marital cunt. To get vengeance on the world, I am going to fuck all of nature. There won't be a virgin left on the face of the earth. Legions of cuckolds will people palaces, cities and fields. I'll exercise my rights even on the Virgin Mary. And when I descend to the paternal arms of Monsieur Satan, I'll fuck the dead.

# MORE EROTIC CLASSICS FROM CARROLL & GRAF

| ☐ Anonymous/ALTAR OF VENUS | $3.95 |
| ☐ Anonymous/AUTOBIOGRAPHY OF A FLEA | $3.95 |
| ☐ Anonymous/THE CELEBRATED MISTRESS | $3.95 |
| ☐ Anonymous/CONFESSIONS OF AN ENGLISH MAID | $3.95 |
| ☐ Anonymous/CONFESSIONS OF EVELINE | $3.95 |
| ☐ Anonymous/COURT OF VENUS | $3.95 |
| ☐ Anonymous/DANGEROUS AFFAIRS | $3.95 |
| ☐ Anonymous/THE DIARY OF MATA HARI | $3.95 |
| ☐ Anonymous/DOLLY MORTON | $3.95 |
| ☐ Anonymous/THE EDUCATION OF A MAIDEN | $3.95 |
| ☐ Anonymous/THE EROTIC READER | $3.95 |
| ☐ Anonymous/THE EROTIC READER II | $3.95 |
| ☐ Anonymous/THE EROTIC READER III | $4.50 |
| ☐ Anonymous/FANNY HILL'S DAUGHTER | $3.95 |
| ☐ Anonymous/FLORENTINE AND JULIA | $3.95 |
| ☐ Anonymous/A LADY OF QUALITY | $3.95 |
| ☐ Anonymous/LENA'S STORY | $3.95 |
| ☐ Anonymous/THE LIBERTINES | $4.50 |
| ☐ Anonymous/LOVE PAGODA | $3.95 |
| ☐ Anonymous/THE LUSTFUL TURK | $3.95 |
| ☐ Anonymous/MADELEINE | $3.95 |
| ☐ Anonymous/A MAID'S JOURNEY | $3.95 |
| ☐ Anonymous/MAID'S NIGHT IN | $3.95 |
| ☐ Anonymous/THE OYSTER | $3.95 |
| ☐ Anonymous/THE OYSTER II | $3.95 |
| ☐ Anonymous/THE OYSTER III | $4.50 |
| ☐ Anonymous/PARISIAN NIGHTS | $4.50 |
| ☐ Anonymous/PLEASURES AND FOLLIES | $3.95 |
| ☐ Anonymous/PLEASURE'S MISTRESS | $3.95 |
| ☐ Anonymous/PRIMA DONNA | $3.95 |
| ☐ Anonymous/ROSA FIELDING: VICTIM OF LUST | $3.95 |
| ☐ Anonymous/SATANIC VENUS | $4.50 |
| ☐ Anonymous/SECRET LIVES | $3.95 |
| ☐ Anonymous/THREE TIMES A WOMAN | $3.95 |

- ☐ Anonymous/VENUS DISPOSES — $3.95
- ☐ Anonymous/VENUS IN PARIS — $3.95
- ☐ Anonymous/VENUS UNBOUND — $3.95
- ☐ Anonymous/VENUS UNMASKED — $3.95
- ☐ Anonymous/VICTORIAN FANCIES — $3.95
- ☐ Anonymous/THE WANTONS — $3.95
- ☐ Anonymous/A WOMAN OF PLEASURE — $3.95
- ☐ Anonymous/WHITE THIGHS — $4.50
- ☐ Perez, Faustino/LA LOLITA — $3.95
- ☐ van Heller, Marcus/ADAM & EVE — $3.95
- ☐ van Heller, Marcus/THE FRENCH WAY — $3.95
- ☐ van Heller, Marcus/THE HOUSE OF BORGIA — $3.95
- ☐ van Heller, Marcus/THE LOINS OF AMON — $3.95
- ☐ van Heller, Marcus/ROMAN ORGY — $3.95
- ☐ van Heller, Marcus/VENUS IN LACE — $3.95
- ☐ Villefranche, Anne-Marie/FOLIES D'AMOUR — $3.95
  - Cloth — $14.95
- ☐ Villefranche, Anne-Marie/JOIE D'AMOUR — $3.95
  - Cloth — $13.95
- ☐ Villefranche, Anne-Marie/MYSTERE D'AMOUR — $3.95
- ☐ Villefranche, Anne-Marie/PLAISIR D'AMOUR — $3.95
  - Cloth — $12.95
- ☐ Von Falkensee, Margarete/BLUE ANGEL NIGHTS — $3.95
- ☐ Von Falkensee, Margarete/BLUE ANGEL SECRETS — $4.50

Available from fine bookstores everywhere or use this coupon for ordering.

---

Carroll & Graf Publishers, Inc., 260 Fifth Avenue, N.Y., N.Y. 10001

Please send me the books I have checked above. I am enclosing $_____ (please add $1.00 per title to cover postage and handling.) Send check or money order—no cash or C.O.D.'s please. N.Y. residents please add 8¼% sales tax.

Mr/Mrs/Ms _____
Address _____
City _____ State/Zip _____
Please allow four to six weeks for delivery.